WALKING THROUGH AND OTHER STORIES

Contributors:

Francine Fleming

Maria Jemmott

Shirley Merith

Manjit Singh

Paula Smellie

ISBN-13: 9781542643726 (CreateSpace-Assigned)
ISBN-10: 1542643724
Library of Congress Control Number: 2017901382
CreateSpace Independent Publishing Platform
North Charleston, South Carolina

To our families and dear friends for walking through with us.

In everyone's life, at some time, our inner fire goes out. It is then burst into flame by an encounter with another human being. We should all be thankful for those people who rekindle the inner spirit.

-Albert Schweitzer

CONTENTS

BUCKETS OF WONDERMENT
By Manjit Singh

Lumps of coal that continued to burn within the tandoor oven cast a soft orange glow across the rooftop veranda, beneath an endless pitch-black sky. Every now and then, bursts of light would flicker and crackle from within the clay vessel like tiny shooting stars, dazzling with their sight and sound, providing an inexplicable comfort, despite a lack of knowledge of what the future would bring.

- Manjit Singh

BUCKETS OF
WONDERMENT

Dear Diary:

When Papa went to live his next life, Mummy was reborn as a tough bull, hard as nails and never the same again. That's what Asha told me a long time ago. Mummy says that I am too much like Papa, and she doesn't want me to be. That's why she's so tough on me, more than with Asha. Mummy says that Papa was too much of a dreamer, believing that we lived under a security blanket of stars. But in the end, not even the biggest of those darned stars, the almighty sun, could keep him safe, but rather, betrayed him. Mummy doesn't want me to chase after silly dreams, or to gaze too high towards the sun, the moon or the stars. She warns me to keep my gaze lowered, so that I too, will not be burned as Papa was. People who knew Papa say that he saw the beauty in life, even where others could see none. Even at the end of a hard day, he would point towards the blackened night sky and tell us how blessed we were to be graced by the light of a million stars. I suppose that's why the dark has never frightened me, not even back then when I was very young and we lived far from the city. When others who didn't know my father ask me what he was like, I simply tell them that he was my Papa, and he gave me vision to see the light, even in the dark.

Naina

━✦ ✦━

E ven at nightfall, the city of Jalandhar is not at rest. Along the outskirts, far from its bustling urban interior, through dusty remote villages and lush green pastures, though the city may seem to be in a state of serenity, it is only the fortunate who truly revel in elusive tranquility – no matter the time of day. In its vastness, Jalandhar is a window to the world. Amidst an ever-growing population, the wealthy live vibrantly alongside the silenced poor. Expansive estates equipped with chauffeur driven foreign cars gleam behind gated communities, sprawling around constricted shantytowns that are dotted with mud and straw huts. Those bestowed with plenty, exist amongst those who live in a chronic state of want. The Grand Trunk Road, an artery running through the entire stretch of the city and beyond, supports the allotted trajectories of its entire people, both 'haves' and 'have not's'. It was on the outskirts of

G.T. Road, in a modest village in India, on a restless night that Naina's story began.

Naina would probably be thirteen or fourteen this year. In her family, as in others like her own, it was common to not know the birthdate of a child. Upon arrival into her present life, the birth of a daughter had been a blessing already bestowed when the wails and cries of first her mother, and then her own, pierced through the rickety walls. The rumble of burden reverberated beyond the open courtyard in which a brown sludge of rainwater rippled and echoed the news into the ears of the working poor. Life here, as in other villages scattered throughout the state of Punjab, was inundated with as much explosive activity as it was with the everyday mundane happenings of slum life.

⊷ ⊶

"Nainaaa, oooh Nainay! Get out of your dream world child and go hang the laundry before those clouds shed their tears!" her mother hollered, indignant to the sacred calm that still hung at dawn.

The blazing August sun had not yet elbowed its way past India's smoggy horizon. Lying on an old woven jute cot draped with a tattered duri, Naina buried her head beneath her pale blue dupatta shawl upon hearing her mother approaching the room where she, along with her older sister Asha, and younger brother Shaan, still lay, partially asleep. While the monsoon climate certainly did not call for any sort of bed covering, the gauzy cotton veil served both as a shield of modesty as well as protection from the tyranny of barsati storm mosquitos.

5

As routine would have it, her mother plunked the plastic bucket brimming with the heavy load of hand wrung garments at the foot of the concrete stairs that lead to the rooftop veranda. *The dreaded morning chore*, Naina thought with despair, still half asleep. Desperate to sustain the most blissful moments of dozing just before daybreak, she slunk deeper beneath the shawl.

"Nuniehhh, are you listening?!" her mother persisted.

With every change of name, Naina recognized the diminishing patience in her mother's voice. Unlike her endearing reference of 'Nunu', it was only when her mother was most agitated with her youngest daughter that she referred to Naina as 'Nainay' or 'Nunieh'. Dozing or not, *this* Naina recognized.

The screech of metal being pushed over concrete, followed by the clangor of water hitting the dented tub, severed any remaining ties to sleep. Her mother's usual barrage of curses spewed out from the bathroom as the water trickled intermittently from the tarnished brass tap. Not much remained unblemished or constant in their small world and time was always at a premium. The day yet barely begun, Naina sighed with her eyes still shut knowing that her mother would bathe hurriedly and that in a few moments, she would have to get up. As far as her mother was concerned, there were no moments to spare.

⚔ ⚔

"A widow with three children cannot luxuriate in the practice of taking her time. Time was for those who could afford it, not for those who were born in a constant struggle to survive, despite it,"

Naina's mother would caution her children. It had been clear to Naina that her mother had worked tirelessly to provide for her children that which her own ancestors could never attain. Born into a low caste family and condemned to live on the margins of society, Naina's mother had made it her mission since the death of her husband, to carve out something greater, something better for her children. Thus, Naina and her siblings attended the local government school whenever their mother could afford to do without their contribution to the familial purse. On occasion, Naina had watched her mother go without eating when food was scarce, claiming that she had already eaten. She had once seen her mother set aside an empty pot, watching her later wipe it clean of any scant remains with her fingers. Her mother had scolded Naina for such spying, just as she scolded her daughter each morning to wake up for school or work. Through it all, Naina and her siblings never doubted their mother's love.

—≕+ +≕—

"Aahhhhh!" Naina screeched as a hand from below reached up to tug at her braided hair.

"Get up lazy witch! It's your turn to hang the clothes!" Asha grumbled from the floor where she lay on her bedroll of two duris. The bedroll adjacent to Asha's lay vacant. Although mice were not a novelty, the sensation of one scurrying across Naina's head during the night was enough to make her abandon her ground level bedroll beside Asha for the security of the elevated jute cot on which Shaan slept. The old wooden frame creaked and wobbled throughout the night whenever Naina tossed or turned, yet both it and her seven-year-old brother seemed to tolerate her added weight.

"Naina, I swear, if Mummy comes out from the bathroom before you're up . . . !"

"Okay, okay!" Naina conceded before Asha completed her ultimatum.

While only a year and a half separated the girls in age, Naina still behaved in a reasonably respectful manner towards her older sister. Though they quarreled at times, Naina knew that she could always count on her sister. It was Asha, after all, who had snuck Naina into a theatre to see her first film. With the little money Asha earned at times, she would buy Naina and Shaan chocolates and spicy crisps from the market. It had also been Asha who sheltered Naina from the mean girls who preyed on the timid and unprotected during recess at the local government school. Primal, a burly 14-year-old in Naina's class, was their bandit leader. By nature, Naina did her best to avoid Primal and any potential trouble. Yet when she learned last year that Primal had stolen a new pink hair clip from Asha's school bag, Naina, who typically feared and avoided confrontation, accosted the girl with an unexpected rage. She retrieved the clip along with a fistful of hair from the girl's head and then pushed Primal, hard, onto a pile of fresh dog poop. Her bottom smeared with the smelly brown paste, Primal was sent home from school, and from that day forward, some of the children had teasingly named her P.P., short for Potty Pants. Since the Potty Incident, those mean girls no longer dared to look in Naina's or Asha's direction.

The water had just been turned off as Naina scurried towards the bathroom. As her mother vacated the tiny room, toweling her dripping hair, a muggy fog enveloped the girl, foretelling of the pending day, laden with uncertainty.

"Naina, how many times do I have to remind you to get started on time? You're not a child. I shouldn't have to chase after you."

"But Mummy, it's Sunday!" Naina proclaimed with her usual weekend defense, eyes not meeting her mother's, knowing full well that the sanctity of Sunday was not a given in their world.

Avoiding her mother's scolding glare, Naina's eyes became preoccupied by a faded sticker plastered on the corner of the small mirror that hung above the sink that stood outside the bathroom. It was not the first time that Naina had become transfixed by the image on the sticker of an hourglass figured woman with a bosom billowing from her tiny mirror-encrusted blouse. Both captivated and envious, she stared at the sultry statuesque beauty who seemed to smile from within a bottled sea of amber Royal Stag whiskey. *What would it be like,* Naina wondered, *to look like that, to appear so stunning, and to be so happy-happy?*

"*Maharani Ji . . . ,*" her mother chastised, addressing her youngest daughter as '*Your Royal Highness*', "this *Sunday-Soonday* business only applies to your fantasy world of castles in the sky. Not for our working people! Do you think Memsaab will have less work for you on the one day of the week when her entire household remains at home? You'll be tending to the entire clan in addition to every drop-by Auntie-Shuntie. Even her daughters-in-law refuse to do much on Sunday apart from calling out orders. They'll have you running around all day!" her mother snapped, forever attempting to keep her dreaming daughter grounded in reality to avoid later heartbreak.

Unbroken by her mother's words or by a reality of which she was fully aware, Naina lowered her gaze to avoid a further dose of wisdom. She snatched and heaved the bucket of laundry, retreating upwards towards the rooftop veranda to begin her day's work. Shaking out each garment before hanging it over the rusty metal line, Naina breathed deeply, taking advantage of the early morning breeze, not yet tainted by a nation of over a billion. One by one, she staggered the articles of clothing, some over the line, and others over the rungs of a weather-beaten bamboo ladder. She reserved the cotton panties and brassieres to be hung over an old plastic chair beneath the veranda's crumbling concrete wall, out of view from prying eyes. While she worked, she was comforted by the tranquility offered by the rooftop. It was a place of solace, a place to contemplate and dream. For the time being, for Naina, it was a place of refuge and escape.

Tranquility would remain for a few hours yet before Memsaab's eldest son, Vicky Gill, would arrive to unlock the doors to his stitching factory on the ground floor, below the third floor flat where Naina's family lived. The quiet of the rooftop would soon be broken with the buzzing commotion from the factory. The hum of Singer sewing machines and the clanking of shears would endure until late evening while the small flock of labourers clipped and stitched patches of coloured leather into sports balls and equipment for foreign markets. It was Rakesh Uncle who, six years ago, had introduced Naina's newly widowed mother to Vicky Gill. Rakesh, a solitary man who had never wed, was Naina's mother's eldest brother. He was initially employed by Vicky as a deliveryman, and had over the years become a permanent fixture in the factory as a trusted production manager and live-in watchman. Rakesh provided Vicky and his family a sense of security and peace of mind, and in exchange, Rakesh was both housed and fed. When Rakesh brought his widowed sister to the factory and told Vicky about the loss of her husband, Vicky hired Naina's mother without hesitation and her family was invited to live alongside Rakesh on the third floor, atop the factory. At the time, demand was high for sports products and Vicky required earnest workers. Naina's mother was a hard worker. Never did she complain about the heat when the fans were shut off to reserve power for the generator when the electricity went out daily during the summer months. Nor did she idle very long during tea breaks like some of the other workers who often lingered to gossip before being directed back to their sewing machines by Rakesh. Before long, Naina's mother had earned Vicky's respect and trust so much so that she was assigned the duty of serving Vicky's growing family, particularly Vicky's mother, Memsaab, in the Gill home. The factory, situated at the foot of a residential colony, was a short distance from the Gill residence to which Naina's mother walked each early morning. After some time, she took Naina along with her, partly to lessen Asha's burden of watching over two younger siblings, but also to ensure that her younger dreamy daughter remained grounded. Although the circumstances behind their move to live in the factory were tragic, the amenities and safety of the colony and Rakesh Uncle's companionship were a timely blessing.

While the factory remained closed, the rooftop was a retreat of sorts for those like Naina who typically knew not of such constructs. While she had the opportunity to dawdle, she glanced about from beneath the gauzy dupatta shawl that partially draped her brow line. By habit, she shielded her face from the rising sun to prevent further darkening of her skin. Her eyes searched the rooftop beyond her own for a familiar gaze. Her hopes were deflated when no one could be seen. Having completed her chore, she lingered for a few minutes more, leaning over the veranda wall, twirling wispy strands of stray hair between her fingers, savouring these rare moments of solitude. Ensuring that there was no one about, Naina slipped her hand in an old rusty trunk which stood in a corner on the rooftop. The trunk was packed with remnants of cloth that were used as rags and worn or broken odds and ends that had not yet found their way into the rubbish. Poking through a familiar path, her fingers reached between the folds of a faded blue towel, frayed and torn throughout. Discreetly, she extracted a leather-bound book and pen from the trunk. Nestling herself atop a mound of discarded garments, Naina leaned back against the veranda's wall and began to write in her secret diary.

⟞⟜ ⟝⟞

Dear Diary:

I'm going to find my own life someday. That's when I'll choose for myself what to do and when to do it. It doesn't bother me when Mummy yells. I know she means well, though she doesn't smile much anymore. And she doesn't like it when we look too happy either, especially in front of others, to avoid the evil eye. I don't really believe in that stuff. It's just easier to do what I'm told rather than upset her. But sometimes she can be confusing. She warns me to pay attention at school so that I can become bigger than she did, yet still scolds me for talking too smart-smart.

I do pay attention at school. I like going to school, mainly to see my friends. Isha and Sonal are my best friends and are in all my classes. We have great fun together but are careful to hold back on our git-mit when our Madams are teaching to avoid being seated apart from one another. Tina Madam is my favourite teacher. I think she's smarter and prettier than the other teachers but she doesn't act too proud. Her hair has shades of both brown and black, like the celebrities in Stardust magazine, and is cut in a steps style just below her shoulders. Every colour she wears seems to suit her creamy-creamy complexion. Isha says it's too bad Tina Madam has that dark mole above her upper lip, not so much because it looks bad, but because it earned her the nickname that some of the girls secretly call her by. Girls like Primal can really be mean. It was stupid Primal 'Potty Pants' who started it one morning with the back row of girls she sat with who started to squirm and scream when a black spider crawled onto one of their desks. Someone blew the spider off the desk and as all eyes searched to see where it had landed, the back-row girls burst into laughter when Primal

mocked under her breath that it had affixed itself to
Tina Madam's face. Of course, it really hadn't. She
was making fun of Tina Madam's mole. Nevertheless,
at that moment, *Spiderwoman* was born. Though Tina
Madam didn't hear her newly baptised name, she
switched P.P.'s seat from the back row to the centre position of the front row, right in front of our seats. Seated
amongst us, Primal became a sulky sourpuss but didn't
let out another peep. Since it was Tina Madam who
had sent Primal home after the Potty Incident, we figured that it must have been a smart move on her part
having P.P. sit in front of us. Since her relocation, our
class has become pretty calm. Potty Pants rarely turns
to face her friends in the back, maybe to avoid looking
in my direction. To be honest, I've always been nervous around those mean girls, especially Primal, so I'm
hoping they won't mess with me anymore.

I want to be like that one day, just like Tina
Madam. She's kind of different from the other
Madams. She's one of the only teachers who never
lays a finger on naughty students yet still has the
most control over them. I suppose she kind of does
have superpowers. Isha says that maybe Potty Pants
named Tina Madam correctly as a superhero. I
hope to have some superpowers of my own someday
so that I can be as strong as Tina Madam whenever
times are tough during my own life.
Naina

—⟩+ +⟨—

Having replaced the diary into the trunk, from her perch above, Naina watched the milk-boy ride by on his Hero Honda motorcycle, his metal milk canisters barely missing a stray dog absorbed in devouring a small casualty strewn on the street below. From a distance, from opposite ends of the colony, loudspeakers echoed the ritual morning prayers, both in Punjabi and in Hindi, as if in melodious harmony, sadly unachievable amongst some of their respective worshipers. In the neighbouring courtyard below, Naina watched in delight as Ramu meticulously stirred a savoury liquid concoction within a clay pot that partially concealed his pot belly. Ramu carefully added spices, a pinch at a time, with his stained, callused fingers. The aroma of ground cumin, coriander, tamarind and black salt powder drifted upwards, teasing Naina's taste buds with the pani-puri he would sell later that day in the main bazaar, bustling with people and traffic. Perhaps this evening she would have a chance to relish in some of Ramu's delights if she were asked to accompany Memsaab's daughter-in-law to the market. Lost in thought, with her elbow resting on the veranda wall, Naina resisted the impulse to scream out as a small pebble shot past her. *Was it him?* Now standing alert, her eyes again searched the rooftop facing her own.

"Nainaaa, hurry up child, you'll be late for Memsaab!" her mother shouted from the ground floor, as if sensing the sudden incident that had diverted her daughter's attention.

"I'm coming Mummy!" Naina retorted, reluctantly severing her gaze from the familiar handsome eyes that had just met hers from a distance.

Naina's body tensed up with the realization that the boy had caught sight of her. Even more disconcerting was the fact that this time, *he* had caught sight of *her* eyes searching for *his*. Impulsively, she turned her back towards him, positioning herself to descend the stairs. If only there was time to build up the courage to face him. She had wanted to for some days. Had she the courage, she would have looked straight into the boy's eyes, just as her favourite heroine Priyanka Chopra had done with her on-screen hero in the film Naina had recently seen with Memsaab's daughters-in-law in Friend's Cinema. Although Naina was taken to the film to mind the children, her attention was consumed by the romance flourishing on the screen. And now, while she may have dreamt of such a moment, never had she thought it would ever happen to her.

Today, however, Naina was forced to turn away, both to appease her mother's growing impatience and to settle the sudden fluttering in her stomach. Still, despite the distance between herself and the boy, Naina's heart could sense more than her eyes dared to confirm. Despite the severed gaze, she could sense a mischievous smile taking shape over his lips. With her back positioned towards him, her lips too curled upward, radiating warmth within her entire body. *What was he thinking?* Naina wondered. *Might he really like me? Could such a dream of being with a handsome boy really come true?*

"Naina, by God, if I have to listen to another complaint from Memsaab about your tardiness . . ." her mother hollered with growing restlessness.

Naina would have to go. She sighed, breathing heavily to keep pace with her racing heart. Before darting down the concrete steps, she could not resist the urge to catch one last glimpse. Success! The boy seemed to know that she would turn to face him, for when she did, their eyes locked, if only for a few seconds. For this, he rewarded her bravado with a playful wink just before Naina bolted down the stairs. This would surely carry her throughout the day, whatever it might bring.

". . . and don't run off without putting some food in your stomach, young lady! God knows you'll need the fuel to keep going for that old woman!" her mother continued even before Naina made it down to the last step, her voice now filled with more concern than annoyance.

"Okay, okay Mummy," Naina reassured from within the bathroom, recognizing the compassion in her mother's words.

She quickly lathered up using the squishy remnants of the Lifebuoy bar of soap, splashing herself with a few mugs of water. Despite the steady murmurs of her mother's chiding, Naina's dimples elevated her blushing cheekbones. Neither cold water nor a disfavored deep brown complexion would easily suppress her current state of exuberance. In her young heart, she carried a sense of hope, a dream, to love and to be loved.

━┽┾━

Dear Diary:

His name is Sanjay. I want to think he likes me. I've never spoken to him though, so I'm not sure. But why else would he come up to the rooftop so early in the morning? Not to do any chores like me,

that's for sure. I don't think he's the type of boy who has ever been given a chore in his life! In fact, I have never seen any of the kids who live in this colony do any work. Why would they when they have people like us to do it for them? At first, I didn't dare look up at him. Then one day he started playing music from his cell phone. When I glanced up towards the sound, I saw that he was staring right at me. It made me feel nervous and excited, all at once. I think I kind of froze and could feel my face get all hot. At that very instant, Asha appeared out of nowhere, and at the same time, Sanjay slipped away, casually running his fingers through his hair. I couldn't stop my eyes from following him until he was gone. Asha gave my arm a sharp pinch. She told me not to be so stupid. That Sanjay was well past my reach and that he was only out for a bargain. She sneered towards him as he vanished. I don't know what her problem is. She is my sister, so I don't hate her or anything. Maybe it's dumb for me to hope to be with someone like Sanjay, but I just wish that I had a chance to meet him. Wish I knew if he really likes me.
Naina

⇌ ⇋

Cool marble met her arrival upon entering Memsaab Prakash Gill's home where Naina slipped off the worn-out flip-flops that matched the condition of her feet. A sense of serenity still lingered throughout the home. A flurry of cockroaches inhabiting the dark stone counter and floor quickly sought refuge as Naina set foot in the kitchen. Without pause or reflection she settled into her daily routine.

The mountainous pile of dishes stacked in the sink usually garnered her attention first. However, in a household still not fully awake on an early Sunday morning, it was also the riskiest of chores. Strategically, Naina selected and gently pulled out one item at a time, every selection threatening to topple the teetering tower of dishes. Intertwined white plastic crockery, chinaware cups and saucers, and an assortment of stainless steel bowls, cups, plates, and utensils, all glistened with the turmeric based lamb curry and sticky, sweet syrup from the gulab jamun that she had served the family the previous evening. Though she had emptied the sink before leaving on Saturday evening, just as she did every evening, a large household assured her that she would be greeted to a full sink the next day. Naina maneuvered her grip carefully, expertly, without hesitation. She had mastered such tasks since the age of seven while working alongside her mother in Memsaab's stately home centrally located within the gated community of Rosewater Colony.

While consumed in work, Naina had the opportunity to let her mind run free. As she washed away the sloppy remains, thoughts of 'Jenga' ran through her mind. She was reminded of the game that Sonia, Memsaab's Canadian granddaughter, who was visiting one summer, had said that Naina would easily grasp.

"You'd be a master at 'Jenga', Naina! I can't believe how you maneuver through that pile of dishes without making them all come crashing down!" Sonia had praised.

"Oh, it's not that difficult when you do it all day," Naina had replied with a shy smile.

"My mom says that my head must be in the clouds when I do the dishes at home. She says that the whole house could be washed with the amount of water I use up," Sonia admitted with a frown.

"*You* do housework?" Naina asked with a look of surprise.

"Yeah, we all do. I mean, someone has to do it," Sonia explained. "Dad cleans the bathrooms and vacuums, Mom takes care of the dusting and laundry and I usually get stuck with the dishes. But only when I don't have a tonne of homework."

Naina very much admired Sonia for her grace and charm. What especially intrigued her was how simple and unpretentious Sonia seemed. Unlike other members of Memsaab's family who were curt in most conversational exchanges with Naina, Sonia would take the time to share and listen. The girls were roughly the same age. Sonia took a true interest in asking Naina about everyday things and happenings while also sharing aspects about her own life. She shared stories about her life in Canada, about her friends, school and home. Sonia talked about her love of books and her dream to be a writer, though her parents were expecting that she would pursue a career in medicine.

"I really don't want to be a doctor," Sonia had shared. "My parents just don't get it, that I can't even stand the sight of blood," she added, to which the girls laughed.

"What about you, Naina, what do you want to be later in life?"

Naina paused and looked intently toward Sonia. Never had she been asked such a question. She was both struck and pleased with the thought that Sonia believed that she, Naina, would decide and control her own destiny. *What will*

I be? Naina ruminated, pleased by the thought. Though only a matter of moments transpired before Naina spoke, she felt herself reply with a newfound inspiration.

"I want to be someone important . . . someone big," Naina confided, for the first time to anyone, even herself. "I want to be happy," she added softly, with a broad smile.

"Me too!" Sonia declared in agreement.

While others napped in the afternoon, Sonia would continue to mill about in the kitchen or on the rooftop with Naina as she completed her chores. "Shall I make you some cold lemonade?" Naina would offer.

"Sure, great idea!" Sonia would say with great delight, and the two would exchange laughs over simple talk as girls could easily do.

Over the years, during each of her visits to India, Sonia had presented Naina with a gift from Canada. Naina had cherished each one, not for its material value, but in the realization that Sonia, an unrelated, privileged young woman from some place foreign, had valued and believed in her. Her most cherished gift from Sonia was a leather-bound journal.

"For you Naina, when I'm not here and you have secrets to share," Sonia explained when she presented the book to her. "It's called a diary. I have one too that I write in almost every day when I get a chance. Just be sure to hide it somewhere safe," she winked.

Since receiving the diary, and concealing it in the old rusty trunk on the factory's rooftop, Naina had used it to put her thoughts, dreams and hopes to words that she could not share with others. The memory brought a smile to Naina's face as she worked. It was not often that she was paid a compliment or was appreciated by anyone outside her own family.

Naina's thoughts were quickly interrupted when Memsaab made her first appearance for the morning, strolling into the kitchen with an empty cup and saucer in hand. Her contact with Naina, as with the other women of the household, was rather mechanical. Having shared in the woman's company for much of her young life, Naina had always regarded Memsaab as somewhat stern, always possessing a steely edge. Despite the obvious luxuries available to her, it seemed that life had somehow hardened the old woman. Any rare smile that she imparted was usually reserved for her grandchildren. Perhaps Memsaab was not much different from her own mother, Naina mused.

"Naina, use the bigger cooker to fit in a few extra potatoes today," Memsaab began, without greeting. "There will be extra mouths to feed for breakfast. And as soon as you finish up in here, I've left the bucket of laundry for you in the lobby. The girls have also left their buckets upstairs. Be sure to hang them quickly before the rain," Memsaab casually instructed, depositing the dirty cup and saucer on the counter as she left.

Memsaab was usually the first to rise each morning. She had usually bathed and had already washed both her and her husband's clothes by hand by the time Naina arrived each day. "These girls today" – meaning both her daughters-in law and the help – "have little sense in how to clean the stains from clothing without fraying and tearing them to bits in that washing machine . . . better to do it myself," Memsaab would complain to Naina.

The grey-haired woman prided herself in no longer having to be familiar with all things associated with the kitchen since she had arranged the marriages of both of her sons. Naina had heard Memsaab declare that all domestic matters were now the concerns of her daughters-in-law, implying that she was above such menial chores. While lounging on her bed, Memsaab would claim ignorance when visiting Aunties would enquire about lunch menus. Naina had heard the woman telling guests that she hadn't laid a foot in the kitchen for years now, leaving such details to those who now possessed such responsibilities. Nevertheless, preparing her husband's early morning chai was not a duty that Memsaab could easily relinquish. Grudgingly, it was a task that only *she* was obliged to execute; a stubborn demand, it appeared to Naina, from the man Memsaab had wed some forty years ago.

Her focus unwavering, Naina continued with the immediate task of washing dishes, acknowledging Memsaab's instructions respectfully with a, "Very well, Memsaab Ji."

"Be sure to hold your tongue young lady; only speak when you are questioned. These bigger people don't have an interest in our little people's chit-chat," Naina recalled her mother counselling her from a young age. She was taught to always address her elders, particularly the '*bigger people*', with the respectful title of 'Ji'. *"Never respond with a solitary 'yes' or 'no',"* her mother would say. *"Always use 'Memsaab Ji' as respectful acknowledgement of Prakash Gill."* 'Memsaab' was a formal title for women such as Prakash Gill who were in a position of authority, and 'Ji' was tacked on as an added measure of deference.

As the household began to stir, Naina remained consumed in her work. Her jet-black locks, pulled back neatly in a waist long braid, glistened from the rays of faint light that fought to penetrate through barsati storm clouds. The light beamed through the kitchen window, illuminating both her coconut oil infused hair and the perspiration already beading on her forehead. Her long-lashed mahogany eyes sparkled and her dark caramel skin glowed, highlighting the chiseled features of her oval face. With her petite frame, Naina tiptoed before the emptied sink, her slender fingers scrubbing away the grease with a sense of confidence that she, otherwise, at times seemed to lack in herself.

From the front gate came the jarring blare of the door buzzer. Naina quickly dried her wet hands against her kameez and dashed out towards the front entrance. Several callers were received throughout the day. Some came to make deliveries such as the milk boy who would fill household steel pots and pitchers provided by residents with frothy milk from tall metal canisters. Others, such as the dhobi man, came to collect garments to be ironed which would be bundled and tied within a dupatta that had been cast away from the wardrobe of one of the women in the household. In this case, however, the face awaiting entry behind the gate was Rahul's. The two greeted one another with a smile. Rahul tipped the messenger hat he wore at Naina and a sense of ease between them meant that no words were necessary. With a nod, Naina directed Rahul to follow her through the courtyard.

With her hand, Naina motioned towards a rattan chair, signalling Rahul to be seated outside the main door. "'I'll be back," she said, though the daily ritual was a familiar one.

Rahul was grateful to rest for a few minutes under the shade of a tall ornamental tree. The tree's branches, heavy with a plethora of pink blooms, diminished the pungency of perspiration that had bled through the underarms of his half-sleeve shirt. As he did each morning, Rahul had come to pick up a thermos of hot spiced chai and biscuits for Vicky Gill. While Naina prepared and parceled the items, he dabbed his face and neck with a cotton handkerchief and ran a small comb through his hair. He quickly returned the comb to the pocket of his shirt as the door to the front entry of the home swung open. Rahul respectfully averted his eyes, avoiding a direct gaze towards Naina as she approached him with a tray in hand.

"I hope it's not too sweet," Naina said playfully as she presented a cup of tea to Rahul, accompanied by a saucer containing a few biscuits.

"Nothing short of perfect every time," Rahul assured her with a beaming smile, after taking a quick sip to validate his point.

Appreciation of the remark was evident in the softness expressed through Naina's eyes. It was always a pleasure to spend a few moments with Rahul. He had been a part of her life since she was a little girl. His presence had always made her feel at ease. They had shared common struggles in life. There was nothing to hide from him. Naina could be herself around Rahul for she knew that he knew all about her, and where she was from. She headed back inside to retrieve the parcel for Vicky. From the periphery of his gaze, Rahul's eyes followed Naina with fondness.

Having lost his own parents at a very young age, he had had great respect for Naina's father, an admiration for a man who very much reminded him of what his own father must have been like, based on his grandmother's stories. Having felt and shared in Naina's grief when her father was no more, Rahul felt a new yearning in his heart for her as she had blossomed into a sweet young woman over the years. How he would ever share these sentiments, he hadn't the nerve to do so thus far. Even if he could muster up the courage to approach Naina with his feelings, what did he have to offer? He was merely a gofer of sorts, running around from here to there to serve others. He would need to make something of himself, become someone before he could ever expect to be seen with respect, Rahul thought, just as Naina returned. Upon finishing his tea and biscuits, Rahul accepted the parcel from Naina. He replaced his hat on his head and the two strolled towards the front gate.

"How are Aunty and the family?" Rahul enquired.

"Just fine," Naina replied, turning her eyes to the ground as she slowly opened the gate for Rahul. His sincerity always made her emotional.

"Glad to hear it. My grandmother always says time heals all. And since I've survived her rolling pins and broom handles over the years, she must be right," Rahul added to end his brief visit with a laugh, as he always did.

Though she smiled, Naina's eyes moistened. There was something very different and quaint about Rahul, something very special about him and how he made her feel. Not quite able to understand, what she did feel for certain was a sense of absence whenever he left. Though she spoke no words in response as Rahul mounted his bicycle with the parcel clutched in his left hand, the sparkle in her eyes expressed the gratitude she felt for Rahul in her heart. How could she not? Were it not for Rahul, who had recounted the details to Naina and her family, they would never have known what had happened to her father.

━━◆ ◆━━

At the time of the fateful event, Rahul was a young sweeper boy. He had worked alongside Naina's father who had been murdered for letting his shadow fall over the owner of the factory. The inebriated owner, who was seated in an open courtyard that day, had shouted at Naina's father to bring him a glass of water. In his drunken stupor, when the glass of water was presented to the haughty man under the midday sun, he became livid and beat Naina's father to death because the lower caste labourer had unknowingly cast his shadow over the higher-class proprietor. *"How dare you taint me with your misfortune!"* the owner had scoffed, unperturbed as the brown earth surrounding him turned crimson with the labourer's blood as the poor man was pounded to the ground, while the sun beat over his corpse.

With a money-lined handshake, as Naina's mother had described it, the *mishap* was written off by the police as an *accident* despite the many eyes that must have witnessed the atrocity. Had Rahul not whispered the details of what he had seen to Naina's family after the incident, they would have never known the truth behind her father's misfortune.

"That wicked bastard has taken everything from me and my children," Naina's mother had wailed, cradling her head in her shaking hands. "You must help me child, you must come with me to the police and tell them what really happened," she begged Rahul in desperation.

With his head lowered to hide the emotions on his face, Rahul murmured, "I can't tell them again, Aunty. I already tried. They didn't listen. They said I must be *confused*. One of them shoved me and told me to go home," he explained with a trembling voice between gasps.

Though Naina's mother had pleaded with Rahul to accompany her to the police station to file a formal complaint, it was to no avail. The frightened boy swore that he would disappear should he be sequestered by the police, fearful of the type of interrogation which would ensue to clear his *confusion*. His reddened eyes, swollen from the tears he wept, told of the remorse in his heart for the dead man who had helped him attain the job that had assisted in feeding his own needy family. Though Rahul had confided in Naina's family about what he had seen, for his lack of courage in pursuing a further attempt to file a formal eyewitness account with the police, he had asked for their forgiveness.

Her face filled with sadness, Naina's mother had bent close to Rahul and whispered what they both already knew. "You are right, my child," she had acknowledged with a heavy heart, "you are right," she had repeated, her eyes pooled with tears. Fearing that Rahul might be endangered by remaining at the mercy of a man who did not hesitate in taking a life, Naina's mother ensured that Rahul was also brought to work for Vicky Gill.

"Why are you giving up Mummy? How can you let that man get away with it? He killed Papa! Don't you care?"

Asha had lashed out once Rahul had left, Naina in tears by her side.

With that, Naina was stunned as she watched her mother's palm meet Asha's right cheek with an unexpected force. The reaction on her mother's face was one of bewilderment, as if she were disassociated from the action her body, her right hand, had taken against her daughter. This was one of the very hands that had massaged their legs when they cried at night from growing pains. It was one of the same hands that had served them food when there was not enough for Naina's mother. This was one of the very hands which had held them tight as no one else could, the very hand Naina had seen Papa so often take into his own, to assure Mummy that things would be alright. Now, Naina watched as her mother's hands shook, as she stood before her daughters in shock. The commotion had at some point awakened Shaan whose soft cries could be heard in the adjacent room where he had been napping. Speechless, Naina's mother took Asha into her arms and held her close. Asha, also still in shock, let herself be held, sniffling soft sounds of hurt. Still by her sister's side, Naina clung onto Asha's kameez, burying her head into the hollow of her sister's back, shaken by it all.

"You must try to understand, there is much that is beyond our control," Naina's mother tried to explain. "Of course, I care. I am as angry as you, and if there was a way, I would kill that monster myself," she had admitted with determination in her eyes. "But that isn't how things work in this world, my child. It's because I care that I have to contain my anger so that I can remain by your side."

"But there were others by Papa's side. Why won't they go with Rahul and tell the police what really happened? Why Mummy? Why?" Naina cried out through tears.

"Because they are scared. Because there is no one to protect them. They won't help because they can't without harming themselves," Naina's mother admitted.

To her children, in the best way she could, Naina's mother had explained that, "*it was understood that people without means had to learn to be blind to survive; blind to feelings, blind to sufferings, and even blind to injustice. Clear sight was reserved for those who could afford to see*," she had especially advised her youngest daughter whose very name worried the widow. 'Naina' – one with clear vision. It was Naina's father's wish to name their youngest daughter 'Naina', hoping that his daughter would forever see goodness. It was now her mother's task to teach her children, and particularly her little girl, when to be blind.

⚓

The cooling effect of the night gone by would linger no more as the intensity of the heat enveloped all within its breadth under a heavy cloak of humidity. The dampness seemed to seep into everything, leaving both the living and nonliving virtually limp. It permeated the packets of sweet and savory biscuits from Lovely Sweets Bakery that Naina had often served the Gill family, robbing them of the crispy strength necessary for withstanding the ritual of tea dunking. It saturated the linens and garments that she folded and stored in the tall gunmetal *Godrej* wardrobes positioned in each bedroom of the home. The humidity also infused the bound stacks of rupees deposited within the wardrobe safe in Memsaab's bedroom, rupees that Naina had many times been presented when asked to run an errand. The humidity even softened the almonds which Naina had occasionally seen Memsaab offer to her grandchildren, clandestinely removing a few nuts from a silk satchel, also tucked away in the wardrobe. Though Memsaab's granddaughter would often give Naina a few nuts from the palm of her hand, in such moments, Naina had learned to look away, not wanting her eyes to impart a sense of longing for that which this present life would not afford her.

Working through a succession of chores, from the rooftop veranda, Naina hung her second, third and fourth bucket of laundry for that morning. By midday, the heat was relentless. The earlier mass of cloud cover had dissipated under the sun's rays that now pulsated down on those who dared to step out from the refuge of shaded interiors. Luckily, she could complete the hanging quickly, having several years of practice. Attentively, she selected the position of each garment according to the familial hierarchy, averting any suggestion of challenge to the matriarch. In accordance, Naina reserved the newest nylon clothesline for Memsaab and her husband's clothing, below the sun sheltered awning and furthest from the veranda's wall.

One by one, the buckets emptied. As usual, Naina hung the unmentionables last. One such item, a pastel coloured *cushioned brassiere,* truly confused Naina when she came upon it for the first time within Rani's bucket of laundry last summer. Rani was Memsaab's eldest and better looking daughter-in-law in Naina's opinion. Never had Naina seen a bra like *that* before. Although naïve, she was sensible

enough to withhold her curiosity about the unusual garment until she got home, for her older sister Asha to sort
out.

"It's called a 'padded bra' stupid! – to make her 'BBC News'
hotter!" Asha had jeered.

When the look of puzzlement lingered on Naina's face,
Asha had offered, *"For her BOOBS, dimwit! To make them a*
hotter broadcast than they are!"

"But why would Rani need such thick padding for extra heat in
the middle of August?" Naina had persisted.

"You're such a dumb duffer sometimes, Naina!" Asha had
continued to mock. *"Do you think your prissy Memsaab,*
Prakash Gill, would have brought Rani home to her eldest son
Vicky as a wife had she known what a 'flato' Rani was?! Rani
has to entice her privileged husband with at least the illusion of
juicy-juicy mangoes over her teeny-tiny God-given boobies," Asha
had smirked.

But, didn't Vicky notice the size of Rani's shrinking breasts when
they met under the covers at night? Did she not remove her pad-
ding when she went to bed? Perhaps Vicky didn't notice in the dark.
Maybe his wife kept the bra on. Now that she thought about
it, Naina recalled that Rani would often still be sporting a
plumped-up bust line even in her sleeping clothes when she
saw Rani in the early morning. Possibilities still sprouting
in her head, Naina dared not question her sister further.
Still, Asha's insight and Rani's transforming bosom stirred
Naina's fascination with the scope of facilities *bigger people*
could draw upon.

Lost in thought, Naina was momentarily caught off
guard by the clip-clopping sound of heeled slippers making
their way up the marble staircase. A well-groomed young

woman wearing a long flowy pink skirt appeared before her. With a quick gesture of a nod, meant more as instruction rather than greeting, the woman, revealing bare white ankles, directed Naina to, "Tell Rani Didi I've arrived." She had addressed Rani with the title of *Didi*, meaning 'older sister' as a customary sign of respect even though the women did not share a blood relation.

"Come on in Pooja," Rani called from her bedroom suite, already anticipating the arrival of her threading girl.

"Naina . . ." Rani continued, but did not need to complete her instruction.

Naina had already acknowledged with, "Of course, I'll be right back," knowing clearly what was being requested. She dashed towards the kitchen, returning with a tray. Naina presented each woman with a stainless-steel cup of sweet red sharbat, a drink of concentrated rosewater-flavoured syrup dissolved in icy water. She often served the Gill family a similar version of the drink mixed with chilled full-fat cow's milk on summer nights.

"No, no, Didi, no need," Pooja gestured dramatically, by way of suitable social convention.

"Please, please, I insist," Rani encouraged with the traditional gracious response, with equal dramatic gusto, as Naina remained standing between the women holding the beverages.

Having served the women, Naina stood by the door with the empty tray in hand, watching as the cups dripped beads of cold sweat from their shiny surfaces onto the marble floor. In her heart, she felt a pang of envy watching as the women partially consumed their drinks, thinking how nothing would go wasted in her own household.

As if reading Naina's mind, Rani offered, "Take the cups down to the kitchen and make some for yourself, Naina." Naina couldn't help notice that as she spoke, Rani glanced first towards Pooja, and then towards her with a contrived smile.

"You've let some time pass since our last visit," Pooja chit-chatted as she started to weave and twirl the thread around her fingers to receive the stray and unwanted strands of hair around Rani's eyebrows.

Naina had slipped back to the room in a quiet manner. From a distance, she watched and listened discreetly with interest.

"What to do with so many duties and a demanding mother-in-law?" Rani both joked and vented.

Both women chuckled as Pooja guided Rani's fingers to stretch out the skin above and below her brow line. Pooja was no ordinary esthetician. She owned the ritziest Ladies' Beauty Salon in the colony and provided an in-home service to her more affluent, willing-to-pay clients.

"Pass me the baby powder by the red bag," Pooja indicated with her eyes to Naina.

Completing Rani's eyebrows with a final snip-snip using tiny scissors, Pooja made the subtle inquiry, "Didi, have you been in the sun?"

"By God, running after these children all day," Rani began, but Pooja interjected.

"No need to worry, I can fix that," she assured. "Would you like me to do the facial? It will bring back your fair glow. You wouldn't want that *darkness* to settle in," she added, furrowing her brow.

"Yes, yes, of course, go ahead, Pooja," Rani acquiesced, as her cheeks turned pink with embarrassment.

Naina was chagrined to have witnessed this exchange between Pooja and Rani. She squatted invisibly along the far wall of the room peering gloomily at her own sun baked complexion reflected from the back side of the stainless-steel tray which lay atop her knees. Still focused on the women, she was mesmerized by Pooja's fingers scrolling over Rani's face, massaging in the magical *Fair and Lovely*. She had seen the lotion advertised numerous times over the various televisions throughout Memsaab's house. She wondered if it would work on her own skin as well. Could it possibly rescript her destiny as the ads promised? Amazed by the thought of the possible transformation, Naina was again struck by the facilities afforded to the *bigger people*. This could make her look more like her Bollywood starlets. Then for certain there would be no need to search for her prince; instead, he would seek her. Naina felt a thrill of excitement radiate through her. The thought of Sanjay, the boy with the handsome eyes, being drawn to her brighter and lighter complexion filled her with extraordinary glee. She twirled a strand of hair that had come loose from her braid contemplatively. Perhaps she would ask Asha about the lotion later that night.

Meanwhile, Pooja's delicate fingers continued to swirl over Rani's face. Naina admired Pooja's fingernails, co-loured in a brilliant coral, which were painted the same colour as her exposed toes. The young woman carried her-self with a confidence rivaled by no other, one that Naina wished to possess one day herself. Naina's focus then shift-ed from Rani's face to her elevated bosom as she leaned back in the chair before Pooja. The lacy border of a lilac brassiere spilled out from beneath Rani's blouse. Judging by the visible cleavage, it must have been a padded bra that Rani was wearing. As she continued to gaze in awe, Naina couldn't help but wonder if Rani's *BBC News* were at least fair, if not juicy – that, however, she would not dare ask Asha.

—≈+ +≈—

Dear Diary:

Asha acts as though she knows everything, or at least way more than me. She doesn't though, and I've told her so. Well, maybe she does, sometimes, about certain things and certain people. Like Sanjay. Some days ago, as I was walking home in the evening from Memsaab's, he was standing by the vacant lot beside our factory. He signaled towards me as I approached. Something about a puppy he had found behind the bushes. I told him that I had to get home, but he said that the pup was so cute, that it would only take a minute. More so than the puppy, I couldn't resist Sanjay's smile and had just started to follow him when Asha screamed out my name from the rooftop, yelling at me to get inside. I was so embarrassed that I charged at her when I got in. She seemed angrier with Sanjay than with me. She warned me to stay away from him. She said that he only wants to use me! Said she would kill him if he ever tried to show me anything again.

I saw Sanjay again in the bazaar yesterday evening. I was out with Rani. Memsaab had asked me to accompany her daughter-in-law to the market. Vicky had sent Rahul with a car from the factory to take us. When Rahul rang the door buzzer, Rani was still getting ready and told me to go wait in the car, that she would be a few minutes. A trip to the bazaar was never a casual outing for women like Rani who always aim to look their best. Outside the front gate, Rahul, sporting his messenger hat, greeted me with his usual smile and opened the back door of the car for me. No explanations were needed. He was accustomed to the ritual of waiting. *I* certainly didn't mind waiting. The air-conditioned car was a welcomed escape in comparison to the sweltering kitchen.

An old song from the eighties had started to play on the radio and Rahul tuned the dial to another station. I protested, told him to go back to the song. He did. He apologized, thinking that I wouldn't care for such old songs. I told him that they were special to me. They reminded me of the days when I was younger, when Papa used to play those old tunes on an old transistor radio he'd gotten from somewhere. The old tunes comfort me. Rahul said that he understood. He felt the same way. We sat in silence as Amitabh Bachchan sang to Rakhee, his secret love who was engaged to another, about the feelings he could never express to her in that old film song. To cut the sadness, I gave Rahul a mischievous smile as he peered at me through the rear-view mirror. He asked me what was so funny. I told him that he was crazy for wearing that hat in this heat. He laughed it off, saying that it added to his boyish charm. He winked and asked me if I agreed. Guess I was kind of sarcastic in my reply, but we shared a laugh. But then Rahul's tone became more serious. He told me that the hat wasn't so bad with the air conditioning, though he realized that he wasn't fooling anyone. Then he admitted that he wore the hat to hide his greying hair. Said he worries about what people will think of him, not even matured and already looking like an old man. Wow! I didn't think guys could also feel so insecure about their looks. I felt so horrible for the feelings I had struck in Rahul. I didn't realize that he had this insecurity. I tried to make him feel better. Told him that the flecks of silver in his hair made his complexion shine. I told him that he was special, one in a million, and that he really didn't need that hat. Rahul laughed. He said that maybe someday he would feel that way. Rahul is the last person I would ever want to hurt, so I was relieved when the smile returned to his face, just in time as Rani approached the car.

Rahul was a savvy driver and had no difficulty weaving through the early evening congestion of traffic and shoppers. Once we arrived in the main bazaar, he parked and remained with the car while I accompanied Rani through a few select shops. Rani wanted to buy some sketching pencils and clothes for the children and new lipstick for herself. While she tried on different shades of red, all of which the salesman claimed looked mind-blowing on her, I sat on a bench by the store's front window holding a bunch of shopping bags. I was simply passing the time, looking out into the evening crowd when my eyes found *him*. Sanjay was on his Bullet motorcycle, his hair spiky and shiny, dressed in skinny jeans and a yellow half sleeve t-shirt with an embroidered horse stitched over his heart. He pulled up to a food stall where a group of girls were gathered, eating dosas. They were dressed all fancy with perfectly straight hair, the kind that only high-fi girls could have with salon treatments in this humid weather. He parked real close to one girl who started to share what was on her plate with him, offering him bits of the potato stuffing from the same spoon she was using. I watched her pull the spoon from him a few times, teasingly. He then clasped her hand and guided the spoon slowly to his mouth. He stared into her eyes as he ate from the spoon, still holding onto her hand. He was kind of smiling but had a serious expression. They left together. The girl straddled herself behind him on the black leather seat. She pressed her chest against his back and gripped him tightly around his waist, not caring who was watching, just like in the movies. Have fun, Simi! That's what her friends yelled out, laughing and waving. Sanjay gave a quick wink to the high-fi girls who giggled in unison as the motorcycle sped off.

Rani had sent me with the bags to the car while she examined some final items and took care of the bill. The car was parked right outside the store. Rahul got out and took the bags from my hand, depositing them into the trunk of the car. I quickly wiped the tears from my eyes which had escaped despite my efforts to contain them. Why was I crying!?

I was being foolish. I hated Sanjay and I hated those stupid high-fi girls! Buried in my own misery, I hadn't noticed the look of concern in Rahul's eyes as he watched me crying in the back seat through the rear-view mirror. I felt embarrassed. Had he seen how I was slighted? How could he know? Even if he did know, it didn't matter, it was only Rahul. He didn't ask anything of me. I turned my head, trying hard to focus my thoughts elsewhere. He tuned the radio to a light-hearted song and began strumming his fingers over the wheel. He said that I might not feel this way right now, but that I was one in a million too. How did he know what I needed to hear? His words have always given me comfort. I tried to smile, but another stupid tear fell from my eye. Just at that moment, Rahul had to leave the car to open the door for Rani.

Initially, I didn't want to share any of this with Asha, to prove her right. She thinks she knows everything. But I couldn't help telling her what I had seen when she caught me crying later that night in bed. I told her how *big* those girls looked, like fashion models, and how good looking that one girl, *Simi,* was. I felt so stupid, thinking Sanjay liked me just because he made googly eyes at me on the rooftop. Guess it was pretty dumb of me, thinking that a rich boy like him would be serious about a girl like me. Asha said that Sanjay was a dog and found his dirty bone for the evening. Better toughen up, she said. There would be worse stuff in life to tackle than the likes of shitty Sanjay.

She told me to grow up and get over it. Under her breath, she also said to not be so hard on myself, that I wasn't so stupid. But if I'm not so stupid, why is my heart still breaking over him?
Naina

⟞⟝

Over the years, there was much to get over, much to get through and to get past. At every stage, life posed new challenges, presented the unexpected, but also contributed in diminishing the frailty which had defined Naina through youth. For every hurdle she faced, she felt herself stronger and more confident for having faced and tackled each obstacle. By her mother's insistence and her teacher's encouragement, Naina had continued with her studies. Tina Madam had often praised Naina on her progress and especially praised her for her beautiful handwriting. Having completed high school, Naina was filled with a yearning to learn and to fulfill her dreams, just as Sonia believed that she could. Naina had grown and began to see and know herself as she had not before. In the process, she found in herself a will to take command of her own destiny.

When the time came, Rakesh Uncle had gone to great efforts to find suitable life partners for his nieces. In a society fiercely patriarchal, without a father, young unwed women were easily taken advantage of or perceived as less than desirable for adoption into a respectable family as new brides. Yet Rakesh, a man whose honourable reputation often preceded him, arranged the marriages for both Asha and Naina, also promising to do the same for Shaan when he matured, overwhelming his sister with tremendous gratitude.

"I think the boy will keep our Asha happy," Rakesh Uncle explained to his younger sister as they completed their dinner one night. They were seated together on the brick floor, with Shaan by their side on a woven straw mat. Unlike the gas cooktop range used for cooking at Memsaab's home, it was a small clay tandoor, a cylindrical vessel fuelled by coal that serviced Naina's family during late night meals on the factory's rooftop. The coal snapped beneath the iron tava on which Asha cooked the rotis that she had formed in the shape of perfect round discs with an old rolling pin that their mother, many years ago, had been given in her trousseau.

Naina assisted Asha in serving the adults and her younger brother. The two sisters would eat together afterwards. She served the rotis, one by one, as they were made, some still puffed like balloons, slowly releasing hot steam from within as they were delivered. As they worked, the girls could hear the conversation taking place. In fact, it was understood that the words were meant to be heard. Naina could see that her mother was listening intently to Rakesh Uncle, not interrupting, allowing him the space in which to complete his thoughts.

"I've spoken to others and they speak well of the boy's parents. He's their only child. There was an older son, but he died some years earlier. Hit by the car of some big shot businessman," Rakesh Uncle continued with sadness in his voice upon sharing the last detail. He paused briefly between bites, taking the time to savour a few spoons of dahl, cradling the small steel bowl in his left palm. Asha had garnished the soupy yellow lentils with fried onions and coriander that grew abundantly in the vacant lot adjacent to the factory. Perceptively, Naina brought a serving bowl over to Rakesh Uncle and ladled some more dahl into both his and her mother's bowl. Shaan, Naina observed, was taking full advantage of the fact that his mother was preoccupied in a discussion, thus gave his comic book more attention than the food on his plate. The faded heroes, having once delighted Memsaab's grandchildren, provided Shaan a pleasurable form of escape from the serious chatter.

"Very tasty," Rakesh Uncle acknowledged. "You girls have added to my waistline, I'll need new pants soon!" he chuckled, both in appreciation and to break the noticeable tension that had taken over. Naina noticed that with Rakesh Uncle's joking, the ever-accumulating lines on her mother's forehead had softened and were less visible.

"He's already earning for his household," Rakesh continued. "One of the workers in our factory, Imran, his brother has worked with the boy. Says the boy is a respectable young man. I think our Asha will be comfortable with him. What do you think?"

With Rakesh Uncle's last remark, his grey eyes traveled towards the girls. Naina saw that he was looking to Asha for a sign of approval. Naina leaned into her sister, their arms touching one another. Naina knew that in this instance, Asha wouldn't push her away. There was a softness to her sister's expression, far from the customary hard edge Asha often displayed. Rakesh Uncle seemed to have such an effect on almost everyone. Naina peered up at her sister and saw that Asha was facing downward, a shy smile taking shape on her face. Both girls then looked toward their mother, their eyes glimmering with anticipation as they awaited her response.

"Varsha?" Rakesh Uncle lightly tapped his sister with his elbow when she did not respond. "Are you uncertain about this?"

Naina's mother lifted her head and looked up, not towards Rakesh Uncle, but to the sky. "My life has been filled with uncertainty, and if God hadn't given us your support, I don't know where we would be right now." Despite her efforts to conceal her tears, they were exposed under the light of the full moon. "It will take me many lifetimes to repay the burdens you have endured for me," she managed to say with a quiver in her voice.

"See children, what a clever woman my sister is, trying to avoid doing me any favours in this life with promises of future lifetimes instead!" Rakesh Uncle jested, quickly succeeding in lightening the mood and coaxing a laugh out of his sister as only he could do. Then, with a serious tone, he added, "You are the strongest woman I know, Varsha. That I know for certain."

Lumps of coal that continued to burn within the tandoor oven cast a soft orange glow across the rooftop veranda, beneath an endless pitch-black sky. Every now and then, bursts of light would flicker and crackle from within the clay vessel like tiny shooting stars, dazzling with their sight and sound, providing an inexplicable comfort, despite a lack of knowledge of what the future would bring.

>≕+ +≕<

And so, Asha was first to go. A mechanic, her new life partner was well-qualified and provided maintenance to many production houses, unfettered by a dependence on a single contract. The wedding was joyous, filled with offerings that were unexpected, and from unexpected sources. The ceremony was a simple one, held in the local temple and arranged by Memsaab who had also insisted on covering all expenses.

On a late Saturday afternoon, Memsaab had just woken from her afternoon nap. On cue, Naina had entered the kitchen to prepare afternoon tea when Memsaab's voice called for her.

"Naina, forget about the tea today. The girls are getting ready upstairs and I want you and Asha to accompany them to the market."

Memsaab was not one for small talk. If she had wanted to elaborate, she would have, but of course, she hardly ever did. And thus, Naina would, usually, simply follow instructions without question. In this instance, however, Naina, with a look of puzzlement, remained standing before Memsaab who was combing out her hair. *Asha?* Naina wondered. Her sister was at the factory, working. She wasn't here.

Noting the confusion on Naina's face, Memsaab continued, "Vicky has asked the driver to bring Asha here in the car from the factory. They'll be here shortly to take you girls to the bazaar . . . to shop for Asha's wedding."

"Shopping? . . . for Asha's wedding?" Naina stammered.

"Yes, of course for Asha. Do you have another sister who is getting married?" Memsaab mumbled with an arched brow as she took a bobby pin from her mouth, securing her hair into a tiny bun.

"Oh . . . Mummy had said that there would be plenty of time to do the shopping later," Naina explained. Of course, her mother had said no such thing, but the words had just rolled off Naina's tongue. There was as much of a convincing look to her expression as she could muster, never allowing her eyes to want for more. This is what her mother had always taught her.

"Your Mummy can shop as late as she pleases," Memsaab replied, craning her neck towards Naina. It was unlike the old woman to offer a direct link to her eyes. Upon noticing the look of demur in Naina's eyes, she added, "Your mother and I, we've both experienced much. We have fulfilled our respective duties, each in our respective roles. Varsha and your family, child, have been a part of us. Contributing to your sister's wedding is not an obligation, it is my moral duty." She paused briefly to apply a shade of burgundy to her lips, and then Memsaab's voice softened in her next remark. "For all that your mother has given, this is gratitude, not charity, Naina."

And so it was. Memsaab had asked her daughters-in-law to accompany Asha and Naina to the market to select and purchase the bridal clothing and artificial jewellery for Asha's wedding, also insisting to pay for the items. Though Memsaab had presented herself as possessing a heart of stone with an attitude of indifference towards Naina and her ilk through the years, the old woman had surprised Naina for the compassion she had displayed. Naina's mother, however, was not surprised by Memsaab's generosity. "No one person is simply all good or all bad," her mother had remarked. In her wisdom, she shared with Naina what life had taught her, that, "it was the conditions in life, the changing circumstances, that continually shape and mould us."

"I suppose you'll sleep in later in the mornings now that I won't be around to harass you to get up," Asha whispered jokingly into Naina's ear after the wedding ceremony, embracing her sister before departing with her husband.

Fighting back the tears threatening to plummet from her eyes, under her breath, Naina retorted, "And I suppose you won't be getting much sleep at all during the night!" Asha gave her sister a loving pinch to her cheek in response.

The sisters embraced tighter than they had ever before. Naina's eyes remained tied to Asha as she accompanied her new life partner into the back seat of an awaiting vehicle. Memsaab had arranged for Rahul to drive the newlyweds to the home of Asha's in-laws in a neighboring village. Before departing, as a sign of respect, Rahul lowered himself to touch both Memsaab's and Naina's mother's feet. He, too, was moving elsewhere. He was taking his ailing grandmother, the only mother he had ever known, closer to an elderly niece who would help the worn woman ease her way towards the end of her life. A cloud of dust rose as the car drove off, but did not diminish the radiance of the golden threads of Asha's maroon chiffon sari that glistened under the bright lights cascading the temple. Though her heart ached, Naina smiled at the sight.

⭑ ⭑

The path forward for Naina, by contrast, was not as simple. Two weeks into her engagement to a young taxi driver, who it was said was well on his way to establishing his own operation, it was discovered one night that the young man was servicing female clientele from the backseat of his Maruti cab. Not unexpected, it was Naina's reputation that was marred by the broken engagement instead of the boy's whose family hastily spread the rumour that it was not their son, but rather Naina who was found to be promiscuous, *'discovered before it was too late, thank God!'* the boy's mother had claimed.

While the gossip settled, Naina was made to wait in the quiet and seclusion of the third floor flat above the factory. No longer was she permitted to venture outdoors. Not to run an errand, not to have a laugh with one of her friends, not to the rooftop veranda that was in plain view of evil eyes, and not even to Memsaab's to work. Naina longed for the company of those who might assure her that all would be made right. She had been barred from visiting anyone. It seemed that all visits from anyone had also ceased. Naina longed for the normalcy that had been taken from her life. But none of it could be helped. Naina's mother was trying to protect her daughter. So fearful was her mother of the puss-puss whispers of shameless scavengers who she was certain were waiting to prey on her daughter whose heart, she felt, had not yet hardened enough to shield away such taunts.

"Mummy, it doesn't matter what people think. It's not what happened," Naina declared to her mother.

"I don't know what past sins I have committed to bring such injustice upon you, Naina," her mother whispered. "My whole life I have tried to keep you, my children, from harm. I tried so hard, Naina. I tried so hard, but failed," she spoke softly, her heart drowning in defeat.

Naina walked over to her mother who stood by the window, solemnly staring upwards to the night sky and placed a hand on her shoulder. "You have never failed us Mummy, not even in the toughest moments. Don't lose faith, we will be okay," Naina consoled, trying her best to use the wisdom she had incurred over the past twenty years of her life.

"How can you be so sure, my child?" her mother questioned, unable to meet her daughter's eyes. "That wretched boy and his mother; what lies they have spread. How will we ever . . . ?"

"Look," Naina interrupted, pointing to the shining stars before them, "Papa's up there, making sure we're safe. He always has, I'm sure of it Mummy."

"Then I suppose I must believe you, Nunu. I must try and see the good that your Papa always knew you would," said the widow, with a slight tremble in her voice, touched by her daughter's strength.

Her mother who had once been a tough bull, hard as nails, with all her might tried hard to conceal any visible anguish from her daughter. She placed her hand over Naina's and shut her eyes. By the light of the full moon, Naina could see the trace of a single tear trickle down her mother's cheek. Naina shot back a strong look of surety towards her mother. Words were needless as her eyes clearly conveyed, "We will be okay Mummy. We will be okay."

⊷⊱ ⊰⊶

Dear Diary:

The morning sun filtered through the haze, casting a soft glow in my room where I checked myself in the mirror. I was dressed in my silky pink salwar kameez, a former gift from Memsaab, almost two years ago, on Asha's wedding. It was an important day, the day of Papa's death anniversary, and I was ready to depart for the temple, even before Mummy. Shaan, on the other hand, was a different matter. I could hear Mummy shooing him into the bathroom insisting that he bathe, despite his usual lazy boy objections. Papa wouldn't care how I smell! I could hear him rant, just as the unmistakable sound of my mother's smack to his backside ended further argument. Didn't matter how old Shaan was, he would always be Mummy's little boy. We will always be her children. I'm happy that Mummy is as fierce and determined as ever. She even smiles more often. The thought brought a smile to my face. It was still early, and so I continued to adorn the stainless-steel plate of offerings with marigolds and jasmine.

Then the unexpected happened. The doorbell sounded from the ground floor and I could hear Mummy's flip flops headed towards the front room window to see who it could be. No one was expected. It was Sunday and the factory below was closed. From the back room, I asked Mummy who it was. Mummy didn't respond and my curiosity peaked by the sound of her hurried steps traveling down the concrete stairs. I followed her to the third-floor landing and crouched to my knees to get a clear view down to the front entry on the first floor.

From that point, my life would change. Without uttering a single word, Mummy quickly unlocked the iron padlock and slid open the metal door restraints. As she swung the door open, a tall dark shadow fell over her. Just as I could make out the figure of a youngish looking man dressed in a white traditional kurta, Mummy had already embraced him. Her arms were quivering, causing the hat that the man wore on his head to topple. He made no effort to retrieve it from the ground. His attire made it obvious. He had come to be with us to remember Papa. His head nestled itself in the crook of my mother's neck. They remained twined for some seconds, the sharp brilliance of the sun behind the young man creating a haloed effect around his head, illuminating strands of silver in his hair. I had remained crouched on the landing of the third floor for a few moments, unable to move. As he stepped past the threshold that morning, once released from Mummy's hug, his eyes met mine, lighting a clear path to my soul, highlighting a destiny which I would shape with a clear vision that had been unshadowed. That vision and inner strength, I realized, had always been with me.

I am certain that when Papa went to live his next life, he left me an angel. It may be that some lives are in jeopardy from the outset, and though pain can never be erased, it need not be constant, unlike the dazzle of a million stars in the blackened sky that will always bring me comfort and clear sight.
Naina

HIGH TRADE
By Shirley Merith

*The beautiful journey of today can only begin
when we learn to let go of yesterday.*

-Steve Maraboli

HIGH TRADE

Camille read the name tags of each flight attendant as she boarded Flight 275 from San Francisco heading to London England. She focused on a young bouncy brunette named Candace, with the toothy smile, who looked like she couldn't save anyone in an emergency. *How old is she anyway? Eighteen?*

Things were not off to a good start. It was bad enough that the flight left late at night, but to be locked into a big metal flying machine for over ten hours would be pure punishment. Walking slowly down the aisles, her eyes skirted from side to side searching for seat 26C. Once found, she struggled to shove her carry-on bag into the overhead compartment.

"Let me help you with that." The offer came from a smooth sounding, insistent male voice. Camille turned to the side to see where the voice came from.

A flash of perfectly aligned white teeth within a wide smile greeted her. "Oh sure, that would be great thanks," she replied while easing into her allocated seat.

She fixed her gaze upon his snug fitting white polo shirt and relaxed fit blue jeans. She watched him secure her bag in the overhead compartment, then immediately put his in afterward.

He slid into the seat across the aisle from her. She flashed a thankful smile as he gave her a nod. *Not bad looking* she thought, though she was hardly in the mood for socializing with anybody. It had been a long day and she was starting to feel a hint of pressure behind her left eye, often indicating the onset of a headache.

Within what seemed to be minutes of her clearing her thoughts and tightening her seat belt, the cabin door slammed shut and her nerves started to tingle. She was grateful to a friend who had told her about taking Gravol before the flight to help with her stomach. She rummaged through her purse to make sure that the pink and white package was still there to be used later on if needed. She grazed her index finger over the package for support.

Camille firmly gripped both armrests giving no consideration to the passenger in the seat beside her. She winced at every bump and thump as the plane rumbled faster and faster down the runway. When the plane started its ascent, she leaned back onto the headrest and closed her eyes. With every jolt, she clenched her teeth and held on tighter. As the aircraft levelled off and the seat belt sign was disengaged, she quietly reached into her purse, slipped the cellophane wrapper off a mint candy and popped it into her mouth. For some strange reason mints always seem to help with her light headaches.

After an hour of flipping through the airline magazine, one that she had hoped would take her mind off the constant drone of the engines, she looked ahead and noticed a line starting to form for the bathroom. She decided to go before the line grew longer.

Quickly getting out of her seat, she collided with the man who had helped with her bag. He was moving to let the passenger in the middle seat out. Stunned for a moment, she couldn't even offer an apology as her throat became instantly dry. His smile clearly indicated that an apology was not needed. He gestured for the ladies to go first then followed them down the aisle.

Camille wondered if it was his breath she could feel on the back of her neck as they stood in line. Somehow, she had switched places with the lady who was beside him, placing her directly in front of the 'carry-on man'. He seemed nice enough helping her with the bag and smiling at her. *Is he going to talk to me?* she thought. She wasn't sure but she had no intentions of speaking first.

"Sometimes these line-ups can be so annoying," he said.

"Yeah," she replied turning slightly to look at him in full. He stood about six feet tall, his perfectly groomed black hair was cut short enough to sit just above the ears. His angular brows were a bit on the thick side, but his warm chestnut brown eyes made up for it. As she straightened back to her initial pose, she felt her shoulders start to stiffen. Hopefully, he would notice her discomfort and stop talking to her.

"You would think that these were the only set of bath-rooms on the plane," he said. "It seems as though everyone is coming here."

"You could say that," she responded while inching forward.

"I guess I'll have to watch how many drinks I have on this flight so I don't have to keep using the bathroom."

She smiled at his comment but did not respond. She felt it would lead to further conversations, which she didn't want to have.

As she noticed his lips starting to move again, the bathroom door opened and it was her turn to go in. She grabbed the door and shut it tightly behind her. She stood in the bathroom with her back to the door and took a deep breath. There was something vaguely familiar about his face, something that she couldn't quite put her finger on. Had she seen it somewhere before?

Looking in the mirror, she checked out her makeup and mid-length hair. She ran her fingers through her sable brown bob trying to fluff up what was already starting to go flat. Then she rubbed her cheeks in a circular motion before adding plum berry lipstick to her full lips.

Her initial decision to not talk to any men on this trip other than for work purposes, was due to an email she recently received from her ex Josh, who insisted they meet to talk about the possibility of getting back together. She was tired of his broken promises and had made a previous commitment to swear off men and focus only on herself for the next year. But boy was this handsome stranger making it difficult.

Taking a bit longer than she expected, Camille double-checked to make sure that she looked decent before exiting.

Returning to her seat she noticed him watching her as she moved down the aisle. She felt his eyes flirt with her body as she settled back into her seat.

Fidgeting around, she finally found the buckle and snapped the seat belt together.

The pilot's voice came on the overhead speakers announcing that they were approaching a small area of turbulence.

'Carry-on man' leaned over and said, "I guess we got to the bathrooms just in time."

Camille's stomach was stirring but she managed a smile. This was the one portion of any flight that she hated the most. It didn't seem like the Gravol had had any effect at all. She tried her best not to look too frightened.

She dreaded the thought of having to sit on this aircraft for another eight and a half hours. She leaned her head back closed her eyes and said a prayer. When the turbulence settled down the pilot announced that he expected a smooth flight from then on.

"I couldn't help but notice your tight grip on the armrest. You look like you could use a drink to make the flight a little easier."

"That obvious eh? I'm not a great flyer, but then I don't know too many people who are," she said feeling a bit ashamed.

"Me neither, but as much as I can, I try to put it out of my mind. Sometimes a drink helps me get used to it," he said. "The flight attendant is on her way down the aisle. Would you like a drink?"

"No, thank-you."

"Are you sure you don't want anything?"

"Mmm… fairly sure."

"Well if you change your mind let me know."

She nodded, then felt down on the floor for her purse.

She pulled out her iPod and plugged in the earpiece. She was getting ready to put the buds in her ear when the plane had another unexpected little bump.

The buds dropped out of her hands. Her eyes closed quickly for a few seconds.

As the plane settled down again, she reopened her eyes and calmly picked up the ear buds.

The flight attendant arrived at their section. Camille decided she did want a drink but a non-alcoholic one and ordered a ginger ale.

She eyed him as he ordered his drink and pulled out his black American Express card to pay. *It appears he has money,* she thought. *But then again money doesn't mean a thing these days. Look at Josh, when she first met him he had money. Then he made a fool of himself and squandered it all away.*

"Enjoy," he said as he raised his glass, then he positioned his earphones for the start of the movie.

Sipping carefully, Camille made sure that she didn't spill anything on her button-down coral cashmere sweater, which she loved and was wearing for the first time. Plane rides can get cold at times so she felt that this sweater would help to take the chill off.

She tapped the screen located at the back of the seat in front of her to make a movie selection. Once she finished scrolling through the choices, she settled on the sequel to a movie she had already seen before. The flight attendant came around again with the meal. Looking at it didn't help her stomach much, but she decided to pick at it anyway since eating something was better than nothing at all.

Watching the movie was uneventful. Who would have known that two and a half hours would go by so fast? Checking her watch, there was still over five and a half hours left in the flight. She removed her earpiece.

She stared forward looking at the tops of people's heads, recanting a silly game she played with herself whenever she flew. She tried to guess the age of people based on their hairstyle. She knew full well that she would never get to find out if she was right or wrong, but it passed some of the time away.

"Since you don't like flying, I gather that you don't travel often?" His comments interrupted her game.

"It depends on what you call often," she replied.

"May I ask what business you are in? Modeling or an actress perhaps?"

Camille felt her cheeks becoming warm.

"No."

"How about a designer or news anchor?"

This guy's too much, she thought. "No again. Actually, I'm in advertising."

"Oh, how interesting. I'm a bit familiar with that industry."

"You don't say. I don't often run into people who know much about it."

"Very true. Me neither. I wonder if you work for an agency that I would know."

"You might know our slogan 'We Take Care Of You Everywhere.' It's plastered all over the place," she replied.

"Oh yeah. You could say I'm aware of it."

She noticed a slight edge in his voice as he leaned closer, but ignored it as the aroma of his lightly scented cologne tingled her nostrils.

"Good. That means our agency advertising works."

"You're probably not going to believe this, but I might know someone who works for that same agency. Are you referring to Inco Advertising?"

"Yes," she exclaimed. "What an uncanny coincidence. We're not a very big agency. You wouldn't happen to know the owners, Ellis Lange or Edward Pinchon would you?"

His forehead wrinkled and his brows pointed downward. "I'm being rude. Let me introduce myself. My name is Kyle and may I ask yours?"

Noticing that he hadn't answered her question she said "Camille. Camille Pryce."

"Nice to meet you, Camille."

"Likewise. So, what leads you to know so much about the advertising business?" she asked.

"Well, you could say that I've dabbled in it for a few years myself."

"How interesting. Then we have something in common. What aspect of the business are you in?" She noticed that she was becoming more and more talkative.

Before he could speak again, the intercom system opened up.

"Ladies and gentlemen, we are going to be coming through with some light snacks. If you are interested, please leave your tray tables down."

"I guess I can continue now," he said.

While he was talking, she could hardly focus as a wave of drowsiness overtook her. All she could remember saying was, "You're a busy man." She then leaned her chair back, threw the blanket over her shoulders and wrapped up. Within minutes she nodded off.

When she awoke, she looked to the side and noticed Kyle was not in his seat.

Her hand immediately went up to her hair to smooth it down. *I must have the worst case of bedhead,* she imagined as she glanced at her watch. She must have been asleep for several hours. The last time she looked it was 2:30 am. Now it was almost 6:00 am.

"You're awake," Kyle said slipping back into his seat.

"Yeah. I was really tired," she responded using her hand again to sleek down her hair.

"It was difficult for me to sleep, though I did nod off for about an hour," he said.

"It must have been the Gravol. It finally kicked in," she replied. The first one didn't do anything, but it looks like the second one I took near the end of the movie really knocked me out."

"I could see that," he answered while buckling back his seatbelt. "So where are you headed when we land?"

"I'm going straight to my hotel to get some more rest. Then I have a meeting tomorrow with clients to cement an account I've been working on for weeks."

"Oh, so that's the purpose of this trip, to gather up more business for your firm?"

"Yes, and also to beat our competitors to the punch. We know they're close on our heels after this account."

"Well, you look like a savvy woman on a mission. I highly doubt that you will have any trouble landing this account."

"Thank you. I think I'll do all right," she said with a slight smirk. "So how about you? Are you going to London for business or pleasure?"

"Neither, actually. London is my home."

"Oh, I didn't notice a British accent."

"Not at all. I moved there a few years ago."

"Interesting. For work I assume?"

"Somewhat. It's a long story. Other than the dodgy weather it's a great place to live."

"If you say so," she said with a smile.

"Have you been to London before?"

"Gosh, it's been years since I've been back. I was there once before with my parents when I was quite young."

"Ahh, then you need to see it all over again."

"Yes, I do."

"Well if you have a few days available after your meeting, make sure you visit the London Eye. It's quite an attraction. The line-ups can be long in the afternoons, so try to get there in the early morning if you do decide to go."

"I'm there for five days, so I'll keep that in mind. Any other suggestions of things to do or see?"

"If you like parks, Hyde Park is rather nice. Then the usual Tower of London, Big Ben or Buckingham Palace are also good choices."

"Thanks for the great information."

"You're more than welcome."

"Also, if you get a chance there's a great restaurant on the north side of town called 'Heleo's.' They serve a delicious glazed pecan salmon and shrimp dish if you're into seafood of course."

"I'll keep that in mind." she replied.

The flight attendant moved through the cabin collecting all the leftover items as they prepared for landing. The captain made his announcement and all passengers strapped themselves in for the final descent.

They heard the wheels of the aircraft lowering down indicating that the runway was now in sight.

"It looks like we don't have much time left in the flight. See you made it. It wasn't that bad, was it?"

"I guess not. I will only say it was a good flight when my feet land back on solid ground," she quickly replied.

She put her seat back into the upright position, took her usual pose with her head back into the seat, and hands gripped on the armrest.

The plane landed without incident and Camille let out a sigh of relief. She searched for some parting words to say to Kyle before they left the plane. After all, even though she initially didn't want to talk, he did help to make the flight more bearable. Clearly, with him being in advertising, it had peaked her interest. As if Kyle could read her mind, he leaned over and thanked her for the good conversation.

"Maybe someday when you return to London we'll meet again," he said with a wink.

"Maybe, but it's a long flight from San Francisco. I can't see me making this trip too often. You though seem like a traveling man. Next time you're in town, don't hesitate to look me up."

She reached into the side pocket of her purse and handed him a business card. Instantly, this action reminded her of her assertive work persona that she was desperately trying to shed. She watched him peruse the card then slip it into his right front pocket.

"You can count on that Camille Pryce," he said.

She once again watched him assist with her carry-on bag. She thanked him and headed down the aisle to the exit.

Camille didn't notice him in the baggage area. *Perhaps he didn't have any checked luggage.* She spotted her blue and white Vanderbilt suitcase and struggled to pull it off the conveyor belt. Once it plunked on the ground the rest was easy. *Thank goodness for the person who invented these roller wheels,* she thought as she made her way outside into the fresh spring air.

As luck would have it, there was Kyle waiting at the taxi stand. He saw her and waved. She waved back while heading in his direction.

"We meet again," he said when she approached.

"Yes, I guess so, I assume this is where the taxi stand is," she replied stating the obvious.

"I'm surprised that it's taking so long. Usually, there are tons of taxi's hanging around."

"Waiting is becoming the norm these days," she said.

"Now that I've seen you again, let me apologize for being so rude."

"What do you mean?"

"It occurred to me after you left the plane, that instead of just telling you about the highlights of London, I should have offered to show you around."

"Oh no, don't apologize. You don't need to do that. I will be fine."

"Actually, it would be my pleasure. Since we are in the same business and all, it would give us something to talk about."

She watched as he reached in his right back pants pocket and took out a pen. He ripped off a corner of the piece of paper he was holding and scribbled on it.

"Here's my cell phone number. I should be free in about two days. That's Thursday. How about I take you to the London Eye, say around 9 am?"

"Look, Kyle, I don't want to inconvenience you in any way."

"Not at all. I could use a break from work anyway. So, can I expect to hear from you?"

She took a few seconds to respond.

"Sure, why not. I'll give you a call to confirm."

"Great I look forward to it."

They continued to exchange small talk about the industry while waiting. He asked her about her pitch for the account. She told him a few things she was working on for her presentation. She added the fact that she had heard the owner, Walter Carnegie, was tough to work with. He gave her a few pointers.

"Mr. Carnegie is a crusty one. I've had a meeting or two with him before. You have to look him straight in the eye when you're talking. If you lose eye contact with him he thinks you're too weak."

"Thanks for the heads up."

"My pleasure. I see a taxi coming now. You might as well take it. I can wait for the next one."

"You're a gentleman."

"See you Thursday. Call me, and by the way, I love the colour of your sweater. It suits you," was the last thing she heard as she got into the cab.

⊨⊨ ⊨⊨

Camille's days in London passed quickly. It was Wednesday and her advertising presentation was over. She could relax a bit and take in some of the sites. With only three days left, she was looking forward to having Kyle take her around. Even though going out with him for the day was breaking her rule of avoiding men for at least a year. He was easy on the eyes and nothing would become of it so why not? She knew that once she left London everything would go back to the way it was, which was just fine with her. Or so she kept on telling herself.

She searched the bottom of her purse until she found the paper with his number on it. She carefully read the instructions for making local calls on the phone beside the bed. Looking at the paper again, she dialed the number. After the fourth ring, it went to voicemail.

"Hi Kyle, it's me Camille, thanks again for offering to show me around. I'll be out and about for a bit. Although I don't use it much overseas, it's best that you reach me on my cell phone at the following number to confirm for Thursday. Bye." She reflected on the fact that she reeled off her number pretty fast when she left the message, but she was not going to call again to repeat it.

It felt a little strange calling a man she didn't know. But in reality, it would be nice to tour around with someone who knew the area. Not that she couldn't enjoy seeing the sights that London had to offer. She was kind of a loner, so doing things by herself was nothing new. Her friends were few and close ones almost didn't exist. Other than Lisa and Claudine, distant friends from high school, and her sister Judy, she truly wasn't that close to anyone.

Camille decided to go to see Covent Gardens. So much had changed since she was last there eighteen years ago. Her father took the family to London on the only trip they went on together. She remembered how big her eyes got when she was ten, as she walked into the National Art Gallery and saw the paintings and artist names she had heard about in school. Now even as an adult she still marveled at the works of art she spent the time perusing.

She ventured next to Somerset House which was a place she had read about on the internet before she left San Francisco. It truly lived up to its name. What a beautiful place it was. She loved the arts and music which this place is known for. She saw a spare spot on a bench and sat down to relax. It was her opportunity to soak in the sights and sounds. Camille watched as the fountains danced in the courtyard to an array of coloured lights. Who would have ever thought that water could be so enchanting? She took the casual tan leather Clarks shoe off her right foot and rubbed it to soothe the dull ache she felt. It momentarily kept her mind off what was bothering her.

She checked her phone every half hour throughout the day to see if he called. Even though her phone would ping if a call came in, she looked at it anyway. As she travelled back to her hotel, she recalled the conversation they had about him taking her around. Then she reflected on the message she had left for him. Was she clear enough; did she speak too fast or did she sound too desperate?

When it got to ten o'clock that evening she grew concerned. The day had come and gone with no response from Kyle. Out of sheer pride, she refused to call him to find out what happened. Hurt, she decided to leave well enough alone.

Camille got up in the morning saddened that he never called. She checked her phone just in case she missed the call. Nope, no such luck.

She decided to go to the London Eye anyway as it was something she wanted to see. She put on her favourite True Religion jeans, which fit rather snug. Then she finished off the look with a thin purple hooded sweater, followed by a light gray scarf.

She took a taxi to the location still wondering why he didn't return her call. All she could think of was that he was married and couldn't get away, or he might just have changed his mind. Either thought wasn't good. But now he had confirmed what she already knew. Men were just jerks.

The night before she was to head back home was the advertising gala event. They were going to announce which company won the account. She felt her pitch to Carnegies and partners had gone well. She had her fingers crossed that Inco would be victorious.

Camille's teal blue low back fit and flare dress hung beautifully as she spun around viewing her curvy five-foot-six frame in the mirror. She rechecked her hair, which was slicked back and pulled into a bun. Then finished off her look by applying black mascara and natural toned lipstick. Her silver sling-back shoes seemed like the perfect comple-ment to the dress. She slipped her feet inside and walked to the window. "Yep, these are comfortable enough," she uttered. Purse and light beige jacket in hand, she left the room for the awaiting taxi.

She arrived late, missing the cocktail hour. A traffic jam caused her to get there just as everyone was entering the ballroom. She quickly found her seat and sat down. The room was buzzing with people affiliated with the advertising industry in some way. Her eyes scouted the room taking in the ambiance of the blue and silver decor. There were even blue and silver trimmed charger plates on the table to match the tablecloth. She was no event planner, but she knew that to get these items to match so perfectly must have taken a lot of time and been fairly costly.

Her mind ran quickly to Kyle, as he had mentioned he was in advertising. She wondered if he was at the event. Even if he was, would she say anything about the cancelled date? Probably not, after all, he owed her nothing.

"Which agency are you with?" the rather plump lady to her right asked.

"Oh I'm with Inco advertising in San Francisco, how about you?"

"Boy, you've come a long way for this. I'm with Parnell of London."

"Wow, this place is lovely, it must have cost a pretty penny to put it all together."

"Yes, I'm sure. But if you know this company well then you know they have deep pockets. Hence the competition they run every other year for their business."

"Oh, I see," Camille replied just as the food service had started.

Over the next hour, the meal service was uneventful. Small talk was exchanged between everyone at the table, but of course, the buzz was about which company was going to pick up the big prize of the night.

The lights dimmed in the room and music played as Mr. Carnegie, a balding well-dressed man about sixtyish, in a navy-blue suit, took the stage. The room hushed to hear him speak. His speech about his organization's success seemed to go on forever. Camille wanted to go to the bathroom but didn't want to leave while he was talking.

Then the moment they were all waiting for arrived.

"Now, I am going to announce the winning company who secured our account and will be managing it for the next two years," the man bellowed into the microphone.

A pin drop could be heard in the room as everyone waited nervously to see if their company was named.

Camille had her fingers crossed under the table. She said a private, pick me pick me, willing him to call her company's name.

"And the company winning the account belongs to 'Lancamp Advertising'. Would they please come up to the stage and join me?"

Camille clapped weakly and showed a fake smile in defeat.

"Oh well, I was hoping it was going to be us, but I guess we'll have to try again another time," the lady beside her said.

"Yes, me too," Camille replied through her clenched jaw and tight teeth.

She picked up the glass of champagne and took a drink. Disappointed by the loss not only for herself but of course for the firm. After all, she was sent there to secure the account, which she failed to do.

When the clapping died down, she focused on the winners on stage. To her surprise, there stood Kyle. Her eyes grew large as she gasped inwardly. *Is this some sort of cruel joke?*

Her head went all fuzzy. She lifted her right hand to the side of her face. This can't be happening. Kyle works for the company that won.

Just then Kyle took the microphone. She had no choice but to listen.

"Wow, I am truly surprised, but thank you, Mr. Carnegie, for this award. My company and I assure you that we will take your business to new heights."

Camille couldn't believe it. She was in shock. Waiting until they came down off stage, she politely excused herself and headed to the bathroom.

No wonder he didn't want to face her. Who knows, he probably took some of the idea's she mentioned to him and used them to secure the account. There was no way she was going back into that room. They might run into each other and she would not be able to control her slow burn.

She retrieved her jacket, looked towards the exit and headed straight out. She took the first cab available back to the hotel and packed for her flight the next day. She cursed the day she met Kyle, as it was obvious now that he was nothing but trouble.

Camille sat in the same pre-blocked seat and continued to sulk the entire plane ride home. A blonde haired elderly lady traveling with a small child who kept referring to her as nana, occupied the seat that had been Kyle's. Every time she looked over to the seat that was his, she got a little more enraged.

The long journey home, plus buzzing thoughts about Kyle, produced another slight headache that made her arrival at the small one bedroom apartment seem like paradise.

She hauled her bag into the bedroom, dumped it in the closet and proceeded to flop onto her bed. After a few minutes, she slid herself off the bed and headed into the bathroom for a shower. As the warm water pelted down, her arms felt heavy and she barely had the strength to scrub herself. Drying off quickly, she slipped on her pyjamas and headed straight for bed. She was feeling the effects of the time change taking its toll on her. "Welcome home," she whimpered then promptly fell into a deep sleep.

⊷ ⊶

"Good morning Ellis," Camille said when she arrived at the office.

"Welcome back," he replied.

"Thanks even though we didn't land the account."

"There will be others. Besides win or lose, you're good at what you do," he added while stroking what was left of his thinning silver hair. "That brings me to an important point. How about joining me at 'Addies' for lunch today, there is some valuable business I'd like to discuss with you."

"Sure. What time?"

"Around noon. I'm meeting a client earlier so we might as well just meet there."

"Great. See you there."

While working intensely on a new account, time flew. Before she knew it, she was rushing out of her office to meet Ellis. When she arrived, he was already seated.

She walked gracefully behind the hostess who was taking her to the table that had been reserved. Ellis stood up, pulled out her seat, then assisted with pushing it in when she sat down. A waitress came by within minutes to take their drink order.

"Ellis, you seemed quite serious when you invited me out for lunch. Is there something going on with the company that concerns me?" She held her breath as she awaited his response.

"First of all, I wanted to thank you again for going after the account and working so hard on it. Yes, we lost out on this one, but there will always be other accounts that we will get."

"Yes, I know but this one hurts. I worked my butt off to land it," she expressed.

"Hey, you win some you lose some, that's how the world works. Anyway, it might not matter as much to you in a few moments."

Fidgeting with the napkin situated perfectly on the plate, Camille gently fanned it out and placed it on her lap. "Oh, so that means there is something up. Out with it Ellis. You know I hate waiting to hear things at the last minute."

"I guess it really doesn't matter when I tell you this so here it goes."

As he was about to start, the waitress came by with their beverages. She placed the glass of Merlot red wine in front of Ellis and the Martini beside Camille. Ellis politely informed her that the drinks were mixed up and she carefully changed them around. He then took up the glass indicating for Camille to do the same. "Cheers to bigger and better things." Their glasses clinked and they both took a sip.

"Camille, we've been working together now for almost three years and I must say your work is exceptional."

"Why thank you, Ellis. It's nice to hear that my work is appreciated."

"Look, I know a few of our competitors have approached you about working for them and I am honoured to know that your loyalties are with Inco."

"Inco taught me everything I know and we are successful. I could never abandon ship."

"That's good to hear because I have a proposal for you and I hope you will give it some thought."

Camille's right eyebrow rose slightly.

"Camille, I want you to listen to me carefully. I have discussed this with Edward and he also thinks that this is the best move for the company. I would like to make an offer for you to become a partner with us in the firm. It would be a 20 percent partnership with an option in two years to make it 25 percent."

Her bottom jaw dropped, as she tried to retain the information that was just presented to her.

"I don't know what to say," she exclaimed.

"Don't say anything yet, just think about it. It's a big decision to make over lunch."

Camille took another sip of her wine. She put the glass down, then quickly picked it up and drank again. She excused herself, walked with slow measured steps to the washroom where she pushed the door open then jumped up and down. She carefully examined herself in the mirror and imagined herself as a partner. She straightened out the sleeveless cream coloured cotton dress she was wearing, clasped her hands in front of her face, closed her eyes and uttered "I did it." She walked back to the table head held up high.

"Everything okay I hope?" Ellis asked.

"Things are great. I appreciate the offer and I will take a day or two to think it over."

"Camille if you accept, I will have Inco's attorneys prepare the legal documents for your review. We will also provide you with a new car of your choice, and a handsome partnership bonus."

"You're making this really hard to even think about saying no. I'm impressed."

"You're worth it and I want to keep you at Inco."

Camille took a few moments to sip on some more wine then thanked him again for his offer.

"Oh by the way, I forgot to mention the name of the company who won the account, she stated. It was Lancamp Advertising and the owner's name was Kyle. I'm still furious about their win. I could swear that he used some of the information he got from me to secure the account."

"What do you mean by that? How could he have possibly known about your presentation? It must just be a coincidence."

"Well, Kyle and I coincidentally met on the flight down. We got to talking while we were waiting for a taxi and I might have said too much. But on the flip side, not once during our conversation did he mention that he owned an advertising agency. I always assumed that he was an account executive like me," she said as her forehead wrinkled.

"Camille, you of all people know how cut throat this business can be."

"Yeah, but I still don't have to like it. He also said he knew someone here."

"Oh. Did he say who?"

"Actually no. And to think that I even took some of the advice he gave me about Mr. Carnegie into my presentation. What a fool I was."

"Look, Camille we've all been conned by the best of them. He's just another one among a dozen others."

"Yeah, I guess but it sure does irk me."

Camille picked up her glass again and finished off the wine. She studied Ellis's stony expression and decided not to push the previous topic any further. Based on his sudden quietness, clearly there appeared to be more to this topic untold.

⚊⚊

Kyle rested his back into the curve of the black office chair placed in front of his desk, at his modestly decorated one bedroom flat. Cupping his face in his hands he rubbed his forehead while reflecting on the chance encounter he had with Camille. He just couldn't get thoughts of her out of his head. The shine of her hair, her warm smile, pillow soft looking lips and that amazing body tucked nicely into the coral coloured sweater and cream pants, left him wishing he had made more of an effort to find her while she was in London. When he tried to return her call, the number she gave him was incorrect. He also had no idea where she was staying. He saw her leave the room at the gala and tried to find her. But no such luck.

Not that he knew if he would ever see her again, but he did know that without any effort things would always remain the same. He was bound and determined regardless of the distance, to go after what he wanted. Even though their meeting was a short one, he felt a definite spark. The name Camille Pryce fluttered around in his mind, and he was determined to reconnect with her.

He took after his mother in more ways than he cared to admit. She never gave up on anything she believed was important to her. Like the time, Kyle was suspended from grade school for taunting a smaller boy in his class. Although he was guilty, his mother put her case together carefully as any good lawyer would, and presented her argument to the principal who had no choice but to back down. After one day off school, Kyle was back in his homeroom seat, well behaved after the scolding he received from his mother. Now it was his turn to put together a case to woo Camille away from his father's clutches.

Drumming his fingers on the glass desk in front of him, he took no notice of the time. He grabbed his cell phone, gave Siri a command and the phone started to ring at the other end.

"Hey, sis what's up?" he said after Tracee answered.

"Kyle? Why are you calling me so early? Is there something wrong?" she asked.

"Early? Come on, sis, it's not that early."

"Okay then, how come you are calling so late? Isn't it after midnight your time? What gives?" she said.

"Yeah, I was up thinking about mom and what the next move will be like for her. It's been two weeks already and dad still hasn't signed the transfer documents."

"Hey, wait a minute. First of all, you are both the power of attorney for mom. So I think you should have discussed it with him as well. In any case, we went up there to see the place. Although it was nice I'm not sure if that's where I want her to be. For one thing, it's much further away than I would like, which makes visiting her more challenging. Second, the room they were going to put her in was too close to an exit door, which made both of us uncomfortable."

"Well, have them move her to an available room that's in a better location. How difficult can that be?" he replied.

"You actually think it's that easy to move people around? Get real. Plus, don't even think you can guilt us into making such a quick decision."

"Oh, so now you're ganging up on me because I considered making a decision that you both were too afraid to make. That's not fair," he said while staring at the art deco picture hanging on the wall facing him.

"No, what you did wasn't fair. Even if you had called to give me the heads up it would have been better instead of just going ahead with it. Now we feel rushed and need some time to think it through."

"Fine. Go ahead, take all the time you need. By then the space will be gone and we'll have to start all over again."

"Well, Kyle, if the space goes then it goes. We will deal with that problem when it becomes one. In the meantime, I'll discuss it with dad again this weekend. When we make a final decision, you will know. In my heart of hearts, I believe Kyle that you did this just to rile dad up."

"It worked, didn't it? From what you've told me he's all pissed off. Now he knows what it feels like when someone does something behind your back."

"Kyle, don't you think it's time to bury the hatchet for mom's sake? You've both made mistakes so call it a draw and move on."

"Look sis, he's controlling and selfish which I can't deal with. No wonder mom lost her mind. It's from living with him all those years."

"That's not true and you know it. He had nothing to do with her getting dementia. By the way, it's too early in the morning for me to listen to your nonsense unless you can back it up with facts, which we both know is impossible."

"I know he didn't cause it but he sure didn't help much when she started to go downhill," he replied grumbling. "What was he doing when she fell before she went into the home?"

"Your comments are ridiculous," Tracee said. "He took care of her when he was not at work for the last three years. Once the nurse left for the evening he was all on his own. He barely went anywhere. You were not around and I was extremely busy with my new job. That day was the first day in a month he actually spent time outside with the neighbours. How was he to know she was going to fall?"

"Well," Kyle started to say and didn't get a chance to finish.

"Well what?" she squawked. "You need to get over it and fast."

"Get over what? The fact that he threw her into a home the first chance he got?"

"Kyle, I'm not going to discuss this with you any further. You're being completely irrational. Somewhere along the line you truly believe that staying away is the best solution to this family issue. If anybody should feel guilty about abandoning mom it should be you. In the meantime, hopefully one day you will come to your senses."

"You had to throw that in didn't you? Maybe I just need some distance and time to process the whole thing."

"Take all the time you need," Tracee replied. "But just remember time slips by fast and any window of opportunity you have to make things right with dad you should take it. Look how quickly mom went downhill. Time was not kind to her."

Kyle paused for a few moments. "Yeah, yeah, I'll think about it."

"I've got to go. You okay otherwise?" she asked.

"I'm good," he responded quietly. "But, before you go, I wanted to ask you about that woman who works at the agency. What's her name again Carol? Candace?"

"You mean Camille," she replied.

"Yeah her. What's she like?"

"Why are you asking about her? You haven't even met her."

"Well actually I have," he replied. "I bumped into her on the plane when I was going home after my last visit. We ended up sitting across from each other."

"How interesting. Look I don't know much about her, but I do know that dad relies on her a lot. He actually credits her with helping to keep the agency going when he needed to take time off to tend to mom. Are you concerned? You're not thinking they are involved in some way are you?"

He thought for a fleeting second before answering, knowing his father's past history.

"No. From what you just told me it seems that she's very talented, so let's just leave it at that."

"Bro, I know you remember? I can tell you're interested. I know she's a very attractive woman."

"It's nothing like that," he replied while laughing lightly. "I know at some stage our paths will cross again, and I just wanted to get the heads up."

"Okay if you say so, but I know you're interested."

"Yeah, yeah, whatever," he said brushing her off.

"Whenever you cut me off like this I know I've hit a nerve so goodbye. Love you," she said then hung up.

Kyle knew he could never put anything past his sister when it came to women. She always knew when he was up to something.

The running of his own advertising company was hectic and kept him busy almost seven days a week. It interfered tremendously with his so-called social life. At thirty, he hoped to be thinking about settling down but somehow that option was eluding him. His previous relationship lasted for two months and ended after he had cancelled three dates in a row due to business meetings. The woman he had been seeing didn't even return his call the last time he attempted to invite her out for dinner. Not to mention that his job and the distance wreaked havoc on his ability to visit with his mother more often.

He reflected on his most recent visit with his mother. Her frame had dwindled down to a woman much older than her actual age of sixty-nine. The glossiness of her eyes always seemed to be looking nowhere and everywhere all the time. Her hands shook gently when holding onto a tattered book that was her comfort just like a blanket is to a little child. It was heartbreaking. He attempted to hug her and she pulled away, yelling at him to leave her alone. Not once did she acknowledge that she knew who he was. Although the nurses tried to calm her down she continued to be agitated, so they suggested that he leave and return another day. His next two visits were not as traumatic, but her lack of knowing who he was caused him great pain. The closeness they had shared for his entire life no longer existed.

Furthermore, it was even more difficult when she kept on asking for her husband. The nurses told him stories about how Ellis seemed to be the only one that truly kept her calm. Whenever her husband arrived which was at least three times a week, she would follow him everywhere he went. If he sat down she would snuggle up to him pleading for him to read her a story. During his readings, she would always start to drift off. Once she was in full sleep mode he would take his time and sneak out of the room.

Boy did it ever burn him to hear how much she was still attached to his father after what he had done to her.

It was a rainy afternoon in June when he had a meeting scheduled at the downtown Hilton hotel. As he rushed out of his car pushing the umbrella open, he noticed a couple passionately lip locked at the entrance of the hotel. From the distance, he could see the woman's arms were wrapped tightly around the man's waist, while the man held her face to secure the lingering kiss.

Sidestepping puddles to get to his destination, Kyle's feet stopped moving when he got closer. It can't be, he thought. There's just no way. But what he saw couldn't be denied. He recognized the man in the tight embrace. It was his father. Kyle watched his father put the woman into a cab, lean in for another long kiss then walk down the street in the pouring rain.

He had not told anyone about what he witnessed. His image of a perfect father and family man was shattered in a matter of a few seconds. Every time he saw his father after that his anger grew. He was even more disgusted when he saw his mother prior to her illness, fawning over his father whenever he visited them. She even believed all of his working late stories. If she only knew what he saw that day, she would have been crushed.

At times, he thought about telling his sister, but just never found the courage. He also didn't want to ruin her image of their father. The idea of confronting his father he believed, would create nothing but lies and he didn't want to deal with it. He knew what he saw and nothing could change that.

Kyle lost his mind when he found out that his father was putting his mother into a home. Granted he knew that the state she was in required around the clock care, probably more than his father could handle, but as far as he was concerned family stuck by family. That's why it cut to the bone when Tracee said that he should feel guilty about running away. He realized that he was no different than the man he had accused of abandonment. By moving to London, he too had distanced himself from the problem.

His mouth twisted as he thought about how selfish he had become. Thinking only of himself and not seeing the other side of the coin where his father was concerned. If there was another side? Tracee was probably right. He needed to do better and at least think about making amends.

He took some time to ponder the phone call he had with his sister, then he began again to turn his focus onto Camille. Based on the few words that his sister had said about her, he was more intrigued than ever.

Even though she might have given him the wrong cell phone number when she was in London, he still somehow felt a connection to her.

She seemed like she was focused and progressive, a trait he admired in a woman. He had to find out more about her, though long distances always made it difficult to get to know someone.

Although he obviously knew where she worked, he still wanted to know more. He would try to connect with her via Facebook if she had a profile. "Heck, she's in advertising. She definitely has a profile," he said.

Grabbing his iPad, he typed in 'Camille Pryce' then hit the enter key. After selecting images, she popped up on his screen. He took a few moments perusing her information to make sure it was the same woman he had met on the plane. When he finished with Google, he looked her up on LinkedIn, then he went onto a few advertising sites. Flipping from screen to screen, he reviewed the several awards and honourable mentions she had received.

She was known in the industry as one of the up and coming magnets in advertising and was described as 'a force to be reckoned with'. "Very impressive," he said aloud. She was giving his profile some serious competition. While her awards were different, they were almost as important as the ones he had won a few years back.

He pulled up his Facebook account and signed in. He searched for her profile, then without hesitating, sent off a friend request. After he pressed the send key, questions flew into his head. What if she doesn't respond quickly enough? Suppose she doesn't accept his friend request at all. What then? "Calm down man," he said as his heart pulsed faster. "Cross that bridge when you get to it."

Signing off the tablet, his eyelids felt heavy. Clearly, it was time to get some sleep. Hopefully, in the morning, he would have a nice surprise by the way of a confirmation from her.

The next day he checked his messages every few hours to see if anything came through. Anxiety built when it got to day three without any response. Refusing to believe that she wasn't interested in staying connected with him, he Googled her again. Not that it made any difference, as the information was exactly the same as before. His mind raced with many reasons for the lack of a reply. Maybe she was out of town on business, or her computer system was down. *No,* he thought, *she probably doesn't want to seem too anxious so she's taking her time to connect with him.* He decided to give her until Friday. If she didn't reply by then she would have made the choice that he would have to respect.

On Friday, the thought of her still not responding consumed him. "She seems to be playing hard to get," he mumbled while scanning through the screens of a local San Francisco flower shop site. Well, I know how to get to a woman's heart, he thought. *A large bouquet of fresh spring flowers should do the trick.* Tapping the numbers into his cell phone, he patiently waited for a response on the other end.

A cheery voice answered. "Good evening, Leave It To Us Flowers. How may I help you?"

"Hello. I would like to order your Spirit of Spring bouquet please," he replied.

"Not a problem sir. Did you want that arrangement in the small or large size?"

"The large one looks good, and I would also like to add one long stem yellow rose with that arrangement as well. Could you let me know how much that will cost?"

"Give me one moment sir. The arrangement including the extra rose will be one hundred and sixty dollars," the voice said.

"Great that sounds like a fair price." At that moment, he dug into his wallet to pull out his credit card that was still shiny from its limited use.

"Where would you like me to send them?"

"Could you have them sent to the following person at this business address, I would like them there by noon tomorrow."

"Would you like to put anything on the card?" she asked

"Yes. Could you please write the following: 'Hope you enjoyed your time in London, Kyle.'

⟫⟫ ⟪⟪

"So, are you going to tell me who sent you these gorgeous flowers?" Wendy, the receptionist asked after she put the bouquet on Camille's desk.

Camille picked up the card and read the message. She showed no reaction. Afterward, she flicked the card onto the desk. "No one exciting. Just a jerk I met on the plane ride to London a few weeks back."

"You mean that trip you didn't want to go on and tried everything possible to get out of?"

"Yes, the trip that turned out to be a total disaster all around."

"I would say based on the look of those flowers, it couldn't have been all that bad."

"Trust me, it was," Camille said, after she picked up the card again and tapped the edge of it on her desk.

"Well jerk or not he has good taste in flowers," Wendy remarked.

Camille was deciding what to do with the flowers. Part of her wanted to throw them out, but they were so beautiful she just couldn't do it.

She was getting ready to respond to Wendy when the office phone shrilled. Glancing over at the screen, she leaned in closer to take a look at the number. Not recognizing it, she waved it off letting it go to voicemail.

"Look I better let you get back to work. We'll touch base later on," Wendy said as she left the office.

Camille put her fingers in her hair then scratched her head as if her mind was itching. *Why would he be sending me flowers after he blew me off in London? To think that he also possibly stole my idea for the account. He has some nerve.*

Picking up the phone receiver she hit the message button. As soon as she heard the smooth voice she knew exactly who it was. She held the phone tightly in her hand while she listened to the message. What was she going to do? Her beating heart was happy to hear from him, but at the same time, her racing mind was not.

She replayed the message once more, hoping that it would give her a clue of what to do next. Finally putting down the receiver she slumped back into her chair and looked up at the ceiling. She deliberately didn't respond to his Facebook friend request from a week ago, as she was still too upset. Now looking at the beautiful floral arrangement she wondered if she was overreacting.

With a push of her feet, the black padded office chair swung around in a full circle landing perfectly back in front of the phone. The decision to call or not to call was taunting her. This would be the perfect reason to tell him off for what he did to her in London. She would call tomorrow. It would give her more time to prepare what she was going to say.

Camille wanted to get back to the work on her desk, but she couldn't clear her thoughts. Believe it or not, she had been so annoyed with losing the account that she never bothered to investigate him further. What was she waiting for? With the click of the keys on the keyboard, she typed in Lancamp Advertising.

A picture of Kyle Lange owner and CEO appeared. Her eyes glared at his rugged profile. It brought back memories of how handsome he truly was. She then focused on the last name. It couldn't be a coincidence that his last name was the same as Ellis'. There had to be a connection.

She continued to read all of the details about the company. Her body burned with disbelief over who he was. She stopped reading and reflected back to her only interaction with Kyle in London. She recalled that he never gave her his last name when he introduced himself. Also, he never revealed who he knew at her company.

Then she recollected her lunch with Ellis. When she mentioned the company name that won the account, the warmth that she previously felt from his body language had changed. She didn't push it, but now she wished she had. What kind of game was being played with her? She had to have answers for her mind full of questions.

She waited for over an hour then got up from her desk and hastily walked to Ellis' office. Once she arrived she noticed that the back of his chair was facing the door. His head was seen just above the headrest and she detected no movement.

"Ellis is everything okay?" she asked.

"What?" he replied without turning around.

"Do you have a moment for me?"

His brows were angled down and his mouth was tightly shut as he spun around to face her. It was almost as if he had aged from the brief time she saw him this morning. She didn't want to add more to his plate than it looked like he could handle. However, her determined nature would not allow her to let things fester.

"You don't look very happy."

"Oh, it has nothing to do with you. I just finished heavy negotiations with one of our accounts and it was tough. But nothing I can't handle."

"Oh. I wanted to talk to you about something that has been on my mind."

"Is it about the new account were working on?"

"No actually it has nothing to do with that account," she replied.

"Okay, then what's it about?"

"It's about Lancamp Advertising. It's owned by Kyle Lange. I just put two and two together. Is he your son?"

She watched him rub the right side of his face with the palm of his hand. He then shook his head from side to side before she saw his lips move.

"Look I'm really not in the mood to respond to that right now."

"Okay, but based on your reaction it appears that I'm correct. At our lunch, when I mentioned the name of the company that won the account, your body language changed. At that moment, I knew something was up. Why didn't you tell me that your son owned the agency?"

"I didn't see the need to tell you."

"Fine, but you did see the need to mention about people being conned. What was that all about?"

"Nothing, just me spouting off."

After his comment, Camille reflected on how many times she heard him speak about his son since she was at the agency, which was very little if any at all. She knew there had been some tension between the two of them, but never felt it was any of her business to inquire as to what it was about. During her time there, she had interacted with Tracee on several occasions. Though she was always cordial, she hardly mentioned him either. Tracee had many similarities in her features and personality to that of her father. However, the resemblance between father and son was more subtle.

"Okay, then I'll leave you to get back to work."

She spun around walking slowly towards the door.

"Camille."

"Yes," she responded with a quick turn towards him."

"Nothing."

She turned around again her forehead wrinkled with discontent. She felt he wanted to tell her more, but decided against it.

Once back in her office, Camille stood in front of her window and shook her head from side to side.

"Men, she mumbled. They always seem to have something to hide." Her mind reflected back to her past relationship.

Josh had moved out unexpectedly over a year ago, leaving her with mounds of debt that he had hidden from her. All she found of his when she got home that day from work was a pair of socks, a comb and a slew of phone calls from bill collectors. In his recent email, he begged her to forgive his rash departure. He knew how much he had hurt her after they had been living together for two years and he was truly sorry. He wanted her to consider giving him another chance.

Did he think she was some kind of desperate fool? After all, he was such a coward not wanting to tell her face to face. Instead, he sent a short text telling her he had gone. Her shock and despair lasted for weeks. At work, she stayed strong, smiling and laughing when required. However, at home, she was broken, often finding herself crumpled on the couch like a well-used throw, wondering how she could have been so blind and gullible.

Suddenly her trance was interrupted by a ping. "What now," she said as she grabbed the phone. Coincidently, it was from Josh of all people.

"I really need to see you. Please respond to my previous text."

"Really? Not if I have anything to do with it," she said as she threw the phone down on the desk.

She barely sat down in her chair when she looked up and saw Ellis at her door.

"Come in and see me in about five minutes. We need to finish our previous discussion."

"Sure," she said now very curious about what he had to say.

She picked up her purse, slung it over her right shoulder then headed for the bathroom. While checking her hair in the mirror she noticed her eyes looked baggy and tired. *I need to get more sleep at night,* she concluded. Just then she looked at her watch which showed it was close to the five minute time frame.

She rushed back to her office, dumped her purse in the drawer and headed to his office.

As she walked in, he got out of his seat, strutted towards the door and pushed it shut.

Ellis started out by telling her that he hadn't seen his son in over three years. Kyle could never forgive him for sending his mother to a home when her dementia got out of control.

It was difficult for him to see his wife of thirty years going through the troubles of the disease. She was a proud woman who made him promise that under no circumstances were the family to be saddled with taking care of her. She was well aware of the damage this disease did to the mind and didn't want them to watch her go through this every day. When the time was right, meaning that she could no longer remember much or manage herself, she instructed them to put her in a facility. Kyle and Tracee said they could never do that. So she left the final decision to Ellis. She reminded him about it every lucid moment she had. Her only request was that they visit her regularly to make sure that she was being properly taken care of.

Ellis had a nurse come in during the daytime to take care of her. He took over in the evenings and on weekends.

Although he kept her home longer than was promised, he knew the right thing to do was to finally honour her wishes.

At the time, Kyle and his twin sister Tracee had a hard time understanding this. Tracee eventually came around and kept in regular contact with him, but his son had yet to forgive him. It tore them apart.

There had been a lot of harsh words spoken and subsequently quite a few words that were left unsaid the last time they spoke. Kyle accused him of wanting to dump her so he could get on with his life. He made it seem like taking care of her was a burden. There were many challenging times and he wasn't perfect, but he loved his wife through thick and thin. He wasn't particularly religious, nonetheless, he had prayed that time would heal the wounds between his son and himself. So far nothing had changed.

While he continued to talk, he took up the picture on his desk. "She was a beauty in her day, wasn't she?" he said as he handed it over to Camille. She noticed that the woman's caramel brown hair was pulled back into a ponytail, with a few wisps flowing on each side of her face.

"She was a mere five feet tall but as feisty as they come," he continued. "Her temper was often a challenge throughout our marriage. I barely ever won an argument. Even when I was right, it was easier to give in for the sake of peace. She would stay angry at me for days if she felt I had done something wrong. It looks like my son Kyle has picked up my wife's trait, except in his case, days turned into years."

Camille continued to listen to Ellis as he described bit by bit the essence of his disagreement with his son. He also stated that he felt there was more going on as to why Kyle was so angry with him, but he had no idea what it was.

Her mind was in a whirl with some of the information she heard. She watched him pound his fist from time to time on the desk with frustration.

He finished half an hour later and during that time she sat very quietly and never spoke a word. It was difficult to try to put her thoughts together. The right words didn't appear in her mind and she was not going to speak until they were formed properly.

"Are you okay? You look astonished," he said.

"Yes, I'm fine. I'm taking it all in. I guess I didn't realize that this was even happening and can tell that it troubles you deeply."

"I've held it in for quite some time, but it's good to finally get it off my chest. It's been on there far too long."

Camille brushed over the top of her teeth with her tongue while thoughts of what to say next came to mind. "While you were telling me your heartfelt story, what came to my mind was that it seemed that you would really like to reconnect with him."

She watched as he stood up and with some hesitation walked over to the brown metal cabinet located to the right side of his desk. His pale blue pinstriped shirt was neatly tucked into his navy-blue pants, which were held up with a black Ralph Lauren belt. She looked down to his black leather shoes, and what else would he be wearing but Ferragamo? He leaned in with his right hand and pulled something out of the drawer and once again, glossed his index finger over what was obviously a picture. A comfortable smile appeared as he handed it to her.

It was of himself and Kyle fishing off a pier, both wearing matching green camouflage vests and baseball caps.

Kyle looked as if he was about twelve years old and was leaning back in a struggle with the white perch dangling on the end of his line.

"You both look like you were having a lot of fun."

"Yes, and he was a great son. I couldn't have asked for anything better. We were as thick as thieves. Even when he grew up we were close. Then my wife got sick and it all changed. To answer your question, I would do almost anything to get my son back in my life."

"Thanks for sharing this with me Ellis. I know it's been tough. They always say that it's a small world. But now I truly know how small it is."

"You can say that again. By the way, I noticed some flowers on your desk. Who are they from?"

She had to think fast as she didn't want to make matters worse. "Ahh, just a past client."

"They're nice."

"Thanks. Look, I think I'll leave you alone for a while. We'll catch up later."

"Sure, sounds good."

Camille returned to her office not knowing what to think. She decided to take some time before making up her mind whether to return Kyle's call or not. Especially after what she had just heard from his father.

⟞⟝

Forty-eight hours had passed since Camille had gotten the voice message from Kyle. After mulling it around over and over in her mind, she decided that today was the day to call him back. She was ready to tell him what he could do with the flowers. While feeling a bit apprehensive about how the conversation might go, she knew that her determination to set things straight far overpowered her discomfort.

"Thank goodness for Saturday mornings," she said as she threw on her light gray and red banded yoga pants and a loose fitting black hooded jacket. She headed out to do some running around and pick up her weekly grocery items. First thing in the morning was always the best time to go out when she wanted to avoid running into people. Besides, the fresh salmon and snapper that she liked always came out at the local fish market around 7 am. By 8 am, the vegetable vendors were finished setting up and she could get the first pick of the items she needed for the week. As much as she loved this recent eating healthy kick she had started a few weeks ago, it could be quite costly at the marketplace. It was just twenty minutes away and the fresh air always gave her time to regroup her thoughts, especially on a day like today when her wit had to be as sharp as ever.

Evening dinner was going to consist of fish, and hopefully tomato salsa with cilantro, asparagus, and corn. As much as she didn't want to spend too much time at the market, the choice of vegetables had to be fresh and firm which took her longer to select.

Upon arriving back home, Camille pulled the vegetables out of the bag smelling each one before they went into the fridge. She then separated the three snapper fishes into single zip locked bags before they reached the freezer. One snapper remained out in a metal bowl as it was going to be seasoned and stuffed with spinach for dinner that evening.

Once finished, she grabbed a tall glass of apple juice and sat down on the couch. Instead of watching the television, she grabbed a book she was still reading and thumbed to the part where she had left off.

Within a half hour of undisturbed reading, she was at the end of the novel. Although it was fairly obvious how the story was going to end, it still held her interest right through. She was hoping that the killer would have tripped up and the protagonist would be the one to catch him, but the savvy detective, as always, came through instead. She thought to herself, maybe someday she would write a book and come up with a wild and crazy unexpected ending for her readers.

The time showed 11 am which would be 7 pm in London England. She looked at the phone number she had written down from the voice message, took a breath and tapped the numbers into the phone. Before she pressed the call key she took another sip of the juice and then tapped it.

She counted the rings and exactly four rings later his voice sounded on the other end.

"Hello."

"Hi Kyle, it's Camille Pryce from San Francisco calling."

"Wow, it's so nice to hear from you. I was beginning to feel as though you brushed me off."

"Oh really, funny you should say that."

"Why?"

"If I recall correctly, it was in fact, you who brushed me off. Remember?"

"What do you mean by that?"

"I thought we were supposed to meet for a tour at the London Eye together on Thursday morning."

"So did I. When I called the number back that you left me, it was wrong. Since you never told me what hotel you were staying at, I couldn't track you down. All I had was your business card, and your cell number was not on it."

"Oh."

"I just figured you gave me the slip."

"No actually, I figured that you didn't want to go after all, so I went touring anyway."

"Why didn't you call me again when you didn't hear from me?"

Camille shrugged her shoulders before she answered. "I don't know. I guess I didn't want to seem desperate."

"You desperate? I highly doubt that."

"Anyway, that's not why I called."

"Oh."

"Look, I have no idea what game you're playing at but I'm not interested."

"What are you talking about?"

"You conned me and I'm furious. I want nothing to do with liars and cheats. If you thought sending me some stupid flowers was going to work you can think again."

"Whoa. Liars and cheats? I take great offence to that. Who lied and cheated you?"

"You think you're so smooth, don't you? First of all, you chat me up on the plane. Then you continue with it at the taxi stand, asking all these questions about my advertising proposal. How do I know that you didn't use some of my ideas for your own selfish purposes? And to boot, you don't tell me anything about who you really are. I was at the gala and saw you accept the grand prize, Mr. Big Shot."

"I think you have this all wrong. First of all, I talked to you on the plane because I found you attractive. Second, I was happy to see you again at the taxi stand so that I could give you my number. When I noticed, you looking a bit stressed, I assumed it was about your upcoming meeting and offered you some advice. In no way, did I use anything you said to win the account."

The pressure in her head started to rise as she listened to him speak. When she couldn't take it anymore, she interrupted.

"Spare me the details. I know the kind of games guys like you play. You even knew about the gala and never mentioned it at all. What was the reason for that? Don't tell me you forgot, right?"

She waited for his response, but none came. Not liking the silence, she continued to talk.

"Aren't you going to say something? Or did the cat catch your tongue?"

"Are you going to let me speak?"

"Actually, no I'm not."

"You asked me a question so let me at least answer it."

"Why bother, I don't want to hear it. You're only going to come up with some story that you expect me to believe."

"What story could I have except the truth? Don't you think you're blowing things out of proportion?"

"Blowing things out of proportion? I don't think so. I don't know you at all, but I don't like what happened."

"Look, Camille, let's slow this conversation down a bit."

"There's nothing to slow down, I'm done."

"Really."

"Yes, and do me a favour. Don't send me any more flowers."

"At least I know you got them."

"Well, you wasted your money."

Then she pressed the end button on the phone.

Her hands were shaking as she put the phone down on the table. The old Camille would have easily allowed him to fill her head with all sorts of excuses. However, the new Camille was in charge of her own destiny. No man was ever going to make a fool of her again.

Her glass of juice was still on the table. She picked it up and gulped down what was left. Next, she sat back on the couch and kicked her feet up on the table. With a short sigh, she put her right hand over her heart and willed it to slow down.

◄═╬ ╬═►

Kyle couldn't believe what just happened. What was that all about? His head shook from side to side in dismay. The only thing she said that he was guilty of was not mentioning about the gala. But that wasn't anything of substance as he figured he would see her there anyways. To think she was that mad about it was disturbing.

How could he have misread the signals she had given him in London? He overlooked the fact that she gave him the wrong phone number. Now she hung up on him. His nostrils flared as he took a deep breath. He rubbed his forehead then shook his head. After a short sigh, he smirked as it hit him that he actually found her feistiness intriguing.

It took him a few moments before he decided to call her back. He picked up his cell phone and looked at the phone number on the screen. Then he changed his mind. Putting the phone back down, he walked into the kitchen and opened the fridge. The first thing that caught his eye was a can of Boddingtons Pub Ale. "Boy, could I use this right now," he said.

Kyle popped the tab, then took a swig. He took a bigger gulp the next time before he walked slowly back to the couch. He figured it was best if he let her cool off. Maybe with some time in between, she would realize that he didn't deceive her in any way. Why would he want to steal her idea in order to get the account? He had already presented his proposal before he even met her.

He had to make her aware of this. But obviously, that wasn't going to be today.

⇥ ⇤

Four days had passed, and no call back from Kyle. She knew he had the number because it would still be on his phone. Not that she had expected him to call. After all, she did hang up on him. But somewhere deep down, she had wanted him to call, if anything to try to prove her accusations wrong. But his behaviour confirmed that what she said was indeed right. It also reconfirmed what his father had previously told her about his stubbornness.

It was her day off, but she wanted to keep herself busy. She put on her pink and white Nike jogging outfit with the pocket at the side. She pulled her hair back into a ponytail, grabbed the iPod and headed out the door.

The fresh air could do her some good. Sitting around the house today would cause her to reflect on all of the bad relationships she had had in her life. What good were those reflections going to do her now? No, she needed to move forward.

Upon her return back home, she released the band from her hair and shook her head.

"Do you think that I need a shower?" she said while walking past the flowers that were still alive from the bouquet Kyle had sent her. As if they were ever going to answer her back.

She put her hand in to test the temperature before she stepped in. Once she was immersed under the pulse of the water, her thoughts started to drift towards Kyle again. Immediately brushing them off she washed her face twice as if the soap was also there to help cleanse her mind.

She got out of the shower, reached for the towel and held it over her face for a few seconds then dried off. Her pyjamas hung on the hook at the back of the door, which she slipped on while walking towards the bedroom. She pulled back the covers and climbed in. Only then did she notice there was a message on her cell phone. It was him. Kyle had called while she was in the shower. She listened to the voicemail.

"Hi, Camille. I hope you're not still upset with me, but I want to clarify the apparent misunderstanding that happened the last time we talked. First of all, I did not steal any ideas from you as I had my meeting with the Carnegies about the account before I left for San Francisco. Second, I didn't dump you on Thursday morning. As I mentioned before, you had given me the wrong number. Maybe by mistake, but nonetheless, it happened. Third, I didn't mention the gala, because I had no intentions of going. It was simply because my business partner could not attend that I had to step in. If we had been able to connect before, I would have told you about it. Fourth, I saw you leave the table at the gala, but you never came back. When I got off stage, I searched for you all evening, but with no luck. I must add that you looked quite beautiful in your blue dress. Please call me back. We really should talk about this. Believe me, I'm telling the honest to goodness truth."

She played the message over again. Even though she was still a bit angry, she had to admit it was good to hear his voice. "What to do?" she said, "should I call him back at all? Obviously, he wants to make amends, but what would be gained by calling him?" She'd have to figure it out in the morning.

Camille woke up twice during the middle of the night. She flipped back and forth so many times that she was still tired when she got up. Luckily it was Saturday and she didn't have to go to work.

She went into the bathroom, stared at herself in the mirror and brushed her teeth. She dragged herself to the kitchen for something to eat. Nothing much appealed to her. The easiest thing to eat was cereal, so she put some frosted flakes in a bowl with milk, grabbed the biggest spoon she could find and sat down.

The whole time she was eating, her mind was occupied with if and when she should call Kyle. Their initial meeting was short lived, but she did find him attractive and fairly interesting. The fact that he still called after she hung up on him so rudely, must mean something.

Camille put the bowl in the sink without washing it. She decided there was no time like the present to call and hear him out. Her cell phone was still in the bedroom, so she got it, sat up on the bed and made the call.

"I'm so happy that you called me back." he said.

"I really don't know why I called because I'm still mad."

"That's ok, I can handle it. Can I assume that you now believe me?"

"I'm not sure yet."

"Let me see if I can convince you. Will you at least give me that chance?"

"Go ahead. I'm listening."

Her full attention was focused on what he had to say about the misunderstanding. He sounded sincere enough that she didn't cut him off when he spoke. Better yet, she didn't feel the urge to hang up on him again. By the time they had finished their hour-long conversation, they had agreed to talk again the next day.

⇒ ⇐

Kyle leaned forward and picked up the remote from the chestnut brown ottoman his feet were resting on. He clicked through the channels until he found his favourite sport. One of the top seeded tennis players he so admired was down one set by a tenth seeded player. What he liked the most about tennis was that even when the losing player was down to the last play of the match, they could still rally back and win the game. That's how he felt about the advertising business. Any firm had a chance of landing an account even if they were not at the top of their game, as long as they had a winning pitch. Potential relationships could also work the same way. Could they not?

While watching the ball bounce back and forth, Kyle's mind was doing the same thing changing between the conversation he had with Camille and the match on the TV. Yes, he had somehow managed to change the tone of their phone call around which could mean that he won the set. But he was not convinced that he had won the match as far as she was concerned. There was still a whole lot of work to be done in that arena.

When a commercial came on, he pressed the mute button and started to contemplate how to move forward. He had already decided that he wanted to move back to San Francisco within a year. As much as he had enjoyed his time in London, he wanted to start a branch office and felt there was no other place for it to be but back home. Besides he wanted to be closer to his mother so he could visit more often.

Setting up the office though would be a challenge considering he was so far away. He needed to have someone on the ground in the new location to run the place until he arrived permanently. That's where Camille could fit in. But would she even remotely be interested? After all, she worked with his father, and from what Tracee said she was quite instrumental in the success of the company.

Maybe now was the time to put his little plan in motion. How great would that be to see his father's expression if and when Lancamp Advertising shot to number one in the business, with his ex-employee in tow?

All of this though was a pipe dream unless Camille agreed to be a part of it. It would take a hell of a lot to win her over, and in his heart of hearts, he knew it wouldn't be about convincing her with money. She was the type of woman that would need to have a vested interest in the business.

Realistically though what did he know about her work ethics, attitude, or business sense? Yes, from what he read on the internet and their brief conversations she seemed dynamite and on the ball, but he would have to personally see her in action before considering any type of partnership. This, of course, meant that pulling her away from under his father's wing would take some time and careful planning.

Although he was thinking about her for his business, his interest was not only a professional one. It was also one that dealt with matters of the heart. He genuinely fancied her and while she had made a few barbs about past relationships, she never clearly said that she was not interested in pursuing one. But then again, they had just met and it was highly unlikely that anything could work considering the distance between them. So, if they ended up only being friends then so be it. Just like a switch had been flipped back on he immediately thought with a sheepish grin, *No I think I'm interested in pursuing more than just friendship, but how will I convince her of that if I mention the business. It could come across as if I am just using her. I might have to rethink my strategy.*

⇤ ⇥

Camille tossed the idea around in her head about when she was going to bring up the topic of Ellis to Kyle. At first, she felt it would be best to approach it head on and get it out of the way. But after thinking it through, she thought it would be a good idea to wait until a few phone conversations had passed before she brought it up.

They spoke again the next day, exchanging more pleasantries. She wanted to know more about the advertising business in London and compared it to how things operated in San Francisco. He wanted to know more about why she selected advertising as a career. Their conversations were never long as one of them was regularly being interrupted by phone calls relating to work.

After the third day of them talking and avoiding the topic of his father and family, Camille finally swallowed deep, took a breath and asked him the question.

"Kyle, I have not heard you mention anything so far about your father. Why?"

"I figured you are aware that Ellis Lange is my father."

"Yes, I'm fully aware of that."

"My father and I are not exactly on speaking terms right now."

"Okay, that doesn't sound so good. Can I ask you what happened?"

"Well it's rather sensitive so I don't think I'm ready to discuss it yet."

"Does it have something to do with your mother?"

"Maybe. Why do you ask?"

"I know that she's in a home and it's hard for the family. I can respect that you don't want to discuss it, but I must say that I truly admire how much devotion he has to his wife. Uhm, I mean your mother."

"Really, you mean he actually cares? I wouldn't know."

"You should know."

"Possibly, but now is not the time for this." he said.

Not wanting to pry too much she politely said, "Okay, I hear you. I hope I didn't upset you by bringing this up."

"No actually, I'm fine with it."

Camille could tell by his quick response and elevated pitch that he was slightly bothered by her intrusion into the relationship with his father. She tapped her fingers nervously on the glass coffee table deciding whether to push forward with more questions, or to let things rest with the hopes that another window would open and she could revisit the topic. She went with the latter.

"Why spoil the momentum we had going? he said before she had the chance to say anything else. Let me continue on with our previous conversation. What makes Camille Pryce tick?"

"A quick change of topic. Smooth," she stated making a full note to leave well enough alone. "I like to watch old movies, love to cook and enjoy a good stroll on a beautiful summer morning," she replied.

"Sounds good. I like what I hear so far."

"Is it safe for me to assume that you also like some of the same things?"

"Somewhat," he replied. "However, since I've been in London, beautiful summer mornings don't come up all that often, so walking is not always high on my list."

"Well it's not for everyone, but any type of exercise as I see it is always a good thing."

"That's true. I try to get out and play a round of tennis as much as I can. It's one of my favourite sports."

"Good to hear that you're not the traditional sports fan who likes football and or baseball," she replied.

"I watch those occasionally but not that often. On another note, do you have family in the San Francisco area?"

"Actually, I have one brother who lives about twenty minutes from me and a sister who lives in Boston. Both my mom and dad have passed away but the three of us are fairly close," she said.

"Oh, so sorry to hear about your parents."

"You don't have to be sorry. They have been gone for over eight and ten years now respectively. They were great parents and I still miss them both very much, but what keeps me going is that we had a great relationship right up until the end, so I have no regrets."

She heard Kyle sigh before he spoke.

"Oh, so no regrets eh? That's great to hear. Hopefully, when it gets to that stage for me I will be able to say the same thing."

"You will reconcile in time, I'm sure. After all family unity is always important, especially when the time comes that you need them the most."

Once their conversation concluded, Camille took a moment to reflect on the broken relationship that had occurred between her brother and father. They never truly reconnected before her father's passing. To this day, her brother still has regrets about not working harder at mending the relationship. It would be a shame if Kyle and Ellis suffered the same fate. She was determined to help in any way she could to push them both towards a reconciliation.

⇥ ⇤

Camille and Kyle spoke either on the phone or through Skype almost every day over the next two weeks. They worked out a schedule of times when it would be best to connect. She basked in their regular conversations, probing but never directly asking about his relationship with his father. Whenever the opportunity presented itself she would include a positive comment or two about his father's work ethics. Hoping it would help to keep him top of mind. Furthermore, she believed that Kyle would open up as soon as he was ready if she managed to lay the groundwork properly.

By week three Kyle was ready to open up.

"It seems like you want to get something off your chest," she said.

111

"Well, we've been talking so well about everything under the sun over the past couple of weeks and I'm feeling more comfortable with you. So, it might be just the right time to tell you what happened between my father and me."

"Only if you're sure about it. Then I'm all ears," she said while pouring Pinot Grigio white wine into a glass.

Once again, she sat and listened to as much of his story as he was prepared to share. Throughout, she refilled her wine glass and put together a small plate of sliced carrots, celery, and cheese. Every now and then she would cross and uncross her legs, finally pulling them both up on the couch underneath her bottom. Kyle's voice grew stronger. He sounded angrier than hurt at the circumstances surrounding his mother while telling his story. This led her to believe that he allowed his anger to cloud his vision of what might really have happened. After almost twenty minutes of him sharing, he suddenly became silent.

She jumped right in. "Wow that sounds deep and I admire the love you have for your mother. However, the man you describe doesn't appear to be the man I work with. While I know people are different when they are out of the office, his love for your mother is very touching. He visits her at least three times a week and spends at least four hours there every time. As a matter of fact, we have to plan our meetings with clients around his visits as he doesn't want to miss even one of those days."

"Oh," he replied.

"Also, he makes sure she has everything she needs, including special meals, clothes, bedding amongst other things." She was trying to make Kyle understand what had been happening in his absence.

"I've met your sister a few times at the office and she's always telling me how your mother would be far worse off than she is now without your father. If you want my opinion, you should be grateful that he's around. With you being in England you can only do so much."

Kyle gave no response.

"Are you still there?" she asked.

"Ahh, yeah, I am just thinking a bit."

"Look it's none of my business, but this whole thing with you and your father sounds like a big miscommunication and two proud men not wanting to give in. I think you should seriously reconsider your stance."

"Maybe."

"As I mentioned before, I firmly believe in family and connections."

Nothing but silence came from the other end of the phone. She decided to leave it up to him to talk first.

"Leave it with me. It's a lot to take in right now," he finally replied. "But I will tell you that it seems as though you are determined to get us talking again. Also, knowing how you feel about family confirms to me that I do want to get to know you better. Besides, I've already put a plan into place to open up a small agency in San Francisco."

"Oh really? That's good to hear. What made you decide this?"

"I truly need to be closer to my mother and believe it or not, I had been thinking long and hard about making an effort to reconnect with my father. My sister has been after me for quite some time and she's right. It's not good for the family to be at odds like this. Believe me, it's really been weighing on my mind."

"I hope then that this conversation was beneficial."

"Actually, it just helped me to realize what I already knew but didn't necessarily want to accept."

"Good to hear. That makes me feel better." She took a larger sip of her wine this time. "When you move back to San Francisco what's going to happen with your London office?"

"Oh, my partner will run the branch here. But that won't be happening for some time as I still have to go back to San Francisco to find a suitable location to set up an office. Then I need to find a capable person to run it for me until I move back."

"Looks like you got a lot of work on your plate." she replied.

"Hey, I've got a great idea. You wouldn't want to work for me, would you?"

"Yeah right," she replied with a sarcastic laugh.

"No really, I could use someone like you in my company. You're smart, well versed and successful in the business."

"Nice try. But I'm staying put."

"Camille, don't think of this as just jumping ship. This new agency is going after a totally different market base than what your servicing now. With my agency, it will allow you to open up new avenues that deal more with women and the changing digital trends in the business. You would have free reign to run it any way you like."

"Yeah until you come back from London and want to change everything around. No thank-you."

"Look maybe I'm not explaining myself very well. So let me try this again. I'm fully aware of your dedication to your current job and I respect that. But if you had the opportunity to be solely in charge of running an agency would that not interest you?"

Camille took a few seconds to contemplate what he said to her before she responded. Of course, being in control of an agency appealed to her, but not this one. She could never leave Ellis to work for his son. That would be unethical. Besides she was just promoted to partner.

"Kyle that all sounds well and good but I can't see me doing that. I'm a partner in your father's firm right now. It wouldn't make sense to leave and run another office. What would be in it for me?"

"I've thought of that and if things work out then a mutual partnership would be a part of the deal. I'll also beat whatever salary my father is currently paying you."

"This is beginning to sound more like a competition than a genuine offer," she said as her voice grew stronger.

"That's not at all what it's about. Advertising is in my blood. Obviously, when I return home I want to continue in the business. My father's company is his and I already have my own. Whether you come on board or not, it's going to happen. Initially, I wanted to compete against my father but not anymore. We would be servicing two different markets. I just thought this would be an opportunity for you to branch out and in many ways, do your own thing. Even when I return to the states, my focus will not be on that portion of the business. I want to spend my time on ramping up the social-media end of the business."

"Kyle, I still don't think it's what I want."

"Look, just think about it. It's going to take me some time to get this all done so there's no rush. But I will tell you regardless of what you decide, I think you are a strong and beautiful woman. I also believe that we were destined to meet. So, I'm still very interested in getting to know you better even at a distance."

Camille felt a warm glow invade her body. She knew he was awaiting a response from her, but she wanted to let the word 'destined' flutter around in her mind for a few more seconds before she spoke. Internally she was still fighting with herself about spending so much time talking with Kyle. But knowing that he was so far away made her commitment to herself to not getting involved again for a year seem attainable. Then it dawned on her, the year was almost up.

Before her words would form to respond to his comment, the doorbell echoed. Ignoring it she heard Kyle ask if that was the doorbell in the background. Within seconds it echoed again.

She told Kyle that she was going to answer it as she walked towards the door with the phone in her hand. Once there she placed the phone face down on the ledge beside her keys.

Her body tightened up and her chin dropped down towards her chest. Her nostrils flared before words started to form. Not in her wildest dreams did she expect to see Josh standing in her doorway. He had aged a bit since the last time she saw him but still stood tall and strong. His neat short brown hair that was always on point now appeared untrimmed and begged for attention. She further noticed a distinct stomach bulge over the top of his jeans, clearly indicating he was not taking care of his once well-muscled body. In his hand was a stunning bouquet of her favourite flowers, white calla lilies, yellow roses and red chrysanthemums. Tucked under his left arm she could see a box of the Godiva Belgian chocolates that they used to eat together when they watched movies. Leaning up against his right leg was the largest card she had ever seen.

"Before you say a word, I know this is a surprise to you but I've realized what a screw up I've been. You were the best thing that ever happened to me and I messed it up. Flowers, chocolates and a card will never be able to make up for the mess I've made of our relationship, but I had to start somewhere."

"Josh this is crazy. What are you doing?"

"We need to talk and you wouldn't return my calls or texts, so here I am and these are for you."

"There's nothing to talk about. You walked away from me and our relationship. What you did was inexcusable. A text message as a goodbye. Really Josh, how weak."

"I know. I also know that it will take some time for you to forgive me, but I'm prepared to work hard at getting you back."

"Josh, you will be working hard for a long time if not forever."

"If that's what it takes."

Suddenly she remembered she had not hung up from speaking with Kyle and although the phone was face down, he might be hearing her exchange with Josh.

"Look, I can't speak with you now I am on the phone long distance."

"No problem, I didn't think I would get anywhere on the first try anyway. These items are yours." He handed her the flowers and chocolates, then bent down to pick up the card. "There will be more like this to come. Believe me. I'm not trying to buy your love back, but I'm prepared to show you at all cost how much you mean to me."

Camille watched still stunned as he gave her a slight nod of the head, then turned around and reluctantly walked down the hall. She took the items inside, shook her head, laughed nervously to herself then picked up the phone.

"Sorry about that, I hope I wasn't gone too long," she said hesitantly.

"No, I'm good, but I do have to run. Can we catch up again maybe tomorrow?"

"Yeah sure."

"Camille, I meant what I said about the business and getting to know you better."

She smirked before replying, "Okay I'll keep that in mind. We'll talk soon."

From what she could tell, it didn't seem that Kyle had overheard her conversation with Josh.

She was quick to hang up the phone and leaned the card against the ledge not even interested in opening it. There were obviously going to be words of love and devotion written in there, that she didn't want to read. He was a master at writing words that cut deep to the heart. Every card she had received from him in the past made her forget about how much of a jerk he truly was. It was not going to work this time. That card was never going to be opened.

She took the box of chocolates and flowers into the kitchen and laid them on the counter. Then she wondered what were the odds of something like this happening to her. Two months ago, she had been a single woman vowing to stay as far away from men as possible. She meets a handsome stranger on a plane who turned out to be her boss's son. Not only did he make her reconsider her commitment to herself, but he made her an offer that could be something worth considering, both personally and professionally.

Then out of the blue, the nightmare ex-boyfriend who could charm his way into the White House, showed up looking as determined as she had ever seen him. Although a reconciliation was still out of the question, his sincere approach was nothing like she had ever seen before. Could he truly be sorry about how he ended the relationship and honestly want to make a second go of it?

She started to mellow a little as she ripped open the chocolate box and tasted one. Her mouth was in sheer delight as she savoured the chocolate and held onto the flavour as it slid down her throat. *After all,* she thought, *we did have some amazing times together.* Somewhere deep down she still vaguely cared for him.

"Pull yourself together, Camille," she said out loud as she walked into the living room to search for a vase. She knew however that Josh was like a tick and was going to continue to try to wear her down. She also knew that if Kyle was determined enough he was going to push to have her work at the new company with him. To wrap everything up in a tidy bow, she also believed that there was no way Ellis was going to let her go without a fight.

⊷ ⊶

Josh was true to his word. Every third day over the next three weeks she had received a different bouquet of expensive flowers and a box of chocolates. Her apartment was beginning to look like the local flower shop. She had strategically placed each set of flowers in different areas including her bedroom but was fast running out of space. To think of it, he didn't spend this much money on her during their entire relationship.

On several occasions, she texted or called Josh to tell him to stop spending his money as she didn't need or want the flowers and chocolate, but he kept sending them anyway. She even resorted to calling his brother to have him convince Josh to stop, but he was of no help. They had gotten along tremendously well before the break-up, so he was egging Josh on to win her back. Eventually, she figured he would run out of money, or find someone else to spend it on. Until then she would just have to grin and bear it. Better yet, she could take the flowers to the local senior's home and drop them off. At least someone there could enjoy them.

As she walked towards the door the big card still stood by the ledge sealed as tight as the day she received it. She knew that if she touched it in any way, she would be compelled to open it, so every day she walked by and tried to pretend it just wasn't there.

Finally, after a month, the flowers and chocolates stopped arriving. It looked like Josh got the message. Relieved, Camille was now free to close that chapter of her life. She shuffled through the drawer in the kitchen for a pair of scissors. Once found, she headed straight for the front door, picked up the card and started cutting it up. Whatever words were written in there would never be read by her.

Kyle did not pressure her as much about his offer. He made sure though that every time she said something about advertising, he complimented her on how brilliant the idea was and how well it would go with his plans for the new company. She figured this was his way of keeping it in her mind without always mentioning it. Her mind though was made up and she told him so the last time they had spoken. She also made it clear, that pursuing her would be a long process. She was no pushover and had high expectations of the next man she got involved with. He took the news well but clarified that it didn't change his growing feelings for her.

⚓ ⚓

"You wanted to see me, Ellis?" she asked noticing the excitement in his eyes.

"Yes, I just had to tell you the good news. My son called me this morning, he said he was coming to town within the next three weeks. He thinks too much time has passed between us and we need to work things out."

"Oh, how fabulous. I can tell you're thrilled to hear from him."

"You bet, and if things go well then I want all of us to have dinner together sometime."

"Name the time and place, I'll be there. Ellis. Thanks for sharing your good news with me."

"No. Thank you. He told me about your budding relationship and the part you played in this. I owe you one."

"Ellis, you owe me nothing. Just seeing you this happy is a gift in itself. I wouldn't trade the chance to see you both back together for the world."

She left his office with a kick in her step. Her face was beaming almost as much as Ellis was. She trusted that Kyle would make the right decision and with a little bit of coaxing from her he did. If he was here right now she would hug and kiss him for being the bigger man. Even though he never told her the other reasons why he was mad at his father, it didn't matter. What was important is that he took the first step in reconnecting with his family.

Camille opened up her desk drawer and pulled her cell phone out of her purse. She was so giddy that she almost forgot what she wanted the phone for. She took note of the time and knew it was too late to call, so she turned towards her computer and sent an email off instead.

She typed joyously as though her fingers were playing the piano.

"It takes a big man to take the first step. I trust you felt the same way your father did after you spoke, a great sense of relief. As I said before, there's nothing better than being a part of a united family. Your mother would be proud. Can't wait to see you in three weeks."

As she relaxed her shoulders to breathe a sigh of relief, a new message appeared on her screen. She clicked on it.

"Hi Camille, I'm not giving up. I gave you a short break but I still want you back. Josh."

"Oh no. Not again," she said as she leaned back in her chair, kicked off her heels and laughed.

She then noticed her reflection in the glass of the art deco picture facing her. For the first time in a long time, she was happy with the confident woman she saw. At that moment, she knew it was high time to trade in her old life, and give herself permission to look forward to a new one.

WALKING THROUGH
By Francine Fleming

Her voice was like Billie Holiday's - rich and bluesy.
I returned my gaze to the lady who was
singing the soulful melody....
She opened her eyes and her gaze met mine.
A smile spread across her face.

- Francine Fleming

WALKING THROUGH

"That's my song." The voice that reached my ear materialized from seemingly out of nowhere.

I looked around for its owner and saw an elderly lady seated in an armchair to the right of mine. Fine wrinkles etched her cocoa complexioned skin, though youthful beauty still shone through her aged face. High cheekbones reached up to brown eyes that bore the hint of a slant and her silver-grey hair was swept up in a neat bun. Passing time had not ravaged her features. I continued staring at her, not certain as to whether she was speaking to me or just speaking.

"Pardon me?" I asked when she spoke again.

"What's playing. That's my song."

The velvety voice that flowed through the visitors' lounge of Forest Brook Retirement and Assisted Living Residences came from a portable CD player that stood on a side table next to her chair. I cocked my head to one side while listening to the singer. Her voice was like Billie Holiday's - rich and bluesy. I returned my gaze toward the lady who was quietly singing the soulful melody, *"...walking through, gonna walk on, walk on through..."*

She opened her eyes and her gaze met mine. A smile spread across her face. "Yeah, that's me singing. Recorded that tune back in '66."

"It's beautiful. I'm Megan, by the way. Megan Craig," I said offering her my hand. She took my hand in hers. Her touch was soft and warm.

"My name's Dahlia," she said. "Born and raised in Harlem, New York. How 'bout you, honey? Where you from?"

"I'm from Brooklyn. Born and raised there."

"Brooklyn? For real? That's where I lived before I moved out here to the country."

I smiled. Forest Brook, nestled among a copse of mature oak trees, was located only an hour's drive outside of Brooklyn, not quite in the country but for urban dwellers it might as well have been. I looked out the large west facing windows at the surrounding trees dressed in their spring finery, their budding leaves illuminated by the setting sun.

This pleasant Sunday afternoon, like every Sunday afternoon since my father suffered a stroke and my husband, Bradley, and I moved him into Forest Brook, found me at the retirement residence for my weekly visit with Dad. He had always insisted he would not leave the house where he and Mom had lived since they got married until he was 'good and ready.' But losing Mom a year ago, then the stroke, forced him to be good and ready.

Dad was snoring softly in his armchair. He often fell into a snooze during our visits and I took advantage of the solitude by writing free prose into my notebook. Being an English Literature professor, my father had nurtured my love affair with the written word. His passion for literature poured from him and rained upon me. When I told him of my desire to become a writer, he happily presented me with my first of many notebooks. On the inside cover, in his bold, slanted handwriting, he had written *If you want to be a writer, write.*

Each time I started a fresh notebook, I recorded Epictetus's words on its inside cover. They stayed with me, through my journey to becoming a successful author and freelance columnist until I shared them with my students at the junior college where I taught creative writing.

I returned my attention to Dahlia. "How long have you been living at Forest Brook, Dahlia?"

"I ain't sure, honey. My daughters, they moved me here, last year, I think. I don't know for sure but it sure was a big old family affair."

"I don't mind," she went on. "I miss Brooklyn sometimes but this sure is a pretty place, ain't it?"

"Yes, it is. See the gentleman napping in that chair? He's my father. He moved to Forest Brook just last month. He's happy here and that makes me happy."

Dahlia turned her attention to Dad and smiled. "Oh yeah, I know Slim. So, he's your daddy?"

"Slim?"

"That's right."

I laughed. "Sweet. I like that name." The moniker suited Dad who'd always had a trim physique, made thinner with aging and the stroke.

Dahlia was laughing also. Suddenly, she stopped and re-garded me curiously. "So, you get your light skin from him, huh?"

I paused, considering how much of my lineage I should reveal to her. "Well, I'm adopted," I said deciding on full disclosure. "My birth mother is white and my biological fa-ther was black."

William and Dorothy Flowers became Mom and Dad to me on the snowy winter afternoon when they brought me to the Brooklyn Heights townhouse that would be my new home. They had adopted me, an acting-out five-year old, from a miserable foster care existence. Since that day, they never allowed the word "adoption" to lessen the bond we had formed.

Dahlia nodded. "Ah. So Slim ain't your real daddy?"

I smiled. "Oh Slim *is* my real daddy, the only one I know."

She smiled with me and then suddenly became agitated. She squeezed her brows into a deep frown and gripped the chair's armrests. I heard frustration tinge her voice when she spoke. "What you say your name was? Mabel? Margaret?"

"Megan. It's Megan."

"Megan, honey, reach over here and put my song on again for me, will you? I don't know why they turned off my music. I didn't want it turned off."

"Of course," I said hoping to soothe her.

I went to the side of her chair and pressed the play button, releasing the sultry voice from its metal casing. A CD shell cover lay on the table, beside the player. I examined the cover photo closely. The picture had the look of a copy, as though someone had burned a copy of her song onto a disk especially for her. Dahlia, all sultry

elegance sheathed in a figure hugging red dress, was surrounded by three dapper-looking men, each holding an
instrument – saxophone, trumpet, and upright bass. A
fourth man sat behind a drum kit.

I peered at her face and thought, with a little envy,
of my own features – round, wide set eyes, round nose
sprinkled with freckles, all set in a heart-shaped face.
'Beautifully cute,' was how Bradley had referred to my
looks when we first met. I knew then that there was something special about a guy who could see beauty in a face
I had always considered quirky looking.

I continued staring at the CD cover. The woman in the
picture was the woman with whom I was speaking alright.
She hadn't changed that much, even after all those years.
How did Dahlia feel, I wondered, when she gazed upon her
youthful self?

Dahlia started humming again, softly, soulfully. She
closed her eyes, swaying ever so slightly from side to side.
I studied her as she hummed and swayed, her movement
almost hypnotic. Suddenly, her eyes sprang open and her
gaze met mine.

"What was the name of them boys again?" She asked.

"I'm sorry, boys?" I asked.

"Yeah, I used to sing with them. Jazz. That's what they
played. The Jazz Deliverers, that's it. They played and I sang.
Honey, we made the sweetest sounds."

"I'm sure you did."

"Oh yeah. But if it weren't for Josephus, I never would've
hooked up with them. Least he was good for something.
That, and playing trumpet. That man, he played trumpet like it was the most natural thing in the world. He

made that thing sing sweeter than a Mockingbird in springtime."

My creative motor shifted into high gear. Curiosity piqued, I asked, "Josephus?"

"Yeah, Josephus. He was my man. He got me into the Half Moon Club, you know. All the best Blues and Jazz folk played there."

"The Half Moon Club? Sounds like quite the place."

"Oh, it sure was. I remember the day Josephus come into the dive where I used to sing. I remember that day real good. He come to the club, looking like a cool cat with his pressed hair and wearing his fancy suit."

I leaned toward her, listening intently as Dahlia spoke, her voice alluring while she recounted the day that the man she called Josephus discovered her. She paused and glanced at the notebook on my lap. "What's that?" she asked.

"It's a notebook. I am a writer. Would you mind if I took some notes?"

She shook her head. "I don't mind one bit."

Determined to capture as much as my note-taking would allow, I began to scribble into my notebook as she continued.

"I watched Josephus go to the bar to fetch himself a drink, but not before he looked my way while I was singing and I knew what I saw in them eyes of his. There was a spark there for sure. After my set, he introduced himself and asked me my name. And that's when he invited me to come down to the Half Moon to sing with him and his band."

I'm not sure how long I had been writing when Dahlia's voice trailed off. I searched her eyes for remnants of those days.

"So?" I prodded, eager for more. "What happened at the Half Moon Club?"

Dahlia gazed at me as though she were seeing me for the first time. Then something like recognition crept into her face, lifting the corners of her mouth into a little smile. "Martha, honey, put my music on will you? Somebody turned it off. I don't know why they turned it off. I was listening to it."

Again, I went to the side of her chair and pressed the play button. I looked at Dahlia hoping she would continue but her eyelids looked heavy and her head was slightly tilted forward. A young personal care worker approached her then. The PCW's name badge read "Liz." She smiled at me, and then put a hand on Dahlia's shoulder. Gently, she shook it.

"Dahlia," Liz said. "C'mon dear. Let's get you to your suite now. It's time for your evening medication."

Dahlia looked up and smiled at the young woman. She allowed Liz to guide her from the chair. I went to the CD player, picked it and the disk up and handed them to Liz. "Don't forget these," I said.

Liz shook her head. "Oh no. We keep the player and CD in the lounge's audio cabinet. That way, Dahlia can have her music whenever she's here."

Dahlia reached for my hand and squeezed it. "Where you going honey?"

"I'm going home, but I'll be back next Sunday. I hope we can visit again."

"Sure. Let's do that. But where you going?"

I wondered whether she heard my response as Liz led her from the lounge. Dad began stirring from his slumber. I looked down at him and smiled as I cupped his lined face in my hands. "Ah, you're back with me, huh Dad?"

"I am sorry, Meg. Did I spend most of our visit sleeping?" Dad asked. He spoke slowly, a slight slur to his voice.

"Not really. We had a good visit before your nap." I glanced at my watch. "I should get going. Come, I'll walk you to your suite."

Inside his suite, I hugged him closely. "Love you lots. I'll see you next Sunday. Sure you're okay?"

"Abserlooly," he replied. "Love you too, sweetheart. And give my love to Bradley and the girls."

I nodded.

On my way to the parking lot, I looked toward the evening sky where patches of grey clouds blotted out the sun, eliminating the twilight's golden hue. The rain began falling just as I reached the SUV. Settling behind the steering wheel, I checked my cell phone for messages. Other than an email from my editor, there were none. I sighed and started the engine.

As I drove, I heard the jazzy backbeat to Dahlia's song in the windshield wipers' rhythmic pock-peck, pock-peck sound and I pictured her face, her enduring beauty and the uncanny sharp details that pushed through the haze of dementia or Alzheimer's or whatever cognitive dysfunction she suffered, as she recounted her past. The idea that had already taken root in my mind began to flourish and grow. I decided then that I would write her story.

⟞⟝ ⟞⟝

Bradley came from the kitchen as I let myself in through the front door. My husband of nearly 25 years greeted me with a nod followed by "hey".

A mouthwatering aroma filled the hallway. "You cooked?" I asked.

"Well, if you call taking that tuna casserole from the freezer and heating it up cooking, then yeah, I guess I cooked."

"Tuna casserole sounds good to me." I hung my jacket in the hall closet then followed Bradley to the kitchen.

"How was your visit?" He asked as he slid on oven mitts and took the casserole from the stainless steel gas oven. Our kitchen was state-of-the-art gourmet. Bradley loved to cook. Cooking, he claimed, helped relieve the stress that came with his career as a New York State prosecutor. He'd had the kitchen remodeled shortly after we moved in. It became our favorite room in the house. I recollected the special times we shared in this space, creating meals together, even stealing intimate moments. Bradley and I used to joke that food wasn't the only thing sizzling in the kitchen. Those days felt like a distant past.

"Megan, did you hear me?"

My focus shifted back to Bradley. "Sorry, what?"

"Your visit. How was it?"

"Oh, really interesting."

"Oh yeah? What did you two talk about that was so interesting?"

The smirk I thought I heard in his voice was deflating. "What're you saying? Because Dad is old, that isn't possible? You'll get there one day too, you know."

I heard him draw in a deep breath. "What's with you? I just asked a question."

"Nothing's with me."

"Whatever. If you're ready to eat, I'll dish out the casserole."

A dense fog of silence enveloped us as we sat at the dining room table. It had become our mealtime normal since our two daughters went off to college.

"Actually," I said while peering across the table at him. "I didn't speak with Dad all that much. He had a long nap during our visit. But I met an amazing lady." I searched Bradley's face trying to recognize a glimmer of the flame that once burned brightly between us.

"Her name is Dahlia. She told me she used to be a Jazz singer," I continued.

"Oh, yeah?" Bradley said, barely looking up from his meal.

"Yeah. She was quite beautiful, even in her old age. And she kept humming to this song that was playing on a little CD player she had beside her chair. She said it was her song. It was lovely, really, sort of haunting. But you know what was most intriguing about her?"

"What's that?" Bradley mumbled between chews.

"Well, she told me she was the reincarnation of Billie Holiday."

Bradley's head shot up. "She what?"

I chuckled. "Oh good, I have your attention."

"Of course you have my attention. I can eat and listen at the same time."

"Of course you can. Anyway, this lady, Dahlia, seemed to be struggling with dementia or maybe Alzheimer's but her long-term memory was just incredible. She recalled her past with such detail."

Bradley looked me in the eyes, his expression now one of curious interest. "Dementia or Alzheimer's eh? Are you sure she didn't invent this Dahlia character?"

'Argh, Bradley! Why do you always have to throw that cynical wrench into everything?' I wanted to shout. It was the lawyer in him, I decided. And, had Dahlia not spoken in such detail and had I not seen her picture on the CD cover, I would have to admit he had a point. But there was no question in my mind that the Dahlia with whom I spoke and the Dahlia in that picture were the same, and I told Bradley so.

"There's no way she made up what she told me. She said she sang with a band called The Jazz Deliverers and she recalled names, places, dates, everything, so clearly."

He set his fork down. "Come to think of it my grandmother was the same in the few years before she died."

"Really?" Bradley's grandmother had died the year we met.

"Well, Gran couldn't recall what day of the week it was, or what she'd had for breakfast, but ask her about how she and my grandfather met, or about their wedding day and she'd give you a blow-by-blow account of those memories. Her attention to detail was incredible, just like your Dahlia. Pretty amazing, alright. So, what did you say the group's name was? Jazz Defenders?"

"Jazz *Deliverers*. The Jazz Deliverers."

"Hmm. Guess I'm not the Jazz aficionado I thought was. I've never heard of them. And you say there's a CD of their record? That means, to this day they're cutting re-releases of their album?"

"Oh no, I don't think so. The CD looks like a home-made version. The shell cover photo looks like a good quality copy, from an album cover. I'm thinking someone made a copy of that record for her."

He nodded. "Makes sense."

The warm satisfaction I felt coursing through me was not the result of the delicious casserole only, but because Bradley and I hadn't had such an involved conversation in ages. Silently, I thanked Dahlia for that.

After dinner, Bradley retreated to the den to work on closing arguments for a high profile trial that was about to wrap up. I stacked the dishwasher and went to bed ahead of him. Climbing the stairs to our bedroom, my steps felt a little lighter. That night, in bed, I stared at Bradley's broad back as it moved up and down in rhythm with his soft snoring. His football player physique – broad shoulders, back and tapered torso were features that first attracted me to him; that, and his rich chocolate complexion. Bradley had, in fact, played college football. We had met at one of his games. After a mutual friend introduced us and I complimented him on his prowess on the field, he had shrugged self-consciously and said "truth is, football's not really my thing, but I wasn't going to turn down the scholarship I won."

Fixing my gaze on his back, I reached over to run my hand over the width of him. He grunted, and pulled the covers tightly around him while shrugging off my touch. 'We'll find a way,' I told myself, 'to get back what we once had.'

—⊹ ⊹—

"Baby, every day should be your day." Bradley had uttered those words at my ear, his arms encircling my waist when, years ago, I declared Mondays "my-days." Back then, my days were filled with the demands of raising two elementary school-aged daughters – supervising homework, chauffeuring the girls to extracurricular activities, attending and planning birthday parties – while Bradley worked long days. On Mondays, my schedule, cleared of classes and office meetings, allowed for six blissful hours to myself. Bradley and I found time for each other where we could.

Then, life served up a dose of irony with the change in our family dynamic – the girls went away to college while Bradley and I grew apart.

This Monday morning, seated at the kitchen's breakfast bar, a coffee mug to my right and my laptop and notebook before me, I drew in a slow, deep breath and then exhaled. A single tear escaped my eye and trickled down my cheek. I brushed it away while flipping through my notebook to the page where my Dahlia notes began.

Adrenaline flowed through me, sweeping away my melancholy mood as I turned on my laptop and stared at the blank page that came up on the computer screen. This was where I would begin her story. My fingers tapped the keyboard while I allowed creativity and imagination to take-over where Dahlia did not or could not fill in the blanks.

⇒⇐

Dahlia's Story – Chapter 1

From the stage, Dahlia eyed the dapper stranger who entered the rundown Harlem Jazz joint where she sang on Saturday nights. She allowed her gaze to follow him, a peacock among pigeons, as he made his way to the bar to order a drink. He was different alright. His gaze, his smile, the way he rhythmically nodded his head to the music were clear signs to Dahlia that he was engaged in her performance. Unlike the regulars who often seemed more absorbed in conducting shady business over cheap liquor than they were in her singing. After Dahlia's set, the stranger approached her and invited her to join him for a drink.

He took her hand in his. "Name's Josephus," he said his voice rich and smooth, like a chocolate malt. "Josephus Elroy Jones."

Her eyes widened. "THE Josephus Elroy Jones? The ace horn player over at The Half Moon Club?"

"The same," he answered. "What about you, girl? You got a name to go with that silken voice?"

She smiled. "I sure do. It's Dahlia. So, what brings you to this dive?"

"I come to check out the sax player but looks like I hit pay dirt with you too. My band, The Jazz Deliverers, sure could use a fine looking vocalist like you. Why don't you come check us out next Saturday, honey? I'll make sure they treat you right."

"For sure, I'll be there," she gushed.

Dahlia wanted to pinch herself, make sure she wasn't dreaming. The Half Moon Club on Lenox Avenue was pure class. She had heard that only the best Blues and Jazz folk played there and getting a gig at the Half Moon was not something that happened to ordinary folk like her. That is, until Josephus Elroy Jones graced this dump with his fine presence. A shiver of jittery anticipation rushed through her.

⟞⧗⟝

Sunday afternoon came on a wave of bright sunshine. I grabbed my car keys from the key hook next to the hall closet and shouted a quick 'bye' to Bradley who was in the den working on his trial file. He mumbled a barely audible 'bye' in return. I hurried through the front door happily anticipating my trip to Forest Brook. My visits would now take on an added purpose – my Dahlia project. I hadn't yet discussed the idea of turning her story into a novel with anyone, not even Bradley. My thoughts searched for those days, like someone groping in the dark for a light switch, when Bradley and I shared everything.

At Forest Brook, I found Dad and Dahlia seated outside on a bench at the foot of a beautiful weeping willow tree. Dad, I noticed, held in his hand his cherished copy of Shakespearean Sonnets. He was reading to her, his recitation surprisingly as strong and as clear as I remembered when he recited Shakespeare to Mom and me. "..*but thy eternal summer shall not fade, nor lose possession of those fair those ow'st...*" What course, I mused, would these two lovely souls' friendship take had they not been limited by their impediments?

I paused to allow Dad to finish reading then smiled and greeted them. "Hey, you two."

With the aid of his walker, locked into position, Dad hoisted himself up off the bench. We wrapped one another in a warm embrace. A lopsided smile spread across his face. "Hello sweetheart. You look lovely, as always," he said while patting my mass of curls.

"Thanks Dad. Hello Dahlia," I said while reaching down to give her a hug. Her face registered no sign of recognition. "It's me, Megan. We met last week and you were telling me all about your days as a Jazz singer. Remember?" I searched her face hoping for a hint that she recalled our chat but her gaze was vague.

Then, her lips curved into a little smile. "Oh yeah. Megan. Such a pretty name. My daughters have pretty names too. Slim, tell Megan my daughters' names."

"Anne and Patricia," Dad said, looking pleased.

"Those *are* pretty names. I wish they were here today. I'd love to meet them."

"They must've been here today. Didn't they come here today, Slim?"

"Um no, Dahlia. Your girls were here yesterday. They visit one day during the week and Saturdays." Dad turned to me. "I met Anne and Patricia yesterday, Meg. They are lovely ladies."

"Just like their mother. How about we take a walk around the grounds? It's such a beautiful day. Dahlia, would you like to join us?"

She reached for her walking cane and, with unexpected fluidity, stood up. "Sure, let's walk."

Our stroll took us over well-manicured lawns and past a lawn bowling green where a group of bowlers chatted between turns. Further on, we came upon a Tai Chi class and further still, seated around a long picnic table, another group was engaged in lively debate.

"The book club," Dad explained.

I gave myself an imaginary pat on the back for helping Dad select Forest Brook. I had researched this and other facilities with, I imagined, as much vigor as a PhD candidate researching her thesis. Forest Brook was noted for being a progressive facility; one that nurtured its residents, those who were self-sufficient as well as those who required assisted living. It was pricey, but worth it. Seeing that Dad hadn't lost his habitually upbeat attitude quelled any nagging concerns I had about his well-being.

"Meg," Dad called to me. I glanced around. He and Dahlia were several steps behind me. "Mind if we go inside now? I could use a comfy chair."

"Of course, Dad. Is the lounge okay, or would you prefer we visit in your suite?"

"The lounge is fine. I love the view from that space."

"I'm coming in too, Slim. You mind if I come in too?"

"We were hoping you would, weren't we, Meg?"

I nodded at my gracious father. Tenderness caressed my heart. Inside, I went to the small kitchenette adjacent to the lounge and prepared tea for the three of us. The kitchenette was well stocked with trays of baked goods. We sat, sipped tea, munched on banana muffins and chatted until I noticed Dad's eyelids, like heavy drapery, slipping over his eyes.

"How're you feeling, Dahlia?" I asked.

"I'm feeling fine." She reached for the teapot but her hand trembled when she tried to lift it. I gently took it from her and topped up her tea.

"Thank you, honey." She looked at me but she was frowning. Her eyes seemed pleading. Anticipating her request, I stood up. "Would you like me to put your music on?" I asked.

She nodded and smiled at me.

I retrieved her CD player and CD from the audio cabinet. Dahlia's eyes sparkled as the music started.

"You know," she said. "Josephus always liked the way I fixed his tea, said I sweetened it just right."

"Oh? Did you and Josephus get married?"

"No, we never did, but he always said we would get married and I believed him. After all, he was my man and I was his woman. We lived in the same apartment and had children. We may as well been married, huh?"

I set my teacup down and retrieved my notebook and pen from my purse. "When did you and Josephus get together?"

"Josephus and me, we got together after I joined his band. My friends, though, didn't trust him, said he looked like trouble. But I didn't pay them any mind. I figured they were just jealous. Well, he asked me to join the band after I sang at the Half Moon one Saturday night. I suppose that was like what you call an audition."

"How did you feel? Were you nervous?"

She chuckled. "Nervous? I was downright terrified. But I tried to keep that fear inside me. Why, from the time I got there and talked to the club manager, to the time I got up on stage and started singing, my knees were knocking together like two big ole coconuts. See, I wasn't used to singing in no fancy place like the Half Moon Club. I didn't know what folk there would think about me or my singing. Good thing I had a shot of gin and soda before I got on stage."

I laughed. "Oh no, Dahlia. How did you get through the song?"

Dahlia paused and I tried to read her expression before she continued. "Well I got through that song because it felt right, like I was supposed to be there on that stage with Josephus and his band. When I looked into Josephus's eyes and he smiled at me, and when I started to sing and I saw them smiling faces in the audience, I knew I was gonna do alright. From that night, I fell for Josephus. I fell hard for him and he fell for me."

"What happened then?"

"He invited me to his place one night after a real hot set. From that night, one thing led to another and, well, I never looked back. Honey, things were real good right up until our baby girls come along."

As Dahlia spoke, I fervently jotted down the notes that would become chapter two of her story. Every so often I glanced at her. She had a faraway expression on her face, as though she were seeing that scene at the Half Moon Club being played out on the wall behind me.

꜀ ꜄

Driving home, I squinted into the setting sun that lingered at the horizon like a golden beach ball. On the radio, a twangy-voiced singer lamented her lost love. But my mind remained on the Half Moon Club. As I drove along the quiet road, the characters that made an appearance in Dahlia's story today – Josephus, the band, the club's manager and patrons – all jostled to gain a position at the forefront of my thoughts. They remained with me the entire trip home, their presence palpable, until I turned onto our driveway.

Inside, I met an oppressive silence. The house felt cavernous. Had Bradley taken a break from trial stuff and gone out? I wondered. But, as I walked through the hallway, the clicking sound of fingers tapping a keyboard splintered the silence. A beam of light shone at the slightly ajar den door. Gently, I pushed it open wider. Bradley was seated at the computer desk, typing away, working, I guessed, on closing arguments.

"Hi there," I said quietly. "You been in here all day?"

He looked up and toward me with tired looking eyes. "Pretty much. How'd your visit go?"

"Great. We took advantage of the beautiful day and spent some time outside."

"Cool. How's Dad?"

"He seems to be improving with each visit."

"That's good news. So, no Dahlia today?"

I hesitated. I could always read his attitude in his body language. This time, I read lack of interest. "Yes, we visited with Dahlia also."

"That's nice," he said then returned his attention to the computer screen. "Well, I'd better get back to this."

'No more questions, Your Honor,' he might as well have said.

"Alright, I'll leave you to it. I'm going up for a shower. Oh, any calls?"

"Uhm...yeah. Krystin called. She said classes are going well and she's looking forward to coming home in August. And she said not to worry about Mikayla; they've been in touch through Facebook or Instagram or one of those things."

"Great," I said. Mikayla, our eldest, was spending the summer teaching English in Thailand, and Krystin was staying on at school through July to earn an extra credit. Both girls would be home in August for a short break before returning to school in the fall. Pride welled up within me when I thought of my daughters' stellar work ethics. Yet, part of me wondered whether the tension they must surely have sensed between Bradley and me influenced their decision to extend their time away from home. I turned to leave the den.

"Oh, and your sister, Laura. She called again." Bradley's words were like a brick wall that sprang up in front of me.

I turned and glared at him. "Laura is *not* my sister, and why don't they leave me alone?"

Bradley removed his glasses, rubbed his eyes and stood up. He came toward me and placed a heavy hand on my shoulder. "Megan" he said, his voice soft. I saw concern in his face, an emotion that had been lacking of late. "Laura *is* your sister, albeit half-sister, but still your sister. She said Helen is very ill. The prognosis isn't good. She may have only months left."

I shrugged his hand off my shoulder. "I'm sorry to hear that, but what does it have to do with me?"

Bradley spoke my name through a sigh. "Megan." He ignored my angry frown and continued. "You've let this go on far too long. You've given your time to some woman you hardly know, yet you refuse to give your own birth mother a chance at reconciliation in what could be the short time she has left. That is not the caring, compassionate woman I married."

Damned tears; they prickled the corners of my eyes. I stubbornly pushed them back. "You just don't get it, do you? You know very well what I went through in foster care. That's all down to her tossing me from her life with no consideration of what I could, and did, face without her to protect me."

Bradley's face appeared crestfallen. We'd had this discussion several times in the past, always with the same outcome. "Look," he said. "You know that Helen was a very young woman; facing motherhood alone after your biological father took off. You never forgave him either. And now he's dead. You'll never get that chance. Do you want the same thing to happen with your mother? Why not give her a chance to explain to you why she made what was very likely an agonizing decision?"

"Oh, so now I'm the guilty party eh, Mr. Attorney?"

"You know that's not what I'm saying. I'm just suggesting that you hear what she has to say, before it's too late."

"Listen, Bradley, enough with the lecture. You weren't there in that foster home with me. If it hadn't been for Mom and Dad, who knows what would have become of me."

"Megan, listen to me, I –"

I rushed from the den and raced up the stairs, through our bedroom to the ensuite bathroom where I stripped off my clothes and stepped into the shower. Salty tears rolling down my face mingled with the warm stream that poured from the showerhead. For whom, I asked myself, was I shedding tears - the little girl who had suffered at the hands of a dysfunctional system or the woman who had given me away like an unwanted cat or dog?

After my shower, I quickly dried off, wrapped a towel around my damp hair and slipped into freshly laundered pajamas. Years ago, Bradley had set up the antique desk that was a housewarming gift from his parents in the alcove area of our bedroom. My laptop sat on that desk beckoning me to come to it and continue with Dahlia's story – a needed diversion from this Helen issue. I positioned my fingers on the keyboard and, venturing back to Dahlia's Harlem and the Half Moon Club, began typing.

⊷ ⊶

Dahlia's Story – Chapter Two

The following Saturday night, decked out in her fanciest dress – an emerald green taffeta - Dahlia tentatively entered the heady atmosphere of The Half Moon Club where she sought momentary refuge in the Ladies' room. There, she tucked behind her ear a strand of hair that had escaped from her glossy upswept hairdo. Nervously, she fumbled through her pocketbook for her compact and applied a dab of powder to her nose, then touched up her rouge.

Satisfied that she looked her Saturday night best, she took a deep breath and, head held high, entered the club. Her heels clicked over the hardwood flooring. Her eyes scanned the large room's rich red and gold textured walls, linen covered tables, each adorned with a flickering candle inside a glass holder and the long bar, its varnished wood glistening beneath Victorian light fixtures. The air was infused with the competing scents of tobacco smoke, cologne and perfume emanating from the few patrons who were already seated. The pungent mixture could have been offensive but Dahlia found it intoxicating. On stage, she saw Josephus and The Jazz Deliverers warming up.

She made her way to the bar and lightly tapped the shoulder of a burley, cocoa colored man seated on one of the barstools. "'Scuse me, Mister. You the manager?" Josephus had described him well.

The manager eyed her up and down before answering. "I sure am. What can I do for you, doll?"

"I'm Dahlia, Josephus's friend. He said to ask for you."

"Ah, Dahlia. So you're the doll Josephus can't stop talking about. Ha-ha," he chuckled. "That brother sure do have fine taste in the ladies."

Dahlia felt a blush of heat rise to her cheeks.

"Have a seat, honey. What can I get you to drink? Josephus said to take good care of you."

She took a seat on the padded bar stool the manager held out for her and said, "How 'bout a gin and soda?"

"You askin' me or you offerin', honey?" he asked, another baritone laugh following his question.

The glow in Dahlia's cheeks grew warmer. She smiled at him. "Oh, I'm asking. Definitely asking."

"Then a gin and soda it is." The manager turned from her and repeated her order to the bartender. "Henry, pour this fine lady a gin and soda."

From the stage, Josephus acknowledged her with a wink and a smile that made her heart dance. She shifted her gaze from the stage and focused on the bartender's long, tapered fingers as he mixed her drink. The band started playing, their sweet Jazz riffs carried in sound waves that bounced off the ceiling and back to her ears. Dahlia took a sip of her drink and began to relax as the potent liquid coursed through her. She looked up from her drink and scanned the club. Quite suddenly, it seemed, the large space was filled with fine looking patrons, chatting, laughing, and sipping cocktails.

After the band's third number, Josephus went to the microphone. "Ladies and Gents, we got a real treat for you all tonight. C'mon up here Dahlia honey and give these folk a piece of scat heaven."

Dahlia took a deep breath and chased it with a gulp of her drink. Her heart began to flutter against her rib-cage. She looked around the room at the fine looking men and women sipping fancy cocktails and her heartbeat accelerated. She stood up to make her way to the stage but her legs felt heavy as though protesting her presence there. The Half Moon Club was a palace compared to the hovel that was the joint where she'd managed to score gigs, where she could have been singing butt naked and the patrons would've taken no notice, as if she was just a piece of the shabby furnishings.

"You sure about this Josephus?" she whispered from the stage stairs. He answered her with a chuckle while extending a hand to her as she slowly climbed the stairs. On stage, her eyes shifted to each band member as Josephus introduced them - Carl on upright bass, Ben on saxophone and Oscar on drums.

On stage, she covered the microphone with her hand and said to Josephus "but we ain't rehearsed anything."

"Girl, don't worry your pretty self. We fellows can play anything. Just tell us what you're gonna sing."

She glanced at Josephus, admiring how green flecks twinkled in his brown eyes. "The Man I Need," she said.

He nodded toward the microphone and mouthed 'go on, girl.' The band started playing. Crimson lips to the microphone, she addressed the audience. "How you all doing tonight?" A burst of applause cued her to begin singing. Eyes closed, hips swaying, her velvety voice rippled through the large room like a balmy breeze, mingling with the ambient sound of hushed chatter and ice cubes tinkling in amber glasses. Through the curtain-like haze of cigarette smoke, she studied the black, brown and sprinkling of white faces in an audience apparently enthralled by her performance. Being on stage in this place and unleashing her vocal gift upon such a receptive audience was exhilarating, like this

*was truly what she was meant to do. At the end of the song,
she held the final note allowing it to simmer like a fine stew.
And as though they could taste that fine stew, the audience
was hungry for more. They hollered for an encore. Dahlia
merely smiled, then left the stage.*

*That night, Josephus asked her to join The Jazz
Deliverers. And she happily obliged. But her girlfriends,
whom she had enthusiastically invited to the new club,
didn't share her enthusiasm and expressed their misgiv-
ings. "Dahlia," they warned. "Men that look like that, with
their pressed hair, fancy suits and smooth talk are the most
troublesome kind." But Dahlia didn't pay them any mind.
Her friends, she decided, were just jealous.*

*So Dahlia dismissed Josephus's detractors while she mar-
veled at his musical stylings. Josephus didn't just play the
trumpet; he seemed to have formed an organic bond with the
instrument, as though it were an extension of his hands.
And she reveled in the passion with which he played, eyes
squeezed shut, lips pursed against the mouthpiece, cheeks
inflated, achieving a range that rivalled any of the great
horn masters. And every Saturday night she tasted something magical when the notes from her lips fused with the
notes from his trumpet. Thus began their courtship, and
throughout their courtship Dahlia's vision was clouded by
a romantic haze, distorting the tell tales signs, among them
Josephus's roving eyes, that should have caused her to pro-
ceed with caution.*

*One night, after a particularly electrifying show,
Josephus fixed his eyes on none other than Dahlia. That
night, she was his and he was hers exclusively. He invited
her to his apartment in a brownstone on 135th Street. She*

accompanied him there, without hesitation, where one blissful night melded into another and another after that until they made those living arrangements permanent. A year later, she cradled a rosy cheeked baby girl in her arms and Josephus, the doting father, gushed over them both. The second baby girl came only 15 months later. Their adorable daughters, Patricia and Anne, completed their perfect family, or so it appeared from the outside. Inside, the reality was entirely different.

⇌ ⇌

Bradley's voice jolted me from my work. "I ordered take out, Chinese, if you're hungry."

I spun my chair around to see his large frame fill the doorway. My stomach rumbled, as if on cue. Hunger had taken a backseat to my distress and determination to work on Dahlia's story.

"Thanks," I said quietly. "I'll get some in a moment."

"Working on an article?" he asked.

I nodded.

"Listen, Megan. I'm not trying to force your hand when it comes to you contacting Helen. Whatever you decide has to be your decision. I just don't want you to live with regrets."

"Damn it, Bradley. How many ways do I have to say I don't feel anything toward that woman and I'm not interested in talking to her? Why are you always taking her side?"

"That's just childish. You know it isn't a matter of taking sides."

"Just give it a rest, alright?"

"Fine. Forget I said anything. But don't come crying to me when it's too late and you wished you had done things differently. I'm going to bed."

"Good," I mumbled under my breath. Why did he insist on rubbing salt into my gaping wound and why had I allowed that wound to fester? Any steps that we had taken forward were now moving in reverse. Fresh tears welled up in my eyes.

The weekdays wedged between my Sunday visits seemed to drag by at an agonizingly slow pace. I was on to my third notebook, quickly filling up with Dahlia's story. Last week's excerpt included more on life with Josephus which, according to her narrative, deteriorated over the years since the birth of their daughters.

During this Sunday's visit with Dad and Dahlia, she told us that Josephus became more and more absent from their lives. Her song, like the soundtrack to her story, softly played while she spoke.

"He was gone more than he was home," she said. "Those times, my heart felt thick and heavy, like it was coated with molasses. That's when I used to hear Momma's song in my head."

"Momma's song?" I asked.

"Yeah. 'Walking Through.' It's what my momma used to say. She used to sing it, like a song, '*I'm just gonna keep on walking, walking through 'till I gets through.*' That's how Momma got through, from the time, I expect, that she come up here from Georgia to the minute she breathed her last breath. I learn to walk through from my Momma and I put her words into my own song."

I listened to the familiar lyrics emanating from the CD player. Something about that song, those words, "*walking through*," seemed to resonate deeply within her. What hardships in her own life had her mother's song carried her through? I wondered. I had an acute sense that she would soon share that with me. First, though, she spoke of a heated argument she and Josephus had had, one that became the impetus behind her decision to leave him. Dad was apparently as mesmerized as I, his gaze fixed on Dahlia's faraway expression.

"We fought real bad that night, hollering and raising hell with each other."

She paused. I waited.

"Dahlia," I coaxed. "What did you and Josephus fight about?"

She turned to me. "I was tired, tired of hearing that sorry old line over and over. 'Dahlia baby, I'm gonna make an honest woman out of you, hear?' I used to believe him you know, 'till I came to my senses. When he said it again, after he'd been gone for days and been with Lord knows who, I just didn't want to hear it no more."

"Did you tell him that?" I asked.

"Hell, yeah, I did. And that's how the fight began. Well, he just kept at me, cussing and telling me it was him who got me where I was. But I let him have it too, and we just kept flinging nastiness at each other 'till it got so bad that if my baby girls hadn't of come into the kitchen, I think he would've beat me. I really think so. That's when I figured I couldn't be with that man no more."

"What did you do then?" Dad asked.

She turned toward him. "The next day, I took my little girls and left his sorry backside. I was done with him."

Dad frowned and cast sad eyes downward. To a man who barely raised his voice toward Mom or me, much less raise a hand to us, her words must have been difficult to hear. I was overcome by an urge to hug him, but continued taking notes until Dahlia stopped speaking. The emotions of those memories, I believed, took a toll on her. She became quiet and started humming her song.

I closed my notebook and offered to accompany her and Dad to their suites. That evening, I raced home from my visit, recklessly disregarding the speed limit in my rush to get home and start on the next chapter of her story.

＝◁ ▷＝

One of our house rules was no electronic devices at the dinner table. Despite that rule, Bradley held his cellphone in one hand, scrolling through emails while he ate. His trial had wrapped up and the jury had begun deliberations. Since then, he made sure he was always within reach of his phone. He loathed losing trials and this part of the judicial process always made him anxious. He hardly noticed me studying his face over dinner.

'*Bradley, I'm leaving you.*' The words that invaded my thoughts startled me. That was Dahlia's narrative, not mine. Bradley was no Josephus. I loved him and he loved me. At least I clung to the belief that that would be his answer, were I to ask him.

"Why can't we get back what we had?" I whispered.

"What'd you say?" Bradley asked, his gaze still on his phone.

"Nothing." I rose from the table and took up our plates.

Later, I hunkered down at my desk. Bradley had gone to bed ahead of me. He slept fitfully, mumbling incoherently. The jury deliberations for this pivotal trial, I was certain, stayed on his mind even while he slept. Seeing him looking so vulnerable tempted me to go and try to comfort him. Instead, I turned to the computer screen and continued typing, eager to complete chapter three.

⸻ ⸻

Dahlia's Story – Chapter Three

"Walking through. I'm gonna keep on walking, walking through. Don't know how long it'll take me or when I'm gonna reach, but I'm gonna keep on walking, walking on through." Dahlia hummed the tune of the song she'd written. She sat at a vanity table in the small space that served as her dressing room while dust particles danced in the glow emanating from a row of lightbulbs fastened above the mirror.

The song was inspired by those words passed on to her by her mother and by generations of women before her: "I'm just gonna keep on walking, walking through 'till I gets through." She could still hear her mother's Georgia twang, strong and clear, speaking the words that had accompanied her when she, like one of Moses's people, joined the exodus from the South. The lyrics were simple yet they spoke of a complex struggle. And the times were ripe for her song. On the streets of Harlem, Malcolm X rallied his troops while,

155

in the South, Rev. Martin Luther King, Jr. dared to have
a dream.

Dahlia wanted to call the song 'Momma's Song' but the
record producer, the fancy fellow who'd come from Detroit
to talk record deal with The Jazz Deliverers, said no to the
song title. "Too plain," he'd said, his long fingers curled
around a glass of bourbon. "You want a name that grabs
folk, make them want to hear what you have to say in that
song." So, she called the song 'Walking Through.'

Carl, the bassist, leaned against the dressing room's
opened door while clutching a bottle of beer. "Sure is a
nice sounding tune, Dahlia. That record ex-ec-u-tive," –
he said, emphasizing each syllable as if to highlight the
word's significance – "is gonna be real impressed."

She studied Carl's reflection as he stared at her through
the mirror. "I hope so, Carl. I just feel bad about Josephus.
He started this band, after all."

"You feel bad? Girl, what exactly do you feel bad
about – that Josephus didn't want anything to do with
the Jazz Deliverers no more? That he never showed up for
rehearsals and the few times he did, all he talked about
was going to Chicago to do session work coz he was too
good to be stuck with this dead end house band? Tell me,
when was the last time you saw your man?"

Her sigh was a heavy one. She looked toward the over-
stuffed sofa tucked in the corner of the dressing room where
her daughters lay asleep, curled up, like kittens, at either
end. Carl was right. Josephus hadn't been home in over a
week. In fact, he was gone more than he was home. But her
heart no longer felt as though it was coated with molasses,

thick and heavy with anguish, during his frequent absences. Instead, as their relationship grew more volatile, she began to cherish his absences. "Walk on through it, Dahlia. Walk on through." Of late she found herself increasingly reaching for the lifeline that was her Momma's adage.

She peered into the mirror, past her reflection and Carl's trying to recollect what Josephus had said that ignited their last, and most vicious, quarrel. The lame promise he'd made, one she'd heard too many times, suddenly popped into her head. She pictured him on the night they fought, slumped over the kitchen table, gazing into a flask of whiskey. A thin line of smoke from the cigarette he held between his forefinger and thumb spiraled toward the ceiling. She remembered tensing up at the sound of his voice. He must not have noticed or even cared about her reaction as she stood at the sink, back to him, swishing dishes around murky water.

"Dahlia, baby. I'm gonna make an honest woman of you yet, don't you worry 'bout that, hear?" Too many years had passed since she'd stopped believing in those words, since she'd stopped believing in him and since she'd let go of the sparkling hope that soon they would be a proper, legitimate family. Maybe she should have kept her mouth shut, let him ramble on with his nonsense but that hollow sentence became like an annoying housefly buzzing at her ear, only to be swatted away with her own words.

She had poured herself a drink also and turned to reach for the glass. She took a gulp before speaking. The words she'd shot back at him rattled in her head, her courage probably bolstered by the alcohol. "What you know about honest, Josephus? You ain't got an honest bone in your body."

She remembered every bitter word that followed, the pitch of their voices rising and crashing like angry waves against the brownstone's paper thin walls.

"What you mean by that? Why you gotta be like that huh, Baby?"

"Don't you 'huh, Baby' me. You know damn well what I mean."

"Woman, you best watch your damn mouth. Remember who got you to where you's at, all right?"

"Where's that, Josephus? Where'd you get me, huh?"

"Hell, girl. You better check your head. I got you singing in one of the best Jazz clubs in Harlem and all you wanna do is knock me down. Yeah, tha's right, knock me down."

"Coz you got me into The Half Moon, I'm supposed to put up with all your crap, just look the other way while you play tomcat with all them hussies flinging themselves at you, all the nights you don't come home, and when you do come home you're so stinking drunk or high you don't even make it into bed? Is that what I'm supposed to put up with? Those sweet little girls in there hardly even know you."

"You don't know shit, woman. I know shit, the shit that's going on between you and them Jazz Delivers boys."

"Crazy fool. You know full well ain't nothing going on between any of them boys and me."

"Woman, who you calling crazy? You think I don't see how they look at you and how you look at them? Oh, they's delivering, all right. They's delivering and you's taking."

"You're just resentful after the group kicked you out for not pulling your weight. All you're doing is trying to cover up your own stinkin' guilt, that's all."

"*Guilt? I'll show you guilt.*" *She could still feel his steely grip on her arm after he rose from the table and lunged toward her.*

She'd gasped but her gaze met his, challenging the rage she saw in his eyes and in his fist. "*Go ahead, Josephus, go ahead and hit me.*" *She leaned toward him, hissing her words through clenched teeth.* "*You just go on, but it'll be the last time you ever do, hear me?*"

"*Momma, Daddy. Stop.*" *Three little words, a panicked plea hit them like a sobering bucket of ice-cold water. Patricia was standing at the kitchen door, her younger sister partially hidden behind her.*

Dahlia had always tried to shield her daughters from the turmoil that was this relationship. But they had witnessed these flare ups too often. She rushed toward the girls, throwing her arms around them her trembling hands fluttering at their backs. "*Patricia, Anne, go on back to bed.*"

"*But we're scared, Momma,*" *Patricia whimpered.* "*We want you to come with us.*"

"*Go on, now. I'll come directly. Your Daddy's just leaving.*" *She paused and turned to Josephus.* "*Ain't that right, Josephus?*"

"*Yeah, tha's right. I'm going but not before I get a hug from my girls.*" *He shuffled toward his daughters who shrunk away from his outstretched arms.*

"*Uh huh. Don't want nothing do with your mean ole Daddy, huh?*" *He glared at Dahlia.* "*After all I done for you, all I give you, this is how you gonna treat me, huh?*"

"*Just get out, Josephus. Go on.*"

"*Alright. I'm going, but this ain't finished, hear?*"

He turned and left the kitchen stumbling toward the front door.

She hadn't seen Josephus since that night. Carl came to her and placed a hand on her shoulder. "C'mon Dahlia. We're about to go on." She nodded and stood up, then went to give each daughter a gentle kiss before following Carl out the door.

⟞⟞ ⟝⟝

The flu bug struck me like a venomous snake hiding in tall grass. By mid-week, I felt like I'd gone three rounds with a Mixed Martial Arts champion. Wednesday morning, I emailed the college to cancel my classes, emailed my editor to let her know I wouldn't make this week's editorial meeting, and, sadly, called Dad and told him I wouldn't make our Sunday visit.

I detected a note of disappointment in Dad's voice when he said, "Get better soon, sweetheart. Hope I will see you next Sunday. But don't push it."

"Thanks Dad. I'm sure I'll be well enough by next week." I hung up and climbed back into bed. Bradley had gone to work. He would check in on me during lunch he assured me. Seeing me looking so miserable must have triggered that sympathetic gesture, the first he'd shown toward me since our ill-fated Helen discussion.

The telephone's shrill ring startled me. I reached for the phone on the bedside table. "Hello?"

The voice on the other end was tentative. "Megan? It's Laura."

I let out an audibly frustrated breath but said nothing.

"Megan? Are you there?"

"Yes, I'm here. How are you Laura?"

"I'm okay. How're you?"

"I've got the flu."

"Yeah. I can hear it in your voice. Hope you feel better soon. Can you talk for a bit?"

"Okay, for a bit."

"Mom has been asking for you. Please, won't you come see her, or even just call her? We don't want her to go this way."

How dare she? I fumed silently. This was blatant emotional blackmail. I wanted to say so, but held back.

"Megan?"

"Yes, I'm here. Listen, you have to give me a day or two. My head is all muddled with this flu and there's a lot going on with me right now."

"Of course. I'm sorry I don't mean to stress you out. I just thought you would want to know. I understand where you're coming from, but please, think about it and let me know as soon as you can."

Again, I expelled a loud breath into the receiver. "Alright. I will."

Her voice sounded teary. "Thank you. I'll let you go. Take care of yourself."

"Thanks, Laura. You too."

I replaced the receiver. The tears flowed then. Could I allow Helen to go that way? "Stop it, Megan. Stop crying for her," I admonished myself. I wiped away my tears with my pajama sleeve, and then put my hand to my forehead. It felt hot. After retrieving my cold and flu meds from the bathroom cabinet, I pulled on my terry robe, fetched my laptop from my desk and headed down to the kitchen. My conversation with Laura stayed with me. "Damn her for adding this weight to my shoulders," I grumbled.

"A soothing cup of tea will fix everything, Meg." I recalled Mom's words to an adolescent me whenever I went to her with some life altering problem. It was times like this that I missed her most. I pushed my conversation with Laura to a far corner of my mind while making myself that soothing cup of tea. Mug in one hand and my laptop in the crook of my arm, I settled into the comfy armchair in the den and forced myself to focus on my most recent draft of Dahlia's story.

The laptop slowly came to life when I pressed its 'on' button. A series of blinking lights told me it had booted up. My finger hovered over the internet browser icon. I hadn't put any research into Dahlia's story. Her recollections, I reasoned, were research enough. Though tempted to do some digging into her past, I held off, not wanting anything I might find online to bias or influence my narrative so far. Research could wait, I decided. I poured through the pages of her story, satisfied with the draft, completed up to my last set of notes.

⊷⊶

Cabin fever was setting in as one week rolled into another. "I think I should be well enough to make the trip to Forest Brook on Sunday," I said to Bradley during Thursday evening dinner.

He didn't respond.

I forced a smile. "Dad will be happy, and Dahlia too. She must be wondering where I've been."

"Yeah, of course. Gotta look out for Dahlia," Bradley said, his voice terse.

My heart fluttered. "Why...why don't you come with me?"

I stared at him and couldn't decide what expression I read on his face. He stood and, mechanically, began to clear the table. Before leaving the dining room, he stopped and turned to me. "If only you could hear yourself, you'd know how much like an afterthought that suggestion sounded."

I sighed heavily. "What do you want, Bradley? I'm trying, alright!"

"Trying? C'mon, Megan. You want me to come with you as much as you want your flu to come back. I wonder if there even *is* a Dahlia? How do I know *you* didn't invent her, huh? If I were the jealous type, I would wonder what you're really up to during your so-called Sunday visits." He turned and left me, gawking after him.

"*They's delivering and you's taking.*" I heard Josephus's blatant accusation in Bradley's veiled one. I stood and removed the remaining dishes then followed him to the kitchen. "Seriously? You can't be suggesting that I'm having an affair?"

"You're the writer. Read between the lines."

I shook my head. "If that's what you're implying, you're one to talk," I shot back. "How about that Cheryl incident, huh, and what Lenore told me?"

He groaned and rolled his eyes before reaching for the dishwasher door. "You're not dredging up that crap again? I was having dinner with a colleague. I have working dinners with my colleagues all the time. You know that."

Dishes clattered as I clumsily stacked the ones I had cleared from the table into the dishwasher. "Working dinner? According to Lenore, you two were doing anything but working."

Bradley pushed the dishwasher door shut and turned to face me. "Man, you sure have selective memory when it suits you."

My heartbeat quickened. I clutched the kitchen counter. "What the hell are you talking about?"

"Are you going to tell me you don't remember what you'd said then? That Lenore was bitter because of the nasty divorce she was going through? That she directed that bitterness toward you, like she wanted you to know how it felt? Those were your words, Megan. I can't believe you're still holding onto that nonsense."

At that moment I despised him for flinging my words back at me.

"I've never been unfaithful to you," he said, his tone growing angrier. "And you damn well know it." He moved closer to me until inches separated us. "I'm not so sure if I can say the same of you."

My nerves felt as if they sprang to attention, ready to heighten the offensive. I looked up and into his blazing eyes. "You're acting like a jerk, you know that? Why would I want anyone else? You're enough trouble!" A sharp jab in my chest accompanied a quick intake of breath. For seconds, we both seemed immobilized. Inside, I winced at the irrational words that had slipped passed my lips before I'd had a chance to rein them in.

Bradley's face clouded. He stood before me, like a wounded bear, unsure of what to do with the arrow I had just shot at him. "Oh, I'm the jerk, am I? Why don't you look in the mirror? Go on to your Dahlia or whoever. I've had enough of this bullshit!" He turned from me and with a few angry strides was at the kitchen door before I could formulate a response.

"Fine! Go then!" I yelled at his retreating figure. The sound of the front door being opened and then slammed shut triggered a flood of tears. I angrily wiped them away, went to the kitchen's built-in wine rack, selected a merlot and poured myself a large drink. Still teary eyed, I sat sipping the wine until only a drop of the blood red liquid remained in the wineglass. I placed the glass in the sink, opened the kitchen window blinds and stared out at a sky that resembled Van Gogh's *Starry Night*. I pictured that masterpiece on display at the Museum of Modern Art and Bradley and I standing before it, admiring it.

"Oh Bradley," I sobbed. "What's happened to us?" Slowly, I closed the blinds and headed upstairs, the wine and our argument pulsing in my head.

⏤✦ ✦⏤

Bradley returned at 12:15 a.m. according to the clock radio's red numbers. I pretended to be asleep when I heard him come into our bedroom and head to the bathroom. Familiar bathroom noises escaped from behind the closed door – a stream of pee hitting water in the toilet bowl, the toilet's flush, running water, and then teeth being brushed. I waited for him to climb into bed, to feel the warmth of his body heat and his muscular arm reaching across me while he snuggled close to whisper that he was sorry. Instead, I heard his footsteps heading toward our bedroom door, then the door being closed behind him. The sound of his footsteps faded as he walked away. Our bed felt too big and too empty without him beside me. I lay awake until sleep finally came, hours later.

Over the following days, an uncomfortable chill settled between us like frost on a cold autumn morning. We spoke to each other only when necessary. And, when necessary, only in utilitarian sentences: "I'm working late tonight." "The dry cleaner called, your dress is ready." "I'm taking my car in for an oil change." We even avoided being in the same room together, until bedtime when we settled into bed, back to back, like enemies forced to share accommodations.

⊷ ⊶

Sunday morning, I awoke to the sound of Bradley rummaging around in the kitchen. The clock radio read 8:00 a.m. I slipped my feet into my slippers, pulled my robe around me and hurried to the kitchen, curious as to why this early start to the day. By the time I made it down the stairs, I heard him go through the front door and pull it shut. I was alone and lonely and wanted him to come back to me. I glanced at the coffeemaker and saw he had made enough coffee for both of us. As I went to pour myself a cup, a folded piece of paper on the kitchen counter caught my attention. A bubble of hope floated through me. Bradley had left me a note, his effort to make up. He was sorry, I guessed, but couldn't say so in person, so he put it in a note. It was a start. I took the paper from the counter, opened it and read *"Playing 18 holes today. 9:00 tee off. Having lunch at the Club. Not sure what time I'll be home."*

The hope bubble burst. Head bent, I took my mug of coffee and went upstairs to shower and get dressed.

⊷+ +⊶

The drive to Forest Brook was a welcome relief from the stifling atmosphere that permeated our home. But as I steered the SUV along the highway, neither Dad nor Dahlia were on my mind. At the forefront of my thoughts were my husband and our troubled marriage. I missed Bradley terribly; the Bradley with whom I had fallen in love. I missed those intimate moments that had held our marriage together, like dabs of glue – little kisses 'hello' and 'good-bye', preparing meals together, sharing anecdotes from our day, feeding off of each other's laughter, or the comfortable silence when we were in the same room, each working on our own thing, but happily aware of the other's presence.

I thought about our fight and what Bradley had said before he stormed out of the kitchen - "look in the mirror." I couldn't, I thought, because I wasn't sure I would like the person I saw there. That person would self-righteously dismiss Bradley's remarks as unreasonable jealousy and resentment, even claim that there's a bit of Josephus in every man.

I pictured myself standing in a courtroom before an unsympathetic judge as he read aloud a long list of accusations: "Megan Craig you are accused of neglecting your already fragile marriage; of effectively committing the sin of omission by not telling Bradley about your Dahlia project; of delegating him to a minor role in your life; and of allowing Dahlia and her story to become your number one priority, even usurping your father. How do you plead?"

"Guilty," I wanted to scream. "I am guilty of all of it."

Ahead, the narrow road, leafy trees, and powder blue sky all blurred into one. Eyes filled with tears, I pulled onto the shoulder of the road and turned off the engine, then wept and wept until I felt I had spent my reservoir of tears. I pulled a Kleenex from my purse and wiped my eyes, then started the engine and steered the SUV onto the road. My imaginary judge's accusations were true and I *was* guilty. I had become consumed by Dahlia and her story. Now it was time to pause and try to piece my life back together.

Her story, I believed, was nearing its end at least as far as her career with the Jazz Deliverers. At times, she spoke about "being done with singing" or "after I stopped singing." Curiously, she sometimes referred to herself in the third person. I longed to call Bradley and ask him his opinion. He would likely encourage me to dig deeper, research their histories – Dahlia's and The Jazz Deliverers'. He would probably suggest that I search for their *Walking Through* album and experience it in its entirety. "Nothing like hearing a recording on vinyl," he always said. I longed to have him share that experience with me. Bradley and I needed to fix things, fix us. But would he be open to working things out or had he truly had enough?

The grounds of Forest Brook came into sight.

⚬

Dad wasn't in the lounge when I arrived. In his suite, I found him in the bedroom, still in his pajamas.

"I've been feeling a bit under the weather," he explained.

My heart sank. "Dad, I hope you're not coming down with that nasty flu. Has the doctor seen you? Maybe you should be in the hospital."

He shook his head and gave me a little smile. "No, it isn't the flu, yes the doctor has seen me and he confirmed that. And I am in no hurry to go back to the hospital. You know what can happen to us old folk in there. We get swallowed up in the abyss that is that quagmire of germs, never to return."

I shook my head. "Oh Dad. You're incorrigible."

"Better incorrigible than, well, you know. I'll be fine. I'm not as frail as I look."

"I know, that. But your body is still healing from the stroke."

He stood up and came toward me. "Listen, why don't you go on to the lounge? I'm sure Dahlia will be there. I'll be along soon."

"We don't need to visit in the lounge. Why don't we stay here? I'll arrange lunch for us and we can watch some old movies like we used to - you, Mom and me. Remember?"

He smiled. "Sure I remember and that sounds fine, Meg. But I've been cooped up in here for days. I really wouldn't mind a change of scenery from my suite. Go on to the lounge. I will join you there soon. Just tell me one thing before you go."

I frowned. "Sure. What is it?"

"I don't mean to pry, sweetheart, but is everything okay? You know...at home?"

I sighed. "Is it that obvious?"

"Well, I can always tell when something is troubling my little girl."

I folded my arms around him and buried my face in his chest. The tears that slid down my cheeks settled on his pajama top and I felt him gently patting my back.

"Meg," he said. "I was at the church, right near the altar when you and Bradley were married. I saw your faces when you exchanged vows and I know you didn't make those vows lightly. Talk to him, honey. Bradley is a good man and a wonderful father. Your marriage has a strong foundation."

"I don't know if he wants to talk, Dad. We had a bad argument, said some hurtful things to each other."

Dad cupped my chin in his hand. His gentle eyes met mine. "Meg," he said. *"Love bears all things, believes all things, hopes all things, endures all things, love never fails.* Sure Bradley wants to talk and so do you. Sweetheart, don't throw away nearly 25 years over a rough patch."

"Aw Dad," I sniffled. "I love you so much. Thank you for letting me be your daughter."

"I love you too sweetheart. And thank you for letting me be your Dad. Now go on and see if you find Dahlia. I won't be long."

Before turning to leave, I reached up to give him a kiss on his cheek.

⊷ ⊶

Dahlia was in her usual chair, chatting away with another resident. I took a seat nearby not wanting to interrupt them but she must have sensed my presence because she turned toward me and smiled.

"Margaret, honey. You came back. You been gone a long, long time."

I went to her and we came together in our customary embrace. "Not that long, Dahlia."

"This here is my friend," she pointed to the woman seated in the chair next to hers. "What's your name again, dear?"

The woman smiled and stood up. "I'm Isabelle."

"Nice to meet you, Isabelle. I'm Megan."

"Nice meeting you as well, Megan. I was just going for a swim. Nice chatting with you, Dahlia."

I smiled at her then turned to Dahlia. "So, how have you been?" I asked, settling into the chair that Isabelle had occupied. "Keeping well?"

"Oh yeah. I'm alright, for an old lady," she chuckled. "How come you been gone so long? Did you go somewhere?"

"No, I didn't go anywhere. I had the flu."

"The flu, huh? Nasty business. But that's what saved me, you know." Her eyes grew wide as she spoke. "If I hadn't of caught that flu, I wouldn't be here right now."

"What do you mean, Dahlia? How did the flu save you?"

"Was the touring that killed them. See, if I hadn't of caught that flu, I'd be dead too, just like the rest of them."

I leaned closer to her. "Them?"

"Yeah," she said. "The band. All of them died, except me. After the boys died, she was gone too. Dahlia was no more. I just couldn't do it no more. You see, that crash that killed them, killed me too, on the inside."

My mouth gaped open. "Crash?" I asked.

She stared at me as though she were staring right through me and her voice had taken on a strange, monotone timbre. "Yeah. The Jazz Deliverers was coming home from a bus tour. After we cut our first album,

171

that fancy-man record executive arranged for us to go on tour, a country-wide tour he called it. We would even go overseas, to Europe and them fancy places after we were done touring here in the United States, but it wasn't meant to be."

"Do you remember how it happened?" I asked, my voice just above a whisper.

Dahlia shook her head. "Sure I do. That truck put an end to all them touring plans when it crossed the line on I-95. Rammed into the bus, head-on, like a big old fist…"

They were returning home from their last tour, Dahlia told me. They had reached about the halfway point and still had another couple of days' worth of travelling left when she fell ill with the flu.

"Hit me like a ton of bricks," she said. "Well, Percy, he was our manager, he always come with us on tour. And when I got sick with that flu, he decided to take no chances. He took me to some clinic. And the doctor said I was in no shape to go the rest of the way by bus. So Percy fixed it so that I could fly home."

She paused then and I peered into her eyes, glistening with tears. "So, you made it home safely and the others did not?"

She nodded. "Yeah. That truck showed no mercy, mashed up the tour bus, sent it flying into a ditch on the side of the road. Not one of them on board that bus got out from that accident alive."

Dahlia was weeping softly. I lay my notebook down and went over to hug her. Some forty-five years had passed since the crash and still she mourned the loss of her boys, The Jazz Deliverers and, perhaps, the loss of the Dahlia she once was.

"Oh Dahlia," I whispered. "I'm so sorry. That loss you suffered must have been unbearable. We don't need to go on any longer, okay? Let's leave it at that."

"Dahlia was done after that," she mumbled. "Much as I tried to walk on through, I wasn't able, no how. Dahlia was done after that."

We sat, holding hands, until one of the PCWs came and stood at her side. She placed a hand gently on Dahlia's shoulder. "Dahlia? Let me walk you to your suite. It's time for your medication." She turned to me and said "please excuse us."

I nodded woodenly and glanced at my notes. That tragic accident had wiped out The Jazz Deliverers and tore them from Dahlia's life. No wonder she clung to those pre-accident memories. I looked up to see Dad entering the lounge. We would have lunch together and I would tell him about the tragedy that had struck down The Jazz Deliverers. But as I stood to meet him, I was gripped with an acute sense of urgency to get home and try to make things right with Bradley.

⊷ ⊶

Bradley was at the top of the steps, golf bag slung over his shoulder when I arrived home. He had taken up playing again since the trial wrapped up. The jury had come back with a 'guilty' verdict, allowing him some time before the losing side filed their appeal.

He acknowledged me with a nod.

"Hi," I said softly. I followed him inside.

"What's that?" He asked looking at the box I held in my hand.

"New York cheesecake."

He raised his brows in a questioning arc. "Oh? Something like a condemned man's last meal?"

"No, just cheesecake."

He placed his clubs in the hall closet. "So, you'll feed me my favorite dessert then tell me you're leaving me."

"Bradley," I sighed. "I'm not leaving you. I love you."

He glanced at the floor and for a moment I caught a glimpse of the unassuming young man with whom I had fallen in love. He returned his gaze to me. "I don't know if that's true anymore, Meg."

"Is that how you feel? You don't love me anymore?"

"Yes...I mean no, that isn't what I'm saying. Of course I still love you. We just seem to have drifted so far apart."

"So far apart that we can't find our way back to each other?"

He shrugged. "It feels that way sometimes, doesn't it?"

I went over to him, placed the cheesecake on the hall table and took his hands in mine. "It doesn't have to be that way. We can fix this. I want you back. I want us back. I want them back." I looked toward our wedding portrait. The vintage style black and white photo hung on the hallway wall in the center of a group of family photos. "Please tell me you want that too, Bradley. Please."

He kept his hands in mine. "Yeah, I want that too, more than anything. This may sound cliché, as you writers say, but you're the best thing that's ever happened to me, aside from our children. It just seems like whenever we try to talking, we end up arguing, or worse."

"I know," I said. "Maybe we need some outside help, you know? Like counseling?" I studied his face. I'd mentioned counseling in the past, but he had only balked at the suggestion.

This time, he nodded. "That might not be a bad idea." He pulled his hands from mine. "But why don't we try clearing the air now because, I've got to say, Meg, I've been feeling pretty neglected, you know? And, well, when I felt you didn't really want me to come with you to visit Dad – that hurt. It really did."

I stared at him, hard, as though trying to penetrate his mind, make my way to his point of view. "I know," I said. "And I'm sorry. You're right, Bradley. I've shut you out of a huge area of my life. I think it started with Dad going to live at Forest Brook, then lately, with this Dahlia project."

"Dahlia project?"

I nodded. "Yes. I've been working on a novel based on her life. But I've gotten so caught up in it that I put you, us, on the back burner. I haven't even congratulated you on winning your trial. I really am sorry. Forgive me?"

He came to me then and drew me into his arms. "Sure, I forgive you and hope you'll forgive me. I'm sorry, too. You were right, y'know. I really did act like a jerk."

"Well, I was as much a jerk, bringing up that Cheryl thing. It won't happen again, promise. So, what do you think? Can we try to move toward what we had?"

"I'll do whatever it takes to make that happen. Let's do it - let's try counseling."

I smiled at him. "How about we try one session, then take it from there?"

"You arrange it and I'll be there. Promise. Listen, I'm going to have a shower. I'll come back down and we can talk some more. I'd like to hear more about your Dahlia project, maybe over cheesecake and coffee?"

My smile widened. "I'd like that."

A flood of joy rushed through me. We had made it through the impasse in our marriage and emerged, if not quite fresh and new, at least somewhat cleansed. We were walking through, headed back to where we once were. Bradley leaned in to kiss me and we clung together as though tasting the goodness in each other for the first time.

"You know I love you, right?" he said as he turned to climb the stairs.

"Yes, I know and I love you, too," I called to him then went to fetch the cheesecake from the hall table. As I passed the family photos, I paused at the portrait of Mom and Dad and whispered "thank you, Dad."

⊷⊷ ⊷⊷

Bradley and I sat at the kitchen table. The air in the house felt lighter like a fresh breeze blew through it breaking through the smog of disparity. As we enjoyed the cheesecake and coffee, he told me more about the trial and I told him about the Dahlia project.

"Sounds like an intriguing idea," he said when I paused to take a bite of cheesecake. "But do you think it might be a bit exploitative? You know? Likely, she's not aware of what you're doing."

I nodded. "Yeah. I have thought about that and I want to contact her daughters, let them know about this novel and maybe see if we can collaborate on this work based on her life story. I'd like to discuss with them how this could maybe bring more awareness to dementia and Alzheimer's."

"Good idea. I'll support you in any way I can, Meg."

"Thank you. That means a lot. I'm so glad you see it as worthwhile. Dahlia's story really is intriguing. In fact, I didn't expect to become so captivated by her and her story. It's been addictive, like a kind of drug."

Bradley whistled, long and low. "Holy cow! I wish I had that effect on you. So, what's so addictive about Dahlia?"

I laughed. It felt good. "Addictions aren't healthy, you know. But, Dahlia, there's something alluring about her. She has this aura where you just feel enveloped in warmth, as if you're wrapped in a thick duvet."

He smiled. "Spoken like a writer. So? What's next?"

"Well, we've come to the end of her time as a Jazz singer. In fact, the band ends up perishing in a fatal accident." I recounted details of the accident.

He stared at me, wide eyed. "So, they all died?"

I nodded. "All of them, except Dahlia."

"Oh my God! How tragic."

"Yeah, it sure wasn't the end to her story I had envisioned. Now, I need to do more research."

Bradley tapped his index finger against his chin. "You know," he said. "Finding The Jazz Deliverers album might be a good place to start. We'll play it on my turntable. That way, you could experience them as close to the real thing as possible. Remember that store in Manhattan, in The Village, where I found that record I'd been searching for?"

"Hmm hm. Tito Puente, Live in Paris, right?"

"Right! I bet that store has their album in stock. Why don't we go check it out; maybe next Saturday?"

Bradley had said 'we'. He'd used that precious little pronoun that had become scarce in our life narrative; he and I, making plans, together. I could have cried but this time my tears would taste sweet, like nectar.

"Great idea," I said. "We can have dinner in the Village, make a date of it."

He scraped the last remnants of cheesecake from his plate and, like a child, licked the strawberry filling from his fork. "Sounds good. It's a date."

⚬

June in New York brought with it a heatwave that, ten days into the month, refused to let up. Entering the tiny record store felt as though we had walked into a sauna. I paused momentarily while waiting for my eyes to adjust to the dimly lit interior. Either the store had no air conditioning or, if it had air conditioning, it surely wasn't working. The whirring noise from a small fan perched on the front counter was amplified in the high-ceilinged space. The fan, blowing warm air around the store, provided little relief from the heat.

Bradley and I walked slowly through aisles of bins stacked with records. I scanned the index cards at the front of each bin searching for the Jazz category.

"Here it is," Bradley said pointing to a card. It's thick block letters read 'Blues and Jazz'.

Just as we were about to start rifling through the albums, the wide-plank floorboards creaked, followed by the sound of footsteps. We turned to face a wrinkled-face gentleman. The line where his wiry grey hair met his forehead was beaded with sweat. He pulled a handkerchief from his pocket, removed the glasses that were perched on the end of his nose and dabbed his forehead and face.

"I'm really sorry about the heat in here folks. AC's been on the fritz for days and the repairman said he's had so many calls, he won't be able to get to us until tomorrow."

"How awful for you," I said. "I heard this heat should break soon, though."

He wiped his face again. "I sure hope so. Folks, my name is Simon, proprietor of The Old Times Record Store." He directed his gaze toward Bradley. "Ah, I remember you, sir. Last year, you came in looking for, hmm, what was that album? Oh yes! Tito Puente Live in Paris." He smiled. "We had a nice chat then. Good to see you again."

Bradley reached his hand toward Simon who accepted it and they shook hands. "Wow! Good memory. I've enjoyed that album a lot since then. This is my wife, Megan."

"Good meeting you, Megan. How can I help you folks today?"

"We're looking for an album called *Walking Through,*" Bradley said. "We thought your shop would likely stock it."

Simon's face brightened. "Ah, yes. *Walking Through* by Dahlia Baker and The Jazz Deliverers. Not too many folks ask for that one lately, but it's still a classic in the Jazz world." He reached for a spot near the front of the bin, pulled the album out and handed it to me. "Here you go."

I took the album, a tangible piece of their history, from him and with my fingertips traced the faces that smiled at me from the picture on the cover. My eyes widened as I gazed at the Jazz group I had come to know so well.

Bradley looked at the album. "I'm ashamed to say I'm not familiar with them."

Simon nodded. "Well, do you know about the accident? Seems their music faded from the Jazz scene after that."

I shifted my gaze from the album to Simon. "Yes, we know all about it. Such a sad ending to a group with so much promise."

"Indeed. It was a tragic ending. I believe they were never allowed to reach their full potential."

"And poor Dahlia," I said looking down at the album cover. "All that great talent wasted when she couldn't go on performing after losing the guys."

"Excuse me?" Simon said.

I looked up at a face that was staring at me as if I had grown a second head. Simon's reaction to my comment sent a chill running through me. I looked at Bradley. He was frowning.

"Is…is something wrong, Simon?" I stammered.

Simon's brow was squeezed together in a confused-looking frown. "Megan," he replied. "Dahlia Baker couldn't continue performing because she died. She was killed in that accident along with the rest of the group. There were no survivors."

The chill became intense, like ice water injected into my veins. I felt Bradley's arm slide across my shoulders, his hand gripping my upper arm. I stared at Simon. "What? No, that can't be. I've met Dahlia. She lives at Forest Brook. It's a retirement and assisted living residence. There has to be a mistake."

"With due respect, Simon, are you certain your facts are correct?" Bradley asked a bewildered looking Simon.

"Because according to the Dahlia my wife knows, she, Dahlia, wasn't on that bus when it crashed."

"Yes," I added. "There must be some mistake. There's got to be. I met Dahlia over a month ago while visiting my father. I've seen her every Sunday since. We've had some great conversations. She told me all about her life with Josephus Jones and her time with The Jazz Deliverers, the accident, everything. Only the person who had lived that life could know all those intimate details, right?"

"Megan," Simon's voice oozed astonished concern. "I don't know what to tell you. Whomever you visit with can't be Dahlia Baker. Honestly. I have the newspaper clipping in my archives. I keep important news stories of all the artists whose records I stock. It's good to know what became of them or what's going on with them. Give me a minute. I'll get it for you."

Dumbfounded, I stood, leaning against Bradley and still clutching the album while Simon disappeared through a door at the back of the store. Bradley and I were exchanging hushed chatter when he returned holding a manila file and retrieved from it a yellowed newspaper clipping. He laid the article onto the counter and called us over.

"Here you go. This is the article on the bus crash."

Bradley and I bent our heads toward the page. Bradley pulled his reading glasses from his shirt pocket. My eyes were drawn to the small picture of the group, the same one from the *Walking Through* album. The headline seemed to spring from the page. Bradley started reading, his voice low and stilted, like a first grader learning to read, "Jazz band killed in accident on I-95. *Popular Jazz band, Dahlia Baker and The Jazz Deliverers, were killed when the tour bus in which*

they were travelling collided, head on, with a truck that crossed the
Interstate's center line. Members of the group identified as Carl
Smith, Ben Taylor, Oscar Wilkins, Eddy Brown, Dahlia Baker,
and manager, Percy Smith, all perished. With their crisp, yet soul-
ful sound, the group exploded onto the Blues and Jazz scene in
1966. Many compared Miss Baker to Jazz great Nina Simone. The
group's untimely and tragic demise is a great loss to the country's
Blues and Jazz community and the music industry, as a whole."

All perished...all perished. Nothing else registered beyond
those words. The heat in the store became more oppressive.
I must have swayed or staggered because Bradley reached
for me. "Honey, are you okay?"

I stared at him but didn't answer.

Simon spoke softly. "Megan, do you need to sit down? I
have a stool behind the counter."

"No, thank you. I'll be okay. May I have some water?"

"Of course."

When Simon returned with the water, I reached for the
glass and drank down the water in one long gulp.

"You sure you're okay?" Simon's voice sounded far away.

"Yes, I..I think so." I handed him the empty glass.
"Thank you. This is surreal. Dahlia told me that the band
members were killed in a bus accident – everyone except
her. She wasn't on the bus, she had the flu and had to fly
home..." My eyes shifted from Simon to Bradley and back
to Simon, his eyes filled with sympathy, as he listened while
I rambled on.

Simon shook his head slowly. "Like I said, I don't know
what to tell you Megan, but the lady at that place can't be
Dahlia Baker."

"Well then, who? Who could she be?" I mumbled.

Bradley placed his hand on my back. "Meg, we should go. Simon has been very kind but we've taken up an awful lot of his time."

I scanned the store. It was getting busy and Bradley was right; we were monopolizing Simon's attention. I turned to him. "Thank you for sharing that information with us."

"Oh, it's no problem at all. I'm only sorry it came as such a shock. Here," he said handing me a business card. "Please let me know if you find out more. I can't recall ever having a day like this and I sure would like to find out who your friend, Dahlia, is."

I nodded and took the card. "Me too. We'll let you know what we find out."

As we turned to leave, Simon called after us. "'Scuse me, folks, did you still want it?"

"I'm sorry?" Bradley asked.

"The record album. Would you like to buy it?"

Bradley took his wallet from his pant pocket. "Oh. Yes, we'll take it."

He paid for the album and took my hand. We left the heat of the store for the heat of the sidewalk where we stood, neither of us speaking. A jumble of possible scenarios raced through my mind. Nothing made any sense.

I looked up at Bradley. "Who *is* she Bradley? A ghost? No, she can't be. Other people see her and speak to her too. Maybe she doesn't even exist. Maybe I'm losing it. But Dad has met her daughters, right? It's all so bizarre."

Bradley patted my back as if trying to soothe an irritable baby. "Slow down, honey. We'll get to the bottom of this. We'll contact her family and find out what's going on.

Listen, why don't we get something to eat? I sure could use a drink in an air conditioned restaurant."

I nodded. "Yeah. A drink sure sounds good." I gripped Bradley's hand as we walked along the sidewalk but I couldn't let go of the image of a crushed bus, laying on its side, in a ditch on Interstate 95.

⚊◁ ▷⚊

It was Sunday morning, 10:00 a.m. when we crossed the Brooklyn Bridge. As we neared Forest Brook, my heart felt heavy. I gazed out the window at the blur of greenery whizzing by. My friendship with Dahlia or whoever she was, and her story, occupied my thoughts.

She had been on my mind all night – Dahlia, The Jazz Deliverers and the tragic accident that claimed their lives, including Dahlia's, according to that newspaper article. I had slept fitfully drifting in and out of sleep and when sleep came, one dream played out repeatedly, like a DVD in a player stuck on automatic re-play: I wandered, barefoot, through a ghostly mist until I came upon the tour bus lying on its side in a ditch on I-95. Above me, the rising sun's tepid rays crept across dawn's pastel sky. Unidentifiable, tear-drenched faces floated upward, like helium filled balloons, among vapors of hissing steam rising from the bus's mangled engine. In the distance, two little girls ran along the highway's grassy shoulder toward me. I tried to go to them but my feet refused to move. I called to the girls who were crying hysterically. They collapsed to the ground. As I tried to reach out to them, the bus righted itself and was restored to its former state. I looked toward it and through its windows saw each member of The Jazz Deliverers peering out. They were calling to someone. I looked around and suddenly, Dahlia appeared before me. She turned to me and smiled, but her smile was sinister. She waved goodbye and disappeared through the bus's folding doors.

I woke from the dream and lay awake until sleep came, but only a couple of hours before Bradley shook me awake at 8:00 to let me know he had started breakfast.

At Forest Brook, the lounge was busier than usual when we arrived. Two men and two women stood in a semi-circle at the far end of the room. They chatted quietly among themselves. The women's faces were partially obstructed by the men's figures, but something about them seemed familiar.

Bradley took my hand. "Meg," he said quietly. "There's Dad."

Dad was seated in his favorite chair. He reached for his walker and hoisted himself up. "Megan. And Bradley! So good to see you. Sit down you two. Megan, I..."

His eyes, I noticed, were rimmed red. "Dad? Is something wrong?" I interrupted.

"Please, sit down." he repeated.

We sat and I wondered what, if anything, he knew of the truth about Dahlia. "Dad," I said quietly. "Bradley and I have something to tell you. It's about Dahlia. We've discovered something about her. She..."

"Megan," Dad said, interrupting my flow of chatter.

"But this is really important. We need to tell you this."

"Megan, please," Dad said.

I peered into his eyes and saw sorrow there. "Sweetheart," he said. "I know what you've come to tell me. I know about Dahlia, that she wasn't Dahlia. Her name was Mae."

My throat felt dry. "Was?" I whispered.

Dad shook his head. "Yes. The lady you knew as Dahlia is dead. Her name was Mae and she was Dahlia's sister. Mae passed away last night, in her sleep."

I gasped and looked from Dad to Bradley, and then to Dad again. Words finally came to me. "Her sister? Mae was Dahlia's sister? And...and now she's gone too?" I began to cry. Bradley hugged me closely.

"Incredible," I heard him say.

I looked at Dad through my tears. "How long have you known?" Had everyone known but me? "I feel so foolish," I whispered while reaching for a tissue to dab my eyes.

"No, Megan," Dad said, "You mustn't feel like that. I only learned about Mae earlier today. See those women over there?" He pointed toward the group at the far end of the room. "They are Mae's nieces, Patricia and Anne, and their husbands. We spoke for a little bit before you two arrived. The couple of times I had met them, briefly, Mae was present so they couldn't explain then. I suppose they are here to make arrangements and so on. I am so sorry, sweetheart."

"Dad," I said while reaching for his hand. "I'm so sorry too. You were very fond of her. I'm just having such a hard time processing this."

"Of course. That's to be expected," Dad said. "Look, her nieces are coming over here. I am sure they will explain everything."

I cleared my throat and stood to meet them. Bradley stood up also but Dad remained seated. Two elegant women stood before us. In their faces, I saw Dahlia's and Mae's features, but the taller of the two bore the more striking resemblance. They were the picture, I believed, of how Dahlia would have looked had she lived to her middle age years.

"Excuse me," the taller woman said to me. "I'm Patricia Gordon. You must be Megan."

"Yes. I'm Megan Craig," I said. "This is my husband, Bradley."

"I'm Anne," said the other woman, reaching her hand toward me.

We all shook hands. "I am so very sorry to hear of your aunt's passing," I said. "She was a lovely woman."

"Thank you, Megan," Anne said quietly. "And we want to thank you for your friendship with Aunt Mae. We know that you and Aunt Mae had long conversations, but we're not sure how much you knew about her illness or what she told you about our mother. You may have guessed that she was suffering from dementia."

I nodded. "Yes, I did. But I was astonished at her detailed memory recall. She shared so much with me, so many intricate details. The last time we met, she told me about the accident." I glanced at Dad and Bradley who were quietly looking on.

"You must know that I knew Mae as Dahlia. I just learned recently that your mother had died in a bus accident. I must tell you, I was shocked to learn about your aunt and that your mother had died in the bus crash."

"Yes," Patricia said. "And we are very sorry you learned about our mother before we had a chance to meet you and explain the circumstances. You know, we are still trying to wrap our heads around this ourselves. We noticed over the past several months that Aunt Mae began

to assume Mom's identity. Mom and Aunt Mae were extremely close, maybe too close. And Aunt Mae never got
over losing her sister, her best friend, so suddenly and so
tragically. And to add to that, poor Aunt Mae felt responsible for Mom's death."

I frowned. "Responsible? Why?"

"Well, Aunt Mae told us that Mom was very reluctant to
go on that last tour. She was tired of touring, she had told
Aunt Mae, and felt like she was coming down with something. But Aunt Mae encouraged her to go claiming she
could jeopardize her career if she missed the tour."

"Hmm. How sad. Your poor aunt."

Patricia nodded. "After Mom died, Aunt Mae and her
husband, Uncle George, became our legal guardians. We
saw our father briefly after Mom's funeral, then lost touch
with him again. Aunt Mae and Uncle George had no children of their own. I imagine Aunt Mae told you all about
how Mom met Josephus and about the Half Moon Club and
The Jazz Deliverers."

"Yes, she told me those intriguing stories. Were Dahlia
and Mae twins?" I asked. "They looked an awful lot alike, at
least according to the picture on the album cover."

"No they weren't," Patricia replied. "But Aunt Mae told
us that they often got taken for twins."

The gentlemen Patricia and Anne had been standing
with came over to join us. Patricia introduced them as
Lawrence, her husband, and Donovan, Anne's husband.
Patricia and Anne went on to explain the unbreakable sis-
terly bond their mother and aunt had shared. Even after
Dahlia moved in with Josephus, and Mae got married, they
remained closer than ever, sharing in one another's lives.

"Mom and Aunt Mae," Patricia said, "confided every-thing in each other. In fact, after Mom left our father, she took us directly to Aunt Mae's and Uncle George's home. They didn't hesitate to take us in."

"Aunt Mae," I said, "told me about a fight that your Mom and Josephus had. She seemed to know exactly what had happened."

Patricia squeezed her brows into a frown. "Which one? They fought often."

"It was the fight they had the night before Dahlia left your father."

"Oh, yes, that one. Our first night with Aunt Mae and Uncle George, Mom told her what had happened between her and Josephus. They sat up late, talking. Mom repeated what was said, practically word-for-word. I remember clearly because I heard them while they sat at the kitchen table. They didn't know that Anne and I were awake and eaves-dropping on their conversation. I remember Mom started crying. Aunt Mae held her and started singing their moth-er's song *Walking Through*. She sang it over and over, while Mom cried in her arms."

I glanced toward the men. We seemed to have lost their attention. The four of them were chatting among them-selves and I'm sure I heard golf mentioned more than once.

I returned my attention to Patricia and Anne. "If you don't mind me asking, when did you notice your aunt becoming ill?"

Anne took over from her sister. "Over the past few years and since we lost Uncle George, we noticed a gradual change in Aunt Mae, you know, memory loss and so on. She was eventually diagnosed with dementia and we came to the conclusion that she couldn't be on her own. As we mentioned, it was only recently that she began slipping into our mother's persona."

"Do you suppose that had any connection to her dementia?"

"Oh, her doctor certainly thought so. She called it a type of delusional psychosis, brought on by her dementia. We had to ask the staff here, and they agreed, to call Aunt Mae 'Dahlia' because she became terribly upset and agitated when she was referred to as 'Mae'. And with her delusion that she was Dahlia, she believed that Patricia and I were her daughters."

"Yes, she did refer to you as her daughters," I said. "She told me that although she sometimes missed Brooklyn, she was happy here."

"She was," Anne said. "But her doctor strongly suggested that we consider moving her to a facility that could better treat her. We felt so torn about that. And as sad as we are by her passing, we are also relieved that we were spared from having to make that decision." Anne paused then to wipe her teary eyes.

Patricia placed a gentle hand on her sister's shoulder. "You know, she spoke often and very fondly of you and your father, Megan. She told us about the nice, young lady who sat and chatted with her. On her good days, she even re-membered your name. And she always remembered the name she had for your father – Slim. We're so sorry that we didn't get a chance to meet with you and explain Aunt Mae's illness. There was so much going on with both Anne and me that we neglected to contact you."

I smiled at Patricia's use of the phrase that seemed to be a common thread in the lives of so many these days: "so much going on with me." Any sense of my having been deceived by them, or anyone, had totally dissipated.

"I feel privileged to have known your Aunt Mae and, through her, your mother," I said. "In fact, I had been meaning to try and contact both of you also. I don't know whether my father mentioned to you that I'm a writer. And hearing Mae tell your Mom's story prompted me to write about it. I've been working on your mother's story, based on my conversations with Mae, but wanted to consult with you both about this project. Now, with this revelation, I would certainly want to include Mae's life as well."

Anne and Patricia exchanged glances, then returned their attention to me. Both women's eyes lit up. "A novel about Mom's and Aunt Mae's life? Megan, I think that's wonderful and I'm sure Anne agrees." Patricia looked toward her sister.

Anne was smiling. "Of course I agree."

"The manuscript is still a work-in-progress but now that we've met and if you can manage the time, I would love to discuss the novel more and perhaps using it to create a greater awareness of dementia and Alzheimer's."

"Here, please take this," I said handing Patricia my card. "And please let me know once you have made funeral arrangements. Bradley and I would like to pay our respects. And if Dad is up to it, I am sure he would like to as well."

"We'll do that," Patricia said as she accepted my card. "Perhaps we can meet for coffee once things settle down and we can talk more about your project."

"Of course. Let's keep in touch." I glanced at the business card she handed to me. It read *Patricia D. Gordon, LL.M, Family Law Specialist.* I felt my lips curl into a slight smile.

We joined the men who were gathered around Dad's chair. After we said our good-byes to Patricia, Anne and their husbands, I said to Dad, "you were right, Patricia and Anne really are lovely ladies."

"Just like their Aunt," he replied. "And likely their mother, too."

Bradley and I stayed for lunch with Dad and visited with him after lunch until he asked to be excused.

"Still not feeling 100 percent," he explained. "Then again, I suppose I will never be 100 percent."

We accompanied Dad to his suite and hugged him good-bye.

"Why don't you come visit us for a change?" Bradley said before we left.

Dad chuckled. "Gee, I don't think my walker would take me that far."

"Dad," I said. "I think that's a great idea. The change will do you good. We'll pick you up next Friday and you can spend the weekend with us, right honey?"

"Hey, why didn't I think of that?" Bradley joked. "We'll see you then, William."

In the car, I reached over to Bradley and kissed his cheek. "Thank you," I said.

"For what?" he asked.

"For everything."

He smiled and started the engine.

⚬⟞⟞ ⟝⟝⚬

My hand trembled as I placed the turntable needle into the record's lead groove, just as Bradley had instructed. Using his precious McIntosh system always made me nervous and likely him as well, though he'd never said so.

It was Thursday evening. Bradley had called to let me know he would be home by 6:00.

"Why don't we eat out tonight?" He had suggested.

"Good idea," I agreed.

The music started with a static crackle before her voice disbursed through the den. I sank into the armchair, closed my eyes and pictured Dahlia on stage, lips to the microphone, hips swaying, velvety voice filling the Half Moon Club, The Jazz Deliverers' melodic riffs accompanying her as she crooned the lyrics "...*walking through, gonna keep on walking, walking through...*" As I sat, immersed in the melody, my thoughts drifted back to Mae's funeral. She was buried on a humid, overcast day in the plot reserved for her next to her husband's. She may not have walked through her tragedy, but Mae walked through this life to the other, where she and Dahlia would, at last, be reunited.

Bradley's light touch on my shoulder brought me out of my trance. Absorbed in the music, I didn't hear the front door being opened. I stood to accept his kiss.

"Hey," he said. "Did you get reservations at Marty's"

"I did, for 7:00."

"Oh good. Gives me time wash off this day and change. But first," he paused and imitating a magician's fanfare, pulled a white envelope from his suit jacket's inside pocket and handed it to me. "Ta da!"

"What's this?" I asked.

He shrugged. "Open it and see."

Carefully, I tore open the envelope and took from it two rectangular pieces of paper. I peered at them. They were tickets to a five-day Caribbean Jazz-themed cruise. I gasped, then hugged him. "Bradley, this is so awesome! We haven't had a vacation, just the two of us, in years."

"That's right. The cruise is booked for September. Just following the counselor's advice. Remember what he'd said about getting away?"

I nodded. "I sure do - plan special getaways. But a cruise? Wow, special alright!"

"Well, we have a significant anniversary coming up, the girls will be back in school and you and I have a lot to celebrate and be thankful for."

I reached up to kiss him again. "You're the best".

He smiled a boyish smile. "I know. I'm going to get ready." He picked up his laptop briefcase and headed toward the stairs.

As Dahlia's rich voice surrounded me, I thought of Mae. I still hear her voice at times and I think about one sister so bonded to the other, that she refused to let her go. I looked toward the phone anticipating the call I had to, I wanted to, make. The fact that Helen was my birth mother didn't negate the love my adoptive parents and I shared. But Helen and I shared common DNA, common blood flowed through our veins. For too many years I had denied that truth by refusing her request to see me.

Slowly, I went to the phone, picked up the receiver and tapped in the number. Laura answered on the third ring with a quiet "Hello?"

I cleared my throat and took a deep breath before speaking, "It's Megan. When can I see Helen?"

A DECEMBER TO REMEMBER

By Maria Jemmott

A strong woman understands that the gifts such as logic, decisiveness, and strength are just as feminine as intuition and emotional connection.

- Nancy Rathburn

A DECEMBER TO REMEMBER

Tricia Spencer collected her luggage and walked out the door of John F. Kennedy Airport into a sea of relatives and friends waiting to receive their loved ones. She scanned the happy faces while looking for her nephew, Richard, but she could see no sign of him. *Where in the world could Richard be?* She wondered. As she struggled with her luggage, she began to regret her choice to wear high-heeled boots.

She mopped her forehead and barely managed to tuck the tissue into the pocket of her coat when she saw a tall, well-built, middle-aged man looking in her direction. He was smiling and waving as he held up a sign that read, "Tricia S."

"That's me," she said as she walked up to him. "How did you know I'm Tricia?" His big beautiful smile and soft brown eyes warmed her heart, and it skipped a beat. She never expected such a welcome to New York.

"First let me introduce myself," he replied, reaching out his hand. "I'm Carlos DaSilva, a friend of your relatives. Now to answer your question, your nephew, Richard, showed me an old picture of you, but you're ten times more beautiful than your picture. I can't believe that you can have a thirty-eight year old nephew. You don't look a day over thirty-eight yourself."

She held her hands to her face, thankful that her dark complexion concealed her blushing.

"You're a real charmer. Thanks for the compliment," she said, laughing. "I can see that I'm going to like you. Where is Richard? He was supposed to meet me."

"Tricia, Richard and Denise are such dedicated doctors they never leave the hospital on time. Denise says she should be home by the time we reach there. Here, let me take your luggage."

Tricia pulled her coat closer as she started the walk to the car. "I can't believe I'm actually in New York again," she remarked. "It's been quite a while since I've been here."

She recalled her nephew's words that made her decide to make this trip. "Auntie, why don't you spend the holidays here in New York with Denise and me? It's been awhile since you've visited and we'd love to have you," Richard had said to her just a few weeks before. So, here she was after such a long absence, and in the company of a man who made her heart flutter the first time she laid eyes on him.

As Carlos placed her luggage in the back seat of the Porsche, she continued, "Carlos, for some reason I believe I've heard your name before. You're not a movie star are you? Your name is so familiar, and you remind me of someone I've seen on the big screen."

"A resemblance to a movie star? Now that's a compliment if ever I've heard one! Perhaps at some time Denise or Richard may have mentioned my name."

"Perhaps."

It was a long drive from the airport to her nephew's home and they chatted all the way, like old friends.

"How did you and Richard become friends anyhow?" Tricia asked.

"My son, Jonathan, was a friend of Richard's."

"Was? Are they no longer friends?"

"Jonathan passed away suddenly six years ago."

She heard the pain in his response and her heart saddened. "Oh, I'm so sorry about your loss. I can't imagine your pain."

"It was very difficult for a while, but Richard and Denise have adopted me as their father now, and their support has been phenomenal and very comforting. Jonathan was at NYU with Richard, and they lived like brothers. I think Richard was the brother he always wanted."

"What about his mother? How is she doing?"

Carlos bit into his lip before breathing a heavy sigh. He kept his eyes straight ahead. "My wife, Sylvia, passed away one year after Jonathan did. She never got over his death. She was heartbroken and lost the will to live."

"Oh my goodness. That's so tragic. You've certainly had your share of sorrow. How are you now?"

"I'm doing all right. I'm not quite alone in the world. I do have a daughter, but she lives in New Jersey with her husband."

"Do you have any grandchildren?"

"Not yet, but I know that Christina and her husband, Derek, hope to be parents someday and I look forward to being a grandpa. Jonathan was married for a short period and had no children."

Tricia detected a change in his voice as he continued. "He'd just recently moved back to our home when the accident happened. What about you? Do you have a family?"

Tricia frowned. She turned to look at Carlos. She was not prepared for his question and began to fidget with her fingers. She took a deep breath before responding. "I'm the mother of two young adult children, Kirk and Katrina. No grandchildren, yet, as they're both still single. I'm recently divorced, and don't say you're sorry, because it was necessary."

"Then I'm not sorry because if you were married, you probably wouldn't be taking this trip and we would not be chatting like this. I'm glad I got to meet you. Richard told me that you're here for the holidays."

"Yes, my dear niece and nephew decided that I needed to get away, and to be with family during the Christmas holidays. Richard suggested I spend a month, if possible. My children will be away with their dad for his niece's wedding during the holidays, and I would have been alone. My children don't live at home with me, but we have a great relationship, and this will be the first Christmas that we won't be together."

"Have you no other relatives back in Toronto?"

"No. Not anyone that I'd want to spend the holidays with anyway. As you may know, my brother, Julian, and his wife, Theresa, Richard's parents, now live in Australia, and that's a long way and a very expensive one too. One day I hope I can visit them there."

"I do hope you get to go. You'll love it. I've been there twice, quite a number of years ago, and to New Zealand as well. I fell in love with both places. Oh, the memories!"

His voice quivered, and he swallowed hard. On impulse, she reached over and touched his arm.

He offered a weak smile.

Too soon, they arrived at Richard and Denise's home where Tricia would be spending the next month. Carlos helped her with her luggage and together they entered the house where Denise was waiting for them.

"Welcome, Auntie. It's so good to see you again. It's been a long time. Too long. Richard's been counting the days to your arrival. I haven't seen him this excited in a long time."

The two women hugged. "It's good to see you again too," Tricia said. "I'm sorry for staying away so long. By the way, thanks for sending such a handsome gentleman to meet me."

A chuckle escaped Denise. "I think you're making Carlos blush."

Carlos looked at Denise, then at Tricia, and the trio burst into laughter.

Denise continued, "I'm so sorry we couldn't meet you ourselves. Our jobs seem to be taking over our lives."

Carlos turned to Tricia. "I've been scolding your niece and nephew for months now. You know the saying about all work and no play. They work such long hours, I'm worried that they may suffer burn-out sooner or later."

"Thanks for caring Carlos. I'll have a chat with them, don't you worry," Tricia said.

"Good. I'll be rushing off now. It was a pleasure to meet you Tricia. If you need someone to get you around the city, just call me. I'll be your escort. How about that?" he said laughing.

"That'll be so nice, Carlos, and thanks for meeting me at the airport too. I look forward to seeing you again."

"Do you have to rush off Carlos? Can I offer you a cup of tea or something?" Denise asked.

"No thanks. I do have to go."

"Okay, thanks again for getting Auntie here."

"It was a pleasure. Tricia, I hope to hear from you. Say hi to Richard for me."

Carlos gave both ladies a friendly squeeze on the shoulder and he headed for the door. Denise followed and closed it behind him.

As soon as Denise closed the door, the telephone rang and she went to the kitchen to answer it.

"That was Richard calling," Denise informed Tricia. "He'll be a bit late getting home. He says he can't wait to see you."

Tricia and Denise sat around the fireplace sipping hot chocolate and catching up on all that had been happening in their lives. When the conversation turned to Carlos, Tricia said, "It must have been devastating losing his wife and only son one year apart. How did he continue after that?"

"It was tough for him for a while, but he managed. He's a strong man, and he has his faith."

Tricia toyed with her cup. "It's been five years since his wife's passing. I guess he isn't in a serious relationship since he picked me up and offered to show me around New York. Most men don't wait that long to start dating again."

"You're right. Some have even gotten married in less time than he's been widowed."

"Do you know if he's seeing anyone?"

"I don't think he is seeing anyone. He spends a lot of time with his daughter, and with Richard and me, when we are available. I think he still misses Sylvia." Denise's eyes widened and an inquisitive look appeared on her face. "Why do you ask? Are you interested?"

Tricia touched her cheeks and hoped that her embarrassment did not show, but from Denise's mischievous smile, she knew that her face had betrayed her thoughts.

Chuckling, Denise continued, "Auntie, you *are* interested!"

"Not really, just curious."

That night as Tricia got into bed she found herself thinking about Carlos and their conversation. She tossed and turned, her thoughts whirling, as many questions rushed through her head. After several hours she finally fell into a peaceful sleep.

━━✠ ✠━━

The next morning, Tricia awoke to gently falling snow. She turned on the television to check the forecast. It called for two inches of snow, but clearing later in the day. That for Tricia was nothing, compared to the large snowfalls back home. As she was thinking about what her plans would be for the day, she noticed a note stuck under her door. Both Richard and Denise were called in to work early. A flu epidemic had the Emergency Department at the hospital going crazy. Tricia would be on her own on her first day, but she was not too disappointed. She decided that she would use that time to phone some of her relatives.

Her first call was to Aunt Stella, her late mother's only living sister.

"Aunt Stella, its Tricia. How are you my dear?"

"Tricia honey, so good to hear your voice! How are you, and my dearest great niece and nephew?"

"I'm well Auntie, and so are Kirk and Katrina."

"Richard told me you were coming for the holidays; I can't wait to see you."

"I can't wait to see you either."

The two spoke for a few minutes and then Tricia called her cousin, Mavis, who had moved from South Carolina to New York some years before. She chatted with Mavis for at least half an hour. Mavis was the funny one in the family and most thought that she could easily do stand-up comedy. Mavis made Tricia laugh so much and so loudly that morning, especially when, in her Southern drawl, she teased, "Tricia, my dear, what you need is a rich old guy who is just happy with a younger woman at his side to make him look like there's still fire in the fireplace, and I know a few."

"Oh Mavis, that's not why I'm here."

"Never mind that. There's no harm in looking. That ole fool Wesley couldn't appreciate you, but I know some real gentlemen here who would."

At the mention of her ex-husband's name, Tricia's thoughts began to wander back to her empty and emotionally abusive marriage and the circumstances that convinced her to make this trip to New York. She had no regrets for staying in the loveless marriage. At least during those miserable years she'd had a role, if not as wife, as a mother, and Katrina and Kirk made her proud. Still, she could not help but feel resentment for Wesley at times.

"Tricia, are you still on the line?"

"Oh, so sorry Mavis. I'm here."

"What's Wesley doing these days anyhow?"

"Wesley's still the same, and doing the same. As my mother always said, 'a leopard can't change his spots now, can he?"

Mavis laughed. "Your mom was right. What are Kirk and Katrina doing for the holidays?"

"They're accompanying their dad to St. Lucia for their cousin Jennifer's wedding. They'll be spending the holidays there. That's why I'm spending mine here. You know, once you're divorced, you're no longer a part of his family. Anyway, I've got to go now. I've some more calls to make. Talk to you soon again, and I'll see you Christmas Day, right?"

"Of course, honey. I might even pick up Aunt Stella and pop over to visit you some time before the holidays."

"That'll be lovely!"

"You take care now, hear?"

"I will. See you soon. Bye"

The quiet in the house was a bit depressing for Tricia and allowed her mind to wander into places where she'd rather it not go. She propped herself up on the cushions on her bed and stared out the window at the snow as it gently touched the earth, and covered the bare trees. As she sat on the bed gazing out the window, her thoughts whirled and she recalled Pastor Butler's words. "Tricia, live in the present, learn from the past, and look forward to the future. It'll be wonderful, because God has great plans for you."

Tricia thought of Carlos and their conversation of last night. She smiled as she remembered the compliment he had paid her. She got out of bed, showered, dressed and made a light breakfast of scrambled eggs, toast and green tea. After a couple of calls to Toronto, she turned on the television to the news, and then watched some sitcoms. She found herself laughing at times and actually enjoying her day. Later, she surprised Denise and Richard by making them dinner. Denise had left some steaks marinating, so Tricia cooked them, along with baked potatoes, green beans, carrots and a garden salad.

"Thank you so much Auntie," Denise said almost in tears. "My feet are so tired. You have no idea how thankful I am for this meal. It's been years since I've come home to a meal. Did you find everything okay?"

"Yep. I enjoyed doing this for you two. I couldn't just sit here all day and have you come home to make dinner, no way! My dears, while I'm here, prepared to be pampered."

Richard hugged his aunt. "Thanks so much. I love you."

"Love you too. Now get washed up and let's eat."

⟫⟩⟨⟪

Tricia was eager to do some shopping, so was thrilled when, a few days later, Carlos stayed true to his word and made himself available. "I'll be there at ten sharp," he said when they spoke. The doorbell rang just as she was coming down the stairs. Tricia glanced at her watch. It was exactly ten o'clock. She grabbed her coat and raced to the door.

"Hi Carlos," she said smiling, as she fumbled with her coat.

"Good morning Tricia. Here, let me help you with that," he said as he helped her into her coat.

As they started down the steps on their way to the car, he took her arm in his. "It's a bit slippery, wouldn't want you to fall and hurt yourself," he said while guiding her towards the car. Carlos opened the door of the passenger side for her before taking his place in the driver's seat.

She watched him turn the ignition key. "Thank you Carlos," she said.

He touched her hand, "You're welcome."

After shopping all morning they stopped for lunch.

The Maitre'D greeted them as they entered the restaurant. "Good afternoon Madam, Mr. DaSilva. Good to see you again. Just the two of you?"

"Yes, Paul."

"Follow me sir. Your usual table is free. I see you've been Christmas shopping. Ah, it's the one thing I hate about Christmas, too crowded in all the shops."

"Oh, these are the lady's packages. She's the one who's shopping."

Paul escorted them to a cozy table near a window. Tricia allowed her eyes to wander around the beautiful room and decided that it must be expensive to eat here. The Maître'D pulled her chair out for her. Carlos waited until she was seated before taking his seat.

During lunch, Tricia could not help but admire the man she'd just met only days ago, but who was already occupying most of her thoughts.

"Thanks Carlos, this is delicious. Do you eat here often?"

"Often enough."

After lunch, they shopped for another hour or so before Tricia said, "let's call it a day. My feet are starting to hurt."

When they arrived at the house Carlos followed Tricia up the steps clutching her shopping bags in each hand. Tricia pulled the key from her purse and as she opened the door, she asked. "Would you like to come in for a cup of coffee?"

"Sure, thank you."

Tricia passed the cup of coffee to Carlos. "Thank you for today. And for making me feel like a lady. It's been a long time since I've had anyone pay me so much attention."

"Tricia, you are a lady, and a ray of sunshine." He took a few sips of coffee before asking, "What are you doing tomorrow?"

She smiled. "That depends on you."

"You're cheeky and so adorable."

"So I've been told."

Carlos laughed. "My goodness, you really are cheeky, but I like it. Seriously now, shall I pick you up around nine? I want to show you a bit of the Big Apple."

"Yes, that's fine. I'll be ready, and thanks."

That night, Tricia knelt by her bedside and said a simple prayer. "Thank you God for blessing me with this beautiful day, and for Carlos." She slept well.

When she awoke, Denise and Richard had already left for work. She found herself singing in the shower, and smiling as she readied herself for her outing with Carlos.

The day spent with Carlos was everything she hoped it would be. The highlight was their visit to the New York Museum of Natural History, followed by the Museum of Modern Art. They spent hours among the fascinating work. After the visits they walked among the hustle and bustle of Fifth Avenue, purchasing gifts and souvenirs and enjoyed a simple hamburger meal.

They were both quiet during the drive home. It was drizzling and Carlos was concentrating on his driving. As they were driving over the Brooklyn Bridge, Tricia noticed a huge billboard advertisement on a building nearby.

"Oh my goodness! Fiddler on the Roof is playing on Broadway! I'd love to see that musical. It came to Toronto twice and both times I had to miss it. I've always wanted to see a Broadway show."

"So, you like the theatre?"

"Like is an understatement. I love the theatre, and so does Katrina. We go as often as we can."

"Great, we have that in common. I love the theatre also. So does Christina. Our family went often, but since…well let's just say I've not been in a while, that's all."

Tricia noticed a change in his voice. She glanced at him for a moment and the sad look on his face quickened her heart. Gathering her composure, she said, "My being in the big apple again is such a delight. I'd forgotten about all the glamour, the fine restaurants, shows and the shopping; the whole culture of this beautiful city. A few minutes ago I had to pinch myself to see if all this was real, that I could be in New York after such a long time. It has been almost twelve years since I've visited."

Carlos glanced at her. "Why is that?"

"Wesley did not like coming to New York. As a matter of fact he hated travelling and his only love of entertainment was meeting with his friends every weekend to play poker. In the summer, it was golf."

"You did nothing together?"

"Nothing!"

"You must have been lonely."

"Yes, at times, but I had my church family and my job that I love, so I was okay. I love the woman I've become, and my difficult marriage helped to shape me this way."

"Did you ever regret the marriage?"

"There were times when I wondered why I ever did marry Wesley. He was so cold and boring. But he wasn't that way in the beginning. He is a very intelligent man, a chartered accountant, and has done very well in his career, but the more money he made, the colder he became. No, I don't really regret the marriage. When I look at my children, I thank God. He gave me 'beauty for ashes'."

"I admire your faith in God. You are one remarkable lady."

"Thank you. Without God, I'm nothing."

Carlos became quiet and Tricia's mind strayed to those lonely weekends, and the marriage that brought her no happiness. She also thought of the divorce that had shattered her self-esteem and made her feel like a failure. She wondered what she would have done without God and her church family.

Carlos' sudden laugh interrupted her reverie.

Smiling, she asked. "What's all that about?"

"I was thinking, that perhaps you should write a wish list for Santa. Who knows, you may get to see a Broadway show."

"I don't believe in Santa, not anymore, and don't tell me that you do."

"That's the sad part of being a grown up, we lose that simple blind faith, that childlike trust. Tricia, there's a Santa in all good people. It is in those of us who show kindness, compassion, and love to others, not only at Christmas, but all year."

"When you put it that way, how can anyone not believe? I might write that wish list after all." She giggled. "Should I leave milk and cookies by the fireplace too?"

"Ha! Ha! Now that's the spirit."

The drizzling continued and it was getting dark. Carlos pulled a pair of glasses from the console of the car.

"I need these," he said, as he placed the glasses on his face.

"You look even more handsome in your glasses."

"Tricia, have you ever met someone and you felt as though you knew them before?"

"Yes, that's how I feel about you, I can't believe we've just met," she replied turning her face to look at him.

He stole a quick glance at her, and a gentle smile formed as he said, "That's exactly what I mean. I feel like I've known you all my life."

A playful smile spread across her face. She passed her hand along his right cheek. "Maybe you have. Maybe we met in another life?"

Carlos continued driving, paying careful attention as the road was becoming slippery. Tricia closed her eyes and was deep in thought when a sudden jerk startled her. Carlos reached over and touched her hand. "Sorry, that careless cab driver ahead changed into my lane without even signaling."

"I sometimes think that cab drivers are the worst drivers of all. Thank God you were able to avoid an accident there."

"Yes, thank God."

She realized that the near mishap made her a bit nervous. When Carlos gently patted her hand, she knew that he'd noticed. She cleared her throat. "I can't believe that Christmas is less than two weeks away. Will you be spending Christmas with your daughter?"

"I normally would have, but Christina, my sister, Gina, and their husbands are going on a Mediterranean cruise and won't be back until January second. Denise and Richard have invited me to have dinner with you all."

"Oh that's so wonderful. We'll be having a full house, because Denise's parents and some of our relatives will be joining us. It'll be just like the old days, my happier days."

When they arrived at the house Carlos walked her to the door, and when they entered the foyer he kissed her gently on both cheeks. Tricia hoped he did not feel the dancing and hear the music that her heart was rendering.

That night thoughts of Carlos would not leave her head, and she could still feel the burning on her cheeks from his kiss. It was hours before she finally drifted off to sleep.

On the days that Tricia and Carlos had no plans for an outing or shopping, Carlos would call Tricia, and she found herself looking forward to his calls. They talked about current events and whatever came to mind. Tricia realized that, more and more, she was becoming the person she used to be a very long time ago. She found her sense of humour returning, as they shared many jokes and laughed like two teenagers.

⊷ ⊶

Five days before Christmas, Carlos and Tricia went into Manhattan. After hours of shopping and with parcels packed in both arms, Tricia stopped, looked at her watch and said, "It's after five. I'm tired and hungry and I can't go another step. Can we call it a day? That is if you've nothing else to purchase?"

"We can stop now, but how about dinner?"

"Yes, dinner it is, but this time it's on me."

"No Tricia, I'm paying and there'll be no argument."

"But at least…"

"No buts. I'm a DaSilva and no DaSilva man invites a lady to dinner and doesn't pay for the meal. Call us old school, but that's who we are."

Laughing, she said, "My goodness, you *are* old school."

He winked at her. "Good, then it's settled?"

They sat chatting and sipping cocktails while waiting for their meal to arrive. Tricia's cell phone rang. She glanced at the number on the screen. "Carlos, I have to take this call. It's Katrina. Please excuse me."

Carlos nodded and continued sipping his cocktail. Tricia smiled throughout the entire conversation with her daughter.

When the brief conversation ended, Tricia said, "Katrina was calling to let me know that they've arrived safely in St. Lucia and all is well. She said it's a beautiful sunny day – twenty seven degrees Celsius. I could surely use some of that warmth right now."

"So could I."

"Would you like to see pictures of my children?"

"Sure!"

She opened the pictures on her cell phone and showed Carlos.

"Tricia, your daughter is beautiful, just like her mother. I can't imagine someone so beautiful is still single, but then again, it seems to be a choice for many today."

"Well, she was supposed to be getting married soon, but her fiancé cheated on her and she broke off the engagement. She says she'll never forgive a cheater and she sure as heck wouldn't marry one."

"That's too bad for them both. Maybe he didn't mean for it to happen. Perhaps he just made a mistake?"

Tricia looked Carlos straight in the eyes, her own eyes blazing. "Made a mistake? A one night stand could be called a mistake, but an affair that lasted almost a year is cheating, plain and simple, Carlos."

He swallowed hard, and the muscles in his jaw tightened as he ran his fingers through his hair. In a very low voice he replied, "It could still be a mistake, something that just happened."

Tricia shifted in her chair. She did not respond right away, but pulled a tissue from her purse and blotted the beads of sweat that had formed on her forehead. She could feel her hair going frizzy from the sweat and she gave a deep sigh, thinking that she should have worn a hat. She composed herself and spoke slowly as she looked into his face, which was drained of colour. "It didn't just happen. It lasted until Katrina discovered his double life. He obviously didn't love my daughter."

Carlos took a few sips of his drink. "Not necessarily. Just because a man cheats on his wife or girlfriend, doesn't mean he doesn't love her. Men do strange, silly things. We just don't think things through like you ladies do."

Tricia's fiery brown eyes again widened as she stared into Carlos' face. He looked down at his glass and his face muscles seemed to tighten as though in a knot. He took the napkin from the table and mopped his face, as Tricia replied. "That's no excuse. Any man who cheats on me will be kicked to the curb. I'd never put up with that, nor will my baby. Katrina was right to call off the wedding!"

His face folded like a crumpled piece of paper.

"Let's change the subject, please."

She shouldn't have mentioned her daughter's broken engagement, Tricia thought. She hated remembering the pain Katrina experienced because of Brian's infidelity. It opened old wounds for her, too. Carlos' pale face and his taut expression made her realize that he too was uncomfortable with the conversation. But why? Her intuition told her that something was not right, but she was afraid to find out. She could only handle so much in one day and was relieved to be off the subject.

"What are your plans for the next few days?" He asked, his voice almost a whisper.

"I promised Denise that I would finish decorating the house and help with whatever else she needs done over the next couple of days. I also plan to do some gift wrapping and I want to surprise them with some home cooked meals, too."

"So when will I see you again?"

"I suppose it won't be until Christmas day."

Their discussion left Tricia agitated and she was finding it hard to get back to calm. His reaction to her news about Katrina disappointed her. Good thing, she thought, that they would not see one another so soon again.

"I'll miss you, I really will."

She managed a smile as she said "You know you can always call me, but it'll only be a few days. I'm sure you'll survive."

They drove home in silence as she recalled their conversation in the restaurant, and why it made Carlos so uncomfortable. She convinced herself that men always take the man's side in those kinds of situations, and that consoled her.

When they arrived at the house Carlos helped her with her packages and walked her to the door, as usual. Inside, they both placed all their packages on the floor and stood there staring at each other. His big brown eyes softened her heart. She wondered what it was about him that so intrigued her. They stood like that for seconds until Carlos took both of her hands in his and looked into her eyes. She shivered. Carlos then pulled her close to him and kissed her on her forehead. She felt his body tremble as she wrapped her arms around him.

"Tricia, I... have a wonderful night, and sleep well."

"You have a good night also, and thanks for a lovely afternoon, and for dinner."

She closed the door behind him after watching him walk to his car. As she walked away from the door, she rested her right hand on her chest, hoping to control the heavy pounding of her heart.

Tricia spent the next few days catching up on her reading, and doing chores around the house for Denise and Richard. Each day she made sure that they had a healthy meal when they got in from work. She found herself humming carols as she worked. Being in New York with family made her feel loved and appreciated. Richard had been right about her making the trip. She was enjoying the change and was glad she took up his offer to spend the holidays with them in New York.

⊶ ⊷

On Christmas Eve, Tricia and Denise were busy preparing meals for the big day ahead. Richard was at work and was supposed to be bringing Thai food for dinner. When Denise told Tricia that she was craving Thai, Tricia teased, "You know my dear, when I was in the early stages of pregnancy with both my children I had some weird cravings. Is there something you're not telling me?"

"I wish there *was* something to tell. Sometimes I think I'm never going to have a child, and it's causing some stress in our marriage."

Tricia hugged Denise and said, "If the good Lord wants you to have a child you will, in His own time. Is Richard blaming you?"

"Oh, no! I'm the one who feels that it's my fault, and so it's making it even harder. I was adamant that we pay off most of our college debts and have a home before starting a family. Now I wonder if it's too late. I'll be thirty-five soon, and that could be risky. I feel I may have made a bad decision. Richard says I should stop blaming myself, but I can't help it."

"Denise, honey, Richard is right. Worrying will make it more difficult. You must try to relax. Many women have had healthy first babies even at age forty, you know that. I know a couple at least."

Tricia kissed Denise's tear stained face before continuing, "You know you can always adopt. Have you considered that?"

"Yes, we're giving it some serious thought. Auntie, having you here is such a blessing. You've brought laughter into our home again, and I don't feel as stressed since you've been here. Thank you so much. I'm sorry, though, that Richard and I have been working so much that we've not had time for you, but at least we have the next couple of days off to be with you."

"Oh no Denise, I'm fine, I enjoy Carlos' company very much. He's such a gentleman."

"Yes, he is a gentleman. Richard and I really love him and we're glad to be friends."

"We're becoming friends too, and I'm glad that I got to meet him. He's kind, gentle and treats me like a lady. He opens doors for me, and when we stop for a meal he does not sit until I have. He carries my packages, and do you know that at times I have to insist that I pay for my own shopping?"

"I can believe that."

"I have to be honest with you Denise, sometimes I feel guilty because I've been secretly glad that it is Carlos showing me around and keeping me entertained."

"Oh, please don't feel guilty. Carlos is charming and really good company. You two have a lot in common, and I'm sure he's more fun than Richard and me.

"I do love being with him, but there's something that's puzzling me. Do...."

"Denise, Auntie, dinner's here!" Richard interrupted.

"Hi honey, I didn't hear you come in," Denise remarked. "Here let me take those from you. Auntie, grab some plates for me please."

As Tricia proceeded to place the plates on the table Denise asked, "What were you going to say just now?"

"Never mind. It was nothing, really."

At midnight Kirk and Katrina called from St. Lucia to wish everyone a "Merry Christmas." It was the first Christmas Eve in a long time that Tricia had not gone to Candle Light service and hearing her children's voice brought back memories of the three of them all attending the service. She missed that special family tradition.

On Christmas Day, Tricia wore her favourite red dress and fixed her hair in an upsweep which she thought emphasized her best feature, her eyes. Before coming downstairs to join the party, she took a look in the full-length mirror that stood in the hallway. Tricia stared at the person she saw, and loved her. A smile spread across her face, as she, with grace and poise, descended the stairs ready to receive her relatives.

Uncle Mac and Stella arrived first with their special macaroni pie and cornbread. Mavis contributed potato salad and stuffed roast pork, a recipe that she learned from her Trinidadian ex-husband. There was Denise's parents' contribution of grilled salmon, pineapple baked ham and candied plantain. Tricia and Denise cooked a turkey, island spicy shoulder of lamb, and made Bajan styled pigeon peas and rice, braised vegetables, a garden salad and coleslaw. There was also home-made ginger beer, and two special West Indian beverages - mauby and sorrel.

Everyone was dressed in their best clothes and it was just as Tricia pictured it, with all the kisses and hugs and so much love in the room. Joy filled her heart. After acknowledging her relatives in the room, Tricia headed for the dining room and was busy setting the table when Carlos entered the room holding a bottle of wine in each hand. He looked like a handsome prince in his black suit, white shirt and red tie. He approached Tricia just as she looked up from placing the gravy bowl in its place on the table.

"Where shall I put these?" he asked.

"Here, give them to me."

As he passed them to her, their hands touched and they both looked at each other and smiled. Tricia's heart skipped a beat and with unsteady hands, she placed the bottles of wine in their place, and once again faced Carlos.

"Tricia, you look so beautiful today. Red is definitely your colour, and I love your hair up like that."

"Thank you. And you look very dashing. One could almost call you 'Prince Charming'."

"Ha, ha! Then, you'll have to be my princess!"

Tricia smiled and Carlos took a couple of steps closer to her. She turned to face him, and noticed a tremor on his lips, and his face flushed red.

"Tricia."

She trembled as he breathed her name.

"I'm sorry, I behaved terribly last Tuesday. I should have shown some empathy and sympathy when you spoke of your daughter's broken engagement. It must have been a difficult time for her and for you as well. I was insensitive to your pain, and I'm so ashamed of myself. Can you forgive me?"

"Yes, it was a difficult time for both of us. Katrina's heart was broken, and so was mine because I couldn't fix it. Anyway, she's fine now, and we both know that God has someone better for her, and He'll send him in His own perfect time. I *was* disappointed at your reaction, but I forgive you. What kind of Christian would I be if I didn't?"

His jaw relaxed, and he reached out and took her hands. She squeezed his, and smiled.

"I missed you," he whispered.

"Dinner's served!" Denise announced walking into the dining room followed by a parade of relatives. Richard rang the dinner bell to get everyone's attention, and as the room became silent, he said. "We're honoured to have so many loved ones here and most of all to have Auntie Tricia, who came all the way from Canada. We're honoured, too, to have Carlos, a very treasured friend, join us. Now it is our custom to have the eldest person in the room say the grace before dinner, but Dear Auntie Stella has a sore throat and laryngitis, so Carlos will do us the honour today. Let's all bow our heads as Carlos gives thanks to the Lord."

At the end of the prayer everyone joined in a chorus of "Amen"

"What a wonderful prayer Carlos. Where did you learn to pray like that?" Tricia asked.

"As children, our parents dragged us to church, almost kicking and screaming. They taught us love for God and others, and they put the fear of God into our hearts. I've strayed at times, become a lost sheep, one could say, but I always came back to the fold."

"That's great, so what are you now?" Tricia asked.

"A saved sheep; back in the fold."

Mavis cleared her throat. Denise looked at her and said. "Mavis, what's wrong? Are you catching Auntie Stella's cold?"

Uncle Mac spoke up. "No Denise. Mavis is just being Mavis. She doesn't go to church so she can't understand anyone having the need for God. Pass the cornbread please, Carlos."

Carlos continued, "I'm a regular church goer, but Lord knows I'm no angel."

Mavis cleared her throat again.

"Of course you're no angel." Tricia teased.

Carlos' eyes widened. "Excuse me young lady! What are you trying to say?"

"Carlos, my friend, please don't go there," said Richard. "You can never win this one with auntie. She can really dish it out."

"Oh, I had a taste of what she can dish out. Didn't I Tricia?"

"Yeah, and there's more where that came from."

Everyone laughed. Mavis, Tricia noticed, was frowning and rolled her eyes as she stared at Carlos.

"My goodness, look at the food on this table!" Denise's mother, Beulah exclaimed. Her eyes widened as she scanned the table. "What a delightful arrangement of Caribbean–American dishes!"

Uncle Mac agreed, "This is a feast fit for kings and queens."

Austin, Denise's dad, raised his glass in a toast, "To kings and queens."

All laughed, as they raised their glasses, and repeated, "To kings and queens."

The teasing and joking continued throughout the dinner. Everyone was fair game.

After dinner the table was cleared and all went into the family room for trivia about the Christmas Story. Later Richard brought out his guitar and with Tricia on the piano and Uncle Mac piping on his harmonica, they all joined in singing *Silent Night*.

"Mom, dad, sing for us," Denise asked of her parents.

"Oh, yes please do," Richard added. "Bless us with your special rendition of *O Holy Night*. Beulah and Austin met in a summer voice training camp as teenagers, Auntie Tricia, and they've been singing together ever since. They've

blessed many a Christmas congregation with their rendition of *O Holy Night.*"

Everyone started clapping and cheering the couple on.
"C'mon sing for us," they pleaded.

Beulah and Austin moved closer together and with
Denise accompanying them on piano, began singing the
carol. When they reached the high notes, the room exploded with applause.

"Wow, you two are incredible!" Tricia exclaimed. "You
should be singing at Carnegie Hall."

"There's a lot of talent in this room. I feel so blessed,"
Carlos added. "What a wonderful Christmas celebration."

"Amen!" Uncle Mac said.

The group continued singing and laughing.

"This is all so beautiful," Auntie Stella managed to
whisper.

During the singing of *O Come All Ye Faithful,* Tricia's
thoughts drifted to a time long ago, when she was a young
girl growing up in her native Barbados. Her family didn't
have much, but they were so happy. Christmas was celebrat-
ed with family, friends and neighbours for twelve happy
days.

Her mind then took her to another time and place –
her home in Toronto. She saw her children in their pajamas opening their gifts. She could hear their squeals
and laughter as the wrapping was ripped from the boxes
to reveal the toy they'd requested from Santa Claus. She
saw her mom, happy and laughing and enjoying being
with her grandchildren. Her mom had been her best
friend and although it was nine years since she'd passed,
Tricia still missed her.

She wiped her eyes as Richard, looking at her with a frown on his face asked, "Auntie, is there anything wrong? Are you crying?"

"I'm fine Richard, don't worry. My thoughts were miles away, but in a happy place."

Everyone continued singing carol after carol until they were exhausted, and thought it time to leave for their own homes.

"Denise, Richard, thanks for a wonderful Christmas," uncle Mac said as he helped Aunt Stella into her coat.

"You're welcome Uncle Mac," Richard and Denise said in unison.

"Aunt Stella, you take care of that cold. Uncle Mac, make sure that Auntie gets lots of rest," Denise added.

Mavis hugged and kissed Tricia. "It was so nice to see you again. You're still as beautiful as ever. Bye for now."

"And you are still as mischievous as ever," Tricia said.

Mavis laughed. "You said it best a few days ago my dear. A leopard just can't change his spots."

There was lots of hugging and kissing as all thanked their hosts for a wonderful Christmas. Carlos was the last one to leave, but not before Tricia handed him the gift she'd purchased for him. He already had his gift from Denise and Richard in his hand.

"I hope you like it."

"Tricia, I'll love anything that comes from you. Thank you so much."

She walked him to the door. He placed his gifts on the bench in the foyer, took her hands, looked into her eyes, and kissed her fully on her mouth. She wanted to return his kiss, but instead became as frozen as a Popsicle.

"Good night, Tricia."

"Good night, Carlos."

Tricia closed the door behind him and plopped down on a loveseat in the family room. Richard and Denise were lying on the sofa, both looking exhausted. She closed her eyes and thought of the evening and Carlos' kiss. It was the first time his lips had touched hers and it made her heart beat rapidly in her chest. She loved the way he made her feel, but questions raced through her mind. Why didn't she return his kiss when she wanted to so much? What did Carlos think as he walked to his car? She consoled herself that at least she didn't push him away. As the reasons for her not kissing him in return became clear to her, Tricia recited a little prayer. "Jesus, help me to trust again. Please let me see my worth. Work on my self-esteem, Lord." Denise's voice interrupted her thoughts.

"Tricia, there's a gift from Carlos to you, under the tree. We can't wait for you to open it."

"I'll open it right away."

She walked over to the seven- foot tree that was beautifully decorated with white lights and gold ornaments and ribbons. She picked up the small box that was labelled "To Tricia, Merry Christmas from Carlos."

Carefully, Tricia peeled the tape from the box and opened it. Inside was an envelope. She took the same care breaking the seal of the envelope. Her mouth gaped open and tears formed in her eyes when she saw two tickets to the Broadway hit, *Fiddler on the Roof* and the note which read, "Dearest Tricia, I know how much you love the theatre and longed to see this musical. When I saw how your face lit up as you gazed at the billboard ad a few days ago, I knew I had to play Santa, and make your wish come true. I purchased two tickets hoping that you would allow me to be your date for the evening. No one should go to a play alone, especially on New Year's Eve, so would you do me the honour of spending New Year's Eve with me? I've also made dinner reservations for two. Of course, if there is someone else that you'd rather be your date, I'll understand. I just want you to be happy." It was signed, "With affection, Carlos."

"Auntie, what is it?" Richard asked. "We're anxious to know."

"It's tickets to Fiddler on the Roof on New Year's Eve. Oh Richard, Denise, he does the sweetest things. He's so amazing!"

"He's a wonderful man, and so are you Richard," Denise added, giving her husband a peck on the cheek.

Tricia continued, "I've always wanted to attend a Broadway show, and I missed seeing Fiddler on The Roof when it came to Toronto some years ago. It's been a long time since I've had a date on New Year's Eve. This one should be interesting." she said laughing.

"I guess it will be. Do you need a refresher course?"

"Richard, stop teasing your aunt!" Denise said laughing. "It's like riding a bike. I'm happy for you Auntie, and I know you'll have fun."

Very early the next day, Tricia's cell phone rang. "Hello Carlos, how are you doing? I was thinking to call you."

"You were? I guess great minds do think alike. I'm doing well, thank you, and you?"

"I'm fine. Thank you so much for your very thoughtful gift. What a wonderful surprise! You've made me so happy, and of course you'll be my date. I'm looking forward to it."

"So am I. Anyway, I was calling to thank *you* for the gloves. I'm always losing mine, and was thinking of buying another pair. You must have read my mind. I shall think of you each time I wear them."

"I'm glad you like them. I know it's a very practical gift, but I honestly didn't know what else to get you."

"It's a wonderful gift Tricia, and thanks again."

⋙⋘

Tricia kept herself very busy doing chores around the home, preparing dinner for Denise and Richard, and getting some much needed rest, during the days following Christmas. She could not wait for New Year's Eve. Now, she would have someplace to wear the black dress that she'd purchased just days before leaving Toronto. She'd seen the dress while shopping for her children's Christmas gifts and decided to try it on. It fit perfectly, and even made her appear slimmer than her one hundred and forty pounds. The dress featured a high neck at the front, a very low V-back, and sheer long sleeves. It hugged her hips showing off her curvy figure; the one thing that Wesley had found attractive about her in the early days of their relationship. She dressed early and had plenty of time to apply her makeup and fix her hair in the upsweep that Carlos liked. When she was satisfied with her appearance, Tricia descended the stairs like a model on the runway. She presented herself to Richard and Denise who were anticipating her appearance.

"Wow, you look stunning, absolutely stunning! But are you sure you won't be cold in that dress?" Richard teased when she turned, revealing the low back.

Tricia smiled mischievously and winked at Richard. "My dear nephew, I've got my love to keep me warm."

"Denise, Auntie Tricia is back! This is the person we knew and loved. Auntie, you're back to your lovely, funny and somewhat naughty self. I'm so glad to see you this way. Have fun tonight; you deserve it. Denise, I wish you had known Auntie Tricia during my childhood years. Sometimes my family would visit hers in Toronto during summer holidays. She would make up all kinds of funny stories to entertain Kirk, Katrina and me. Once, she got all dressed up in a dazzling gown, and very high- heeled shoes. You should have seen her make-up and hair, adorned with a tiara. She started from the top of the stairs and took her time descending while she sang 'here she comes, Miss America'. Kirk, Katrina and I clapped and laughed. Oh the fun we use to have back in those days!"

"Oh, I wish I'd known her then. It seems like you guys had a fun childhood hanging out with Auntie." Denise responded. "Somehow that doesn't surprise me though. I've seen her slowly letting her hair down these few weeks. Auntie Tricia, I can still remember you having the time of your life at our wedding, even though Uncle Wesley was as stiff as cardboard."

They all laughed as Richard added, "Yes he was a real stuffed shirt."

⟩⟨ ⟨⟩

Carlos arrived about ten minutes before they were scheduled to leave and the four of them had a glass of wine.

"To friendship and a happy New Year," Richard toasted.

They clinked their glasses together. "To friendship. Happy New Year."

As Carlos helped Tricia into her coat, he said to her, "You are *so* beautiful. I'm a lucky man to have such a gorgeous lady as my date."

The compliment pleased her, and she smiled from her heart.

Carlos had a cab already waiting at the house for them, and they drove from there to Petite Fleur restaurant.

"Good evening Mr. DaSilva, Madame," the Maître D greeted them. "It is good to see you again, Sir. Your table is ready. Follow me please."

As they walked to their table Tricia could not help but admire the ambiance of the large room, lavished with Christmas decorations and expensive looking paintings on the walls.

"Carlos, this place is amazing. That Christmas tree is just beautiful and I love the giant chandeliers!"

"This is one of the best restaurants in the city. You're in for a real treat."

Dinner was a feast of onion soup, seared salmon with a dijonnaise mustard sauce, roast duck, in an orange sauce, and triple sec liquor. It was served with seasoned rice, and included grilled vegetables. For dessert, Tricia chose the New York Cheesecake and her choice of wine was a glass of Cabernet Sauvignon. Carlos chose a glass of Chardonnay, but passed on dessert.

Carlos took a sip of his wine. "Wasn't it a wonderful Christmas?" he said. "I'm so glad that I accepted Richard and Denise's invitation to dinner. The food was delicious, and the company heartwarming. I don't remember laughing so much and having so much fun in a long time."

"Carlos that is what a real family dinner is supposed to be like. You know, the love, the teasing and the laughter. We used to have that in my family, a long time ago."

"I know what you mean. I too miss that, but I'm thankful we had this one."

"So am I."

Tricia found herself looking at Carlos and admiring his broad shoulders and his handsome face that showed maturity yet also softness, features that made him so attractive, she thought. She did not realize that she was smiling until Carlos commented, "You've been smiling all evening. Can you tell me what is so amusing?"

She looked into his eyes. "I'm not amused. I was thinking that I'm a lucky gal to be in the company of such a handsome, warm and generous gentleman."

Carlos smiled. "You say the sweetest things, but *I'm* the lucky one."

Her heartbeat quickened as she realized that she loved everything about this man who came into her life at a time when she definitely needed the friendship. "I now know who you remind me of," she exclaimed.

"Who?"

"Tom Selleck."

"Tom Selleck? Ha! I don't know what to say. This time, I'm speechless."

"Carlos, how old are you, may I ask?"

Carlos took a sip of his Chardonnay, then with his head tilted to one side and a boyish smile on his face answered, "I'm sixty-two."

"Sixty-two! Are you serious? You don't look a day over fifty. Wow, you've got great genes!"

"So have you, Tricia. You look young enough to be Richard's sister, *not* his aunt. I won't ask your age though, because a gentleman never asks."

"Thank you. Anyway, I have no problem telling you my age. I'm fifty-five."

"I would never have guessed that. You look very much younger."

He stared at her for a moment and then added "Your eyes are beautiful. They are such a light brown, and sometimes they look green. I love them!"

"I like them too. It's the one thing I inherited from my dad."

They both laughed.

"Carlos, why did you retire so young?"

She looked at him anticipating his response. He ran his fingers through his hair before looking into her eyes. "Tricia," he started, but she noticed the pain in his eyes and she knew then that he was going back to a sad place and time.

She reached across the table and touched his hand. "It's alright. You can tell me another time."

He nodded and squeezed her hand in response.

Carlos beckoned the waiter over. After settling the bill, they left the restaurant, hand in hand, and headed for the theatre.

⇥⇤

Carlos held Tricia's hand at times during the musical. At the end of the performance they jumped to their feet along with the entire audience. A thunderous applause filled the room along with whistling and hooting. Some cast members blew kisses to their patrons. Tricia cheered and hooted as well. Carlos placed one arm around her waist and kissed her on her cheek.

He smiled as he said, "You're having a good time, and that makes me very happy."

As they were leaving the theatre, it was she who took his hand. "Wasn't the show terrific?" She asked. "I enjoyed it so much, I wouldn't mind seeing it again."

"Yes it was great. It was funny and very entertaining. I too, wouldn't mind seeing it again, especially if I have the pleasure of your wonderful company."

"Hmmm, maybe we could arrange for that to happen."

It was just after eleven so they decided to take in the festivities in Times Square. Carlos hooked her arm as they walked towards the square. The closer they got, the louder the music and happy chatter of the crowd grew and the more rapid was her heartbeat. She wondered if Carlos could sense her excitement from just being with him on this special night. Could he feel her tremble, or sense the emotions that were flooding through her? She thanked God that because of the loud music Carlos would not hear the loud pounding of her heart.

"Carlos I love this," she shouted above the noise. "I can't believe I'm going to actually be in Times Square on New Year's Eve."

"I sense your excitement, and I love it. I can't believe this whole evening, either. It's magical!"

At last they stood among thousands, all waiting to welcome the New Year. Music filled the air and a myriad of red, white, gold and green lights and huge beautifully decorated

Christmas trees adorned the whole perimeter of the square. Couples packed every square inch. There was hugging and kissing and joy filled the air. The music and the merriment of excited party revellers were intoxicating and infectious.

Carlos drew her close to him and pecked her on her neck. She turned, tiptoed and kissed his cheek. Her heart was freed as her insecurities melted away. She raised herself on her toes and spoke in Carlos's ears above an overture of noise. "Carlos, this is a dream come true. Thank you."

He hugged her. "You're welcome, sweetie. To be part of this grand celebration is like a happy dream for me too."

At times they both moved to the music and smiles never left their faces. As the ball lowered, she suddenly found herself in his arms. Ba bum, Ba bum. Their hearts beating in unison drummed their own music.

Five, four, three, two, one ....

Their lips touched, and as he kissed her, on the stroke of midnight, life again flowed through her veins and found its way into her sleeping heart. She felt resuscitated, and her heart whispered, "I'm alive, so much alive. Thank you God."

The band led the thousands of revellers in Times Square in a chorus of *Auld Lang Syne*. In the background, the loud musical sound of honking cars, whistles and party horns sent their "Happy New Year" wishes into the cold night. In the excitement of the moment Tricia tightened her arms around Carlos' waist. His lips again found hers and he showered her with gentle kisses. She inhaled deeply taking in the intoxicating fragrance of his cologne, and enjoying his arms around her. It had been so long since she'd felt a man's touch, and it felt good. She realized that she'd missed that all these lonely years. Her response to his kisses was spontaneous and ignoring the crowd around them, kissed him with more passion than she had intended, and with a fervour that she thought had long died.

Pop, crackle, bang, swwwwiiiish, weeeeeeeeeeee dot dot dot spuurrrrrrrrhhhhhhhh, pooooooooooooffffffff A kaleidoscope of dancing colours burst into the air. As the fireworks lit up the night, light began once more to shine in her eyes.

Suddenly Carlos released her waist and cupped her face in his hands while looking into her eyes, which were moist with tears.

"Happy New Year, Tricia."

"Happy New Year, Carlos."

Her thoughts raced again. Something wonderful and unbelievable was happening to her and she wondered if Carlos could sense it. She would have given anything to be able to read his thoughts. After the music stopped, she secretly longed for an encore performance.

As though reading her thoughts, Carlos gently took her hand in his and a warm flow of excitement again rushed through her. Her happy heart refused to be quiet. Pure joy, love and happiness entered into her body, fed her starved heart, and quenched her soul. They remained hand in hand, just taking in the entertainment and the excitement of the evening.

Moments later, as the crowds began to disperse, Carlos placed her in front of him and with both hands around her waist, guided her through the crowded square without saying a word. They were leaving but she did not want the night to end, not just yet.

They made their way through the crush of partiers, away from all the noisy chatter and music. Carlos moved his hands from around her waist and gently took one hand in his as they continued walking into the busy and cluttered street where dozens of taxicabs were waiting.

"One thing's missing from this night, Tricia."

"What's that?"

"Champagne."

"Champagne? Where will we get Champagne at this hour?"

"I know the perfect place.....Taxi!"

They slipped into the cab without saying a word. She did not ask where they were going, and she didn't care as long as she was still with Carlos, and her night was not yet ending.

Carlos gave the driver an address. Tricia rested her head against the back of the carseat and closed her eyes, as Carlos took her hand in his. She kept her eyes closed, afraid to look at him. She was afraid that he would be able to look into her eyes and see right into her heart.

"We're going to my place. I hope you don't mind. I have a bottle of Moet chilling and that's what we need to *really* celebrate this night, and the beginning of a new year," he said. She could hear the smile in his voice.

"No, I don't mind at all. I'm looking forward to that glass of champagne."

Carlos turned the key into the door of his penthouse condominium and upon entering they both removed their shoes. She took a few steps further in and a breathtaking scene greeted her. Tricia's eyes widened.

She gasped, imagining streams of daylight pouring through the soaring windows that offered a magnificent view of the city. In-floor heating welcomed her feet. Her eyes darted about the room to take in all that it had to offer, from the coffered ceiling to the wool rugs. As she followed Carlos in, she caught the faint scent of cedar. That, she deduced, must be the hall closet. The home had all the fine appointments of cutting edge design meets old world charm.

The library housed a floor to ceiling bookcase. Tricia wandered over to get a glimpse of his taste in literature. There were several early editions of Ernest Hemingway, Mark Twain, William Shakespeare and many others in the hall of literary giants. Tricia could not help but to run her fingers across the keys of the white baby grand piano which stood proudly in the room. She turned around and a sumptuous leather sectional in a warm chocolate hue beckoned her. Two accent chairs in a two-tone chocolate flanked the slate fireplace and a large Picasso painting hung over the mantelpiece. She could not help but notice the wooden coffee table, its tempered bevelled glass top adding to the room's ambiance. Both the coffee table and the two end tables resembled a chest with pull out drawers.

Tricia walked a little further into the home and found herself in the formal room which was just as exquisite. A beige fabric sofa and loveseat dressed the room. She was about to peruse further, when Carlos followed her into the room.

"*Magnifico,*" she whispered. "Carlos, your place is absolutely beautiful. I love your choice of colours."

"Thank you. After the two deaths, I no longer wanted to live in our home. It was too large and held too many memories. Christina helped me choose this place."

As he spoke, he took her coat and with Tricia following closely behind him, walked to the hall closet where he hung both their coats. As they continued walking to the room her eyes first saw, Carlos said, "Welcome to my favourite room. This is where I do my thinking and reading."

Tricia stood, her eyes again darting around whole area, still in awe of the beautiful, yet very masculine décor.

"Make yourself comfortable, please."

Tricia sat on one end of the leather sectional and Carlos sat next to her.

"Did you decorate all this yourself?"

"No, my sister helped quite a bit."

"It all looks so professional. Your sister did a great job,"

"That's because she *is* a professional decorator. You may have heard of her, Ginette Da Silva. She's featured in quite a few magazines, in the USA and throughout Europe."

"Ginette Da Silva is your sister? Oh my goodness, you are *that* Carlos Da Silva, the famous architect! I now realize why your name seemed so familiar! I read about your family some years ago in a home decorating magazine. If I remember correctly, you were all in the business of designing and decorating homes, mostly for the rich and famous."

"You are correct. Papa, my grandfather, started a modest company but it has grown to be known worldwide. Papa and dad are both deceased, and of course Jonathan. Gina, Christina and their spouses, along with some partners, now carry on the business and it has really grown. They moved it from New York to New Jersey just recently."

"Yes, I remember that it was, what the article called, a 'family business.' Goodness gracious, I am in the company of a famous person!" She spoke quickly, almost out of breath.

"Tricia, slow down, please!"

She cupped both of her cheeks, shook her head from side to side and continued without catching her breath. "I can't believe this whole day. Carlos pinch me, please, because I must be dreaming! Why didn't you tell me all this?"

He laughed. "Well, first my dear, I couldn't pinch you without feeling your pain. So, instead I'll just confirm that you're not dreaming. Secondly, I never mentioned anything because I figured you would find out soon enough, and I didn't think it was important."

"My goodness, I can't believe I kissed Carlos Da Silva. What's more, I can't believe that Carlos Da Silva kissed *me*! Denise and Richard have never mentioned any of this to me. Now I really need that drink." she said laughing,

He smiled casually. "Yes let's get that champagne, after all it is the reason you are here."

Carlos wandered over to the wine cooler as Tricia allowed her eyes to wander around the room once more, smiling as she did so. The whole evening was like a beautiful dream, like Cinderella at the ball with Prince Charming.

Pop!! The noise startled her and Tricia came down from her cloud. Carlos returned, smiling, with a glass of champagne in each hand. She stood, reached out and took a glass from him. They crossed their hands and their glasses clinked as they touched each other.

"To a beautiful and exciting woman," Carlos said smiling. "Happy New Year, Tricia."

"Happy New Year, Carlos, and thank you for making the start of my new year a very memorable one."

They both took a few sips of the champagne before flopping down again on the sectional. Carlos placed his glass on the coffee table that was so perfect for the décor of the room. He took the glass from her trembling hand and placed that on the table also. She looked at him, a bit confused, but not for long, as he moved closer to her, placed one hand under her chin and placed his lips fully on her mouth.

He kissed her gently, quietly, over and over again. She sat there, almost frozen, eyes closed, as she tried to process the events of the past several hours. Her mind went back in time and she started to cry.

"What's wrong my sweet, do I kiss that badly?"

"Oh, no! It's just that I was remembering another New Year's Eve quite the opposite of this one. I was six months pregnant with Katrina and was forced to spend the night alone, while my husband chose to be out partying with his friends. That night I had a scare and..."

"Shhhhhh, Tricia," Carlos said as he placed his fingers on her lips. "No tears tonight, and no bad memories. That's over my sweet. Tonight, let's just think about good things. It's a new day and a new year. Let the past stay in the past, where it belongs. Losing Jonathan and Sylvia has taught me two things: to live in the present and love without regret. After all the present is all we've got, isn't it?"

"It's just that this New Year's Eve has been so much fun. I never imagined when I booked this trip that it would turn out so well. I'm really happy and I'm sorry for crying."

"Don't be sorry. Just don't cry anymore, or I'll have to keep on kissing you to dry the tears."

"Ha! Ha! Ha!"

"Great, I made you laugh, now isn't that much better?"

He took his hand and wiped the tears from her eyes as she smiled.

"You have a beautiful smile."

She did not respond, but rested her back against the cushions and relaxed. Carlos moved closer to her. So close she could hear his breathing as he took her hands in his.

"Tricia"

"Yes, Carlos."

"I think I'm falling in love with you."

"Oh Carlos, please don't do that!"

"Why? Is it because my love can't be reciprocated?"

"Oh no, Carlos. I do have some feelings for you, but I don't know what they are. You know, I've just recently been divorced and even before the divorce, my ex and I lived like strangers in the same home for years. You're the first man I've actually dated since then. I do enjoy your company and I'm embarrassed to admit I love your kisses and the way I feel when I'm with you. I'm not sure if it is because I've not been with a man in such a long time. Or, that I'm caught up in and being influenced by all the love and happiness that this beautiful season seems to stir in so many of us. I just know it is a very vulnerable time for me, and perhaps even for you."

"Tricia, everyone has been telling me that it's time to start dating again. Christina worries about me being so lonely and has pleaded with me several times. 'Dad, please be happy, find someone to love again. For God's sake, dad, have a life.' However, I did not feel I was ready, and never thought I could love again. That's until I met you. My dear, you've changed all that. I haven't been this happy in a long time. You make me laugh, and each night as I lay in bed I think about you, and I re-live all that we did during the day. There is something very special about you, and I've so enjoyed these past few weeks with you. I'm not ashamed to admit that I find myself looking forward to seeing you. Tricia I want you in my life. I *need* you in my life."

"Carlos, I do love being with you too, but my marriage has caused me so much pain. I think I'm afraid, really afraid to trust again. We also have another problem. We live in separate countries and while you're retired, I'm still a working gal. It's common knowledge that long distant relationships seldom work."

"Well, then we'll have to prove everyone wrong and make this one work, and really Tricia, you're a mere ninety minutes or so away. I can hop onto an airplane and be with you in a couple of hours, that way we can see each other at least every weekend. So, that isn't long distance."

"Carlos, would you do that for me? I mean hop onto a plane every weekend? That'll cost a fortune!"

"Tricia, my sweet, what good is money if you can't use it to make someone happy and oneself at the same time? Maybe sometimes you could come to me in New York. How about that? Your children are grown and away from home, so there's nothing to hold you back now, is there?"

"You have all the answers, don't you?"

"Not really, but I do know that I want you in my life and I will do whatever it takes to make that happen."

"Carlos, this whole night has been so romantic and I'm so happy being here with you, but it is also a lot to process. May I sleep on it?"

He looked straight into her eyes, and she could see disappointment in his, as he spoke in a quiet voice, "No pressure, Tricia. When do you leave for Canada?"

"In six days. On the seventh."

"Goodness, so soon? I guess I'm going to have to make full use of the next few days."

"I guess so. Time does fly when one is having fun, so they say," she replied.

"Okay, my sweet, how about dinner the night before you leave? That'll give you more time to think things over. I'll make reservations and call you with a time to pick you up. In the meantime, let's enjoy the next four days. Are you okay with this?"

"Sounds like a great plan. You know, I'm really going to miss this place."

"Is that all you're going to miss?"

Tricia kissed his cheek as she replied, "and you too, silly!"

He returned her kiss and whispered, "I'll miss you too, very much. Now, let's finish off that champagne, shall we? Are you hungry?"

"Now that you've mentioned it, yes I am."

"What would you like? I could order in a meal, or I could make you a ham sandwich. That's about it."

"I'm tired of ham. How about pizza?"

"Pizza?"

"Yes, pizza! I haven't had any since I've been here, and I've always loved New York pizzas, but can we order in food at this hour?"

"Sweetie, this is the city that does not sleep. What toppings would you like?"

"Pepperoni of course, with double cheese, hold the onions, and the rest is up to you."

He smiled. "Okay, pizza you shall have."

Tricia hugged him as she replied, "thank you."

Carlos placed the order and returned to the sectional. Tricia snuggled closer to him, and they chatted as they waited for the pizza. During their conversation Tricia discovered that one of Carlos' hobbies was to sketch and paint.

"One day I hope to show you my creations, which Christina thinks are worth displaying," he said.

'Oh, I'd love to see them some time!"

They continued chatting until the security buzzed that the pizza had arrived. Deliveries were not allowed to the penthouse floor so Carlos went down to retrieve it. Tricia closed her tired eyes and sat back on a cushion on the chair until he returned. She took a couple of bites and remarked. "This is delicious, and thank you for ordering a thin crust. I'd forgotten to mention that."

He gave her a teasing wink. "See how well I know you already?"

"It could be that you're a mind reader. I have to be careful around you," she replied, laughing.

They ate most of the pizza and finished off the whole bottle of champagne.

Tricia asked to be excused and headed for the powder room to freshen up a bit. When she returned, Carlos arose from the sectional, took her hand in his and guided her towards the piano. He sat on the bench and started running his finger across the keys. She stood over him, listening to the sound he was making on the piano.

"What are you playing?"

"Nothing special, just warming up and thinking of what I *should* play. You can say I'm making love to the keys."

"Okay lover boy, don't let me stop you then."

Amidst loud laughter, he exclaimed, "Cheeky devil!"

"I warned you. Didn't I?"

"Yes, you did. Do you play any instrument?"

"No, but I've always wanted to play one."

"It's not too late to learn. Perhaps I'll get the opportunity to teach you."

"Perhaps. Do you play anything else?"

"Yes, the guitar."

"Gosh, you're talented."

He started to play and Tricia instantly recognized the song, but did not anticipate what came next. Looking straight into her face, his rich mellow voice tugged at the strings of her heart as the caressing lyrics of the song flowed from his lips.

"*You are so beautiful to me. You are so beautiful to me. You're everything I've dreamed of, you're everything I need. You are so beautiful to me.*"

Carlos motioned for her to join him on the bench. She did, but remained silent, as he raised one hand from the piano and ran it along her left cheek, wiping the teardrop that had rested there.

Her heart spoke. "*How can I tell him that he's everything I've dreamed of, and everything I need? Help me Jesus!*"

"You've a beautiful voice," she finally managed to say.

He glanced at her. "I bet you can sing well too. Let me see what I can play that we can sing together. Would you like that? To sing, I mean."

"Carlos, if music be the food of love, *play* on."

"Hmm, a woman who quotes Shakespeare, I love that."

They were both smiling as Carlos started a new melody. They sang together, love song, after love song. After a few songs, Carlos turned his face to her and said, "This last one is for you and very fitting." He sang, "You're *once, twice, three times a lady and I love you*"

At the end of the song, he kissed her on her cheeks, and used his hands once more to wipe away her tears.

"Thank you Carlos. I really enjoyed this."

"I did too. It was great having someone to play for again."

They returned to the sectional. She snuggled close to him and rested her head on his big, strong shoulder. She ran her fingers along his face, enjoying the softness of his smooth olive complexion. She closed her eyes, and smiled.

━◁┼ ┼▷━

Some hours later, Tricia opened her eyes to find herself in Carlos' arms, and he fast asleep. She moved away and took a glimpse at her watch. Her movement stirred him. He opened his eyes and yawned.

"Goodness gracious, look at the time. It's after six. We must have slept for quite some time. Richard and Denise must be worried sick about me!"

"I doubt that they're worried, my sweet. They know you're big girl now and your nephew would never have asked me to take you around New York if he didn't trust me. I'll take you home in a few minutes and pick up my car."

"That's right; I'd forgotten that we took a cab last tonight."

As he left to retrieve their coats, Tricia sat there still not sure if these past few weeks were real or just one long beautiful dream. She muttered, "Lord, if it is all a dream, please don't let it end yet. I've not had so beautiful a dream in a long time."

"Okay. Let's go," Carlos said.

She snapped from her dream as he returned to the room. A soft smile appeared on her face as she looked, admiringly, at him.

Carlos helped her into her coat and they headed for the door. As he turned the handle, she touched his shoulder and he turned to look at her. They gazed at each other for several seconds, and then he kissed her tenderly on her cheeks and neck. Even in her high-heeled boots he still towered over her. She tiptoed and this time, she kissed him on his lips several times. He wrapped his arms around her and it was in that moment that she felt the love he spoke of. It was then, she realized, that he really loved her and she knew, too, that she'd fallen in love again. She said a silent prayer. "Oh Lord, what shall I do? I did not mean for this to happen and I'm scared, so scared. Help me, Jesus."

Finally, she took Carlos' hands in hers, looked up into his warm, brown eyes and with a tremor in her voice, said, "Carlos, thanks again for last night and all the other days. Being with you this unforgettable holiday season, your gentle ways and your kindness, have restored my confidence and my trust in men. You have given me a December to remember, and I will make this first day of 2005 the beginning of the rest of my life."

"You're welcome Tricia, but it is I who should be thanking you for allowing me to be in your company, and for giving me one of the happiest New Year's Eve ever. I'm so glad that I was available to pick you up from the airport that freezing night last month. When I saw you looking around for Denise and Richard, I knew I was going to enjoy your company. You looked lost, but so beautiful. I had a chuckle watching you walk around in those really high-heeled boots," he said laughing, "but I liked you right away."

Laughing also, she replied, "I liked you right away too. So I guess, for both of us, it was "like at first sight.""

Carlos held her hand all the way home in the cab and she was enjoying his touch. She loved being with him and knew she would miss him terribly once she returned to Canada.

They exited the cab, and after paying the fare, he walked her to the door. Inside, he took Tricia into his arms and kissed her over and over again. She liked it, and responded with passion.

"Good morning my sweet. I'll see you later, at the 'Robinsons' for dinner. Now, try to get some rest."

"See you later. Please get home safely."

As she walked toward the kitchen, she noticed Denise already dressed for work. She was seated at the breakfast nook, sipping a cup of coffee.

"Hey Auntie, must have been some night. Do you know what time it is, young lady?" she said laughing.

"Denise, it was really some night. I had the time of my life, and Carlos commented on the great time he had as well. I've so much to tell you. I can't wait until you get in later, but first, why didn't you tell me that he was *the* famous Carlos DaSilva?"

Denise took another sip of coffee. "For us, he's just Carlos, a very nice man and a good friend, and I didn't think it was important."

Glancing at the clock Denise called out, "Richard, come on down, we're running late. Remember, we're taking one car today."

"Hey Auntie," Richard said as he came running down the stairs. "Happy New Year."

He walked over and hugged his aunt and plopped a kiss on her cheek. "How was your date with Carlos? You wild one!" he teased.

Tricia, smiling and as excited as a child, replied, "My time with Carlos was amazing. Dinner was delicious, and the show was delightful, funny and very entertaining. Times Square was magical, and I was in the company of the most interesting, warmest, and kindest man I've ever met. I had the time of my life!"

"From the look on your face, I would say it was heavenly," Richard responded. You've got to fill us in later, but we've got to rush off now."

"Richard," Tricia scolded, "No breakfast, not even a cup of coffee?"

"I'll grab some breakfast from the cafeteria. See you later."

"Yea, see you later Auntie," Denise repeated as she rose from the table. "We'll have that chat later. Now, you get some rest."

"Bye kids!"

"Don't forget we're having dinner at my parents' this evening," Denise said before closing the door.

"I won't forget, drive safely guys."

Tricia yawned her way up the stairs to her room and after showering, she collapsed into her bed and was asleep in an instant.

━━✛ ✛━━

Tricia awoke around eleven a.m. to the sound of her cell phone ringing. She rolled over rubbed her eyes to focus and grabbed it from the night table, thinking it was Carlos.

"Hello," she answered in her softest tone.

"Hellooo Tricia. It's Maaavis," she drawled. Happy New Year!"

"Happy New Year Mavis. How are you?"

"I'm good, Tricia. How are you, and how was your night out with Carlos?"

Tricia wondered how Mavis knew that she was out with Carlos, but just replied, "My night was wonderful Mavis, we…"

"What's going on between you two anyways?"

"What do you mean, Mavis?"

"C'mon Tricia, I've seen the way you look at each other. He couldn't keep his eyes off you all Christmas day. As a matter of fact your eyes were on him the whole time too."

"Mavis, I've no idea what you're talking about. We've become friends. Is that a problem?' Before Tricia could continue Mavis warned, "Be careful my dear cousin. He'll break your heart."

"Break my heart? Why do you say that?"

"Didn't Richard or Denise tell you about his affair that caused his son's death?"

"What are you talking about Mavis? What affair?"

"Tricia, Carlos cheated on Sylvia, and it cost Jonathan his life. I'm surprised Richard or Denise never told you. The man's no saint. Like I said, he'll break your heart."

Tricia's heart pounded. She began pacing the floor and tugging at her hair. "For heaven's sake, Mavis, I don't know if I want to hear this. Not now, please!"

"Well you've got to hear it some time. You'd better talk to Denise about it, that's all I'm going to say."

"Damn it Mavis! I've got to go. I..."

"Tricia, I just don't want to see you hurt," Mavis interjected. "Women throw themselves at Carlos all the time. Haven't you noticed how darn handsome he is? And he's mighty rich too!"

Tricia raised her voice. Agitated, she said, "Mavis, It's always about money for you isn't it? *Please*, no more!"

"Tricia!"

"Bye Mavis!"

Tricia dropped the phone and ran to the bathroom, tears flowing like a river that had burst its banks. She was sick to her stomach. What had she gotten herself into? "I've got to speak with Denise as soon as she gets in." she spoke aloud through sobs. She jumped back into bed. Her tears flowed and her heart felt heavy in her chest. The phone rang several times. Tricia ignored all the calls.

"Auntie Tricia, are you alright?' It was Denise calling out to her. "Carlos called the house a few minutes ago. He is worried sick about you. He said he's been calling you all day and got no answer. I didn't bother to disturb you when I came in. I thought you were just tired. We're going out to dinner have you forgotten?"

"What time is it?"

She heard Denise's voice on the other side of her bedroom door. "Four twenty Auntie. Dinner's at six thirty"

"Goodness, I'd forgotten. Denise, do you mind if I skipped dinner?"

"What's wrong? Are you getting that nasty flu bug?"

"Please come in, I need to talk with you. Oh Denise, why didn't you or Richard tell me that Jonathan's death was the result of Carlos' affair?" She turned her face toward her pillow and sobbed.

"He's told you!"

"*No,* Mavis did!"

"Oh that gold digger and her gossipy mouth. Four divorces have taught her nothing!"

Denise sat on the bed next to Tricia and gently caressed her back. "Auntie." She spoke in a soft, caring tone. "Carlos is a wonderful, loving man who made a mistake and paid a high price for it. He's a good man. Richard and I would not have matched you up. We purposely made ourselves unavailable so you two would be together. We hoped you would fall in love with each other, because we love you both dearly and we know that you are both warm, caring, decent people who deserve a second chance. Talk to him, give him a chance to explain."

"But why didn't he tell me?"

"I guess because it's still so difficult for him to talk about, and especially to you, who I believe he cares for. I do know him though, and I do know that he would have told you when he felt the time was right. Talk to him, ask him about it, and all that's bothering you, but don't torment yourself."

"No, *you* tell me Denise! I need to know, now, and I can't talk to Carlos, not for a while at least."

"Auntie, Carlos loved his wife Sylvia very much, Richard and I know that. One had only to be in their presence to see that. After this whole awful mess, he felt the need to confide in Richard and me. He didn't want us to hear it through rumours, and twisted stories and all that and trust me, there were many. As I said, he loved Sylvia very much but somehow he got involved with a younger woman. It was a short affair, I think he said it lasted only three months. He felt guilty and broke the affair off, but, it was one of those fatal attractions. The woman refused to go away, and one day called the house and spoke with Sylvia. She lied that she was pregnant and that Carlos promised that he would divorce Sylvia and then marry her. Of course, you can understand how Sylvia felt. She confronted Carlos when he got home, and they got into a terrible, loud argument. Sylvia got out of control, sobbing wildly and pounding on Carlos' chest. Jonathan arrived during the argument, and could not handle seeing his mom so hurt. He got back into his car and just sped recklessly onto the highway, until his car slammed into a guardrail, overturned and burst into flames. The police said he had to be going at least one hundred and twenty miles per hour. He was lucky that no one else was hurt during the accident."

"Oh no, Denise, how terrible for them all!"

"Of course, we were all devastated. Richard lost his best friend, and Sylvia, Carlos and Christina had a rough time for a while. Things got better for Christina and Carlos after they all got counselling. Sylvia, however, could not get over the loss of her son, and died one year later. Carlos carried guilt for a long time, but Christina has been very supportive to her dad. I think she understood him better than even Sylvia did. They have remained very close. So now you know Auntie, but I'm sorry you had to find out this way. I think I will have a chat with Mavis. That woman should learn to stop gossiping."

"Denise, how did Mavis know that I was out with Carlos?"

"She called the house to wish us all a happy New Year, and I told her you went on a date with Carlos. I'm now sorry that I did."

"It's okay Denise, I just wondered how she knew."

Tricia stopped crying. Denise phoned Carlos and told him that Tricia was not feeling well and wanted to rest.

"Denise, please give my apologies to your parents, but I just don't want to be in the company of anyone today. I know I'd be poor company anyhow, and I can't face Carlos today. I feel awful, just awful. Please explain to Richard also."

"Sure. I know you feel awful right now, but it will get better. Mom and dad will be disappointed, of course, but I'll tell them you're not well. They will understand."

"Denise, I don't know if I'll ever understand men. How can you cheat on someone you love?"

"That's the million dollar question."

Richard and Denise left for dinner and Tricia slept until the next morning. Her cell phone and the home phone kept ringing. She took no calls and she ate nothing. Early the next morning, she called the airlines and was able to book a flight, without penalty, that same night. She had to take the red eye, but she didn't care. She just could not stay one more day in New York.

"This is an emergency!" She had almost screamed at the ticket agent. "I have to be back in Toronto. Tonight if possible!"

She asked Richard to tell the family that she had to leave earlier than scheduled, and that she would connect with them all once she was back in Canada.

"I must forget Carlos, and the sooner the better!" she'd snapped to Richard and Denise when they told her that she was making a mistake, and that she should at least give Carlos a chance to explain all to her.

"Please don't go like this." Denise pleaded. "Talk to Carlos. You both need to be happy again, and I promise you, in spite of the affair, he's a good man, he really is."

"Denise, I can't talk to him now; maybe in time, but not now. I just wish he'd trusted me enough to tell me. Hearing it from Mavis was awful."

"I'll drive you to the airport," Richard volunteered. "But I really wish you wouldn't leave like this."

"Oh no, Richard, it's a late flight and you have to be at work early in the morning. I'll take a cab."

"You'll do no such thing. I'll take you, and no argument! I'll be worried about you all night. Please. I'll feel better!"

Richard rose and threw his arms around his aunt. He hugged her tightly.

"Thanks Richard, I really needed that."

Tricia sat, frozen, on the airplane that was taking her back to Toronto, feeling as empty as she had when she left one month before. Tears slid down her cheeks. She was glad it was a short flight.

The evening of January 4th she checked her cell phone and saw that there were two voicemail messages from Carlos. She listened with dread to the first message she heard. "Tricia, how are you? I spoke with Richard and he's told me that you are back in Canada. Please call me. I'm very worried about you."

Hearing his voice was painful. Thankfully, there was no one around to see her tears. She checked the second message, her heart pounding. "Hey Tricia, it's Carlos again. Richard told me why you left so suddenly. Sweetie, I'm so sorry. I know you are hurt and also angry with me, but at least give me a chance to explain. I can't be happy if you're not. I love you, I really do. Please call me."

She knew that she could not speak with him, not yet. She decided to text him. "Carlos, I don't even know what I'm feeling at the moment. I, too, value your friendship, but I can't talk to you, not yet. I need time, and will call you when I'm ready."

Days after her return home, Tricia still felt numb and sick. She could not eat or sleep and tossed and turned for nights. When she did eventually fall asleep, it was intermittent. She missed Carlos, very much, and wished that she never knew about that fatal night, or the affair.

"Tricia, you don't look yourself. You've dark circles under your eyes and you've been very quiet since you returned from New York. What's wrong?" her co-worker and friend asked.

"It's nothing, Merle. I just haven't been sleeping. I think it's menopause."

"Yeah, could be. You and I are both taking a pause from men."

"Tee hee hee!"

"Oh my, so glad I could make you laugh."

Tricia eventually saw her doctor, who prescribed sleeping pills. They helped with her sleep, but not the ache in her heart. The only bright spot in her life now were her conversations with Katrina and Kirk, who gave her day- to- day accounts of their vacation in St. Lucia, including Jennifer's wedding.

One day when they visited Katrina commented on how tired she looked.

"Partied too much in New York," Tricia responded.

"So, did you meet anyone special?" Katrina asked.

The question caught her off guard and she stumbled for an answer. "Katrina I met lots of people. New York is a big place."

"Okay, mom," Kirk chipped in. "We know when you're stalling. That will be a "yes." Katrina, no more questions now. Mom's not ready to talk about it, yet."

Tricia smiled. "You know your mom so well," she said.

That night she prayed, "Thank you God for not allowing Kirk and Katrina to realize how miserable I am right now. Oh why did I fall in love with him? God, I miss him so much. Help me, Father!"

The weeks went by. Tricia refused to return Carlos' calls. On Valentine's Day, realizing she was going to be late for work, she pulled off the road and stopped to telephone her co-worker Merle. Up popped the text message. She opened it and read, "Happy Valentine's day Tricia. I love you, and I am missing you terribly. You asked for time, so I'm honouring your wish. I just hope you will have the desire to call me soon."

That night as she laid in bed, she imagined herself out to dinner with Carlos, and then dancing the night away. Only her pillow knew how much she cried.

Two days later, her phone rang. It was Richard calling.

Tricia answered, "Hello Richard, how are you, and Denise?"

"We're both well, but we have some bad news, and before I go any further, Carlos is okay."

"Thank God."

"It's Aunt Stella. She passed away late last night. She never got over the flu and developed pneumonia. At age eighty-nine her immune system was too weak to fight any longer."

"Oh Richard. Dear Aunt Stella. I'm so glad we spent some precious moments together during the holidays."

"You will come back for her funeral, won't you?"

"Of course."

After her conversation with Richard ended, she prayed again. "Dear Lord, how can I face Carlos? I know he will attend the funeral. Oh God, please strengthen me."

⚬⚬

On February 22nd, Tricia again walked through the doors of John F. Kennedy Airport. Again, she looked for Richard or Denise. They had said one of them would pick her up. She was careful this time to wear lower-heeled boots. She continued walking, mumbling as she went along "Oh no, oh no, this can't be happening again! Knees stop shaking. Richard, Denise, where are you?"

She stopped to grab a couple of tissues from her purse and gently dabbed her forehead. She then ran her fingers across her forehead and through her hair. Just as she thought, her hair was beginning to go frizzy. "Awful hot flashes." she mumbled.

Tricia started walking again, her eyes scanning the area. Her heart pounded loudly in her chest as she walked. She could feel the hot flashes getting worse. All kinds of thoughts rushed through her mind. *Richard and Denise have so much to do with the funeral and everything. I hope they haven't forgotten, after all I did change the date. Perhaps they've been delayed at the hospital. Oh no, the captain did warn us of the snow and that it was supposed to get worse. I hope they didn't have an accident!* Suddenly, she had a sinking feeling that they had sent someone else to meet her.

She continued scanning the crowd. Then, she saw the familiar face and the hand waving. Her legs felt wooden as she wobbled over to him. "Dear Lord, how do I handle this?" She silently prayed. Ba bum, Ba bum. She was sure those around her could hear the loud beat. Mixed emotions flooded her heart as he started towards her. Anger, sadness, and, perhaps most surprisingly, a sense of familiar comfort and love, which she tried to ignore as her heart continued to pound in her chest.

"Hello," said Carlos.

"Hello," said Tricia, tears beginning to stream down her cheeks.

He reached for her luggage. "I've missed you."

⟞⟞ ⟝⟝

October 17, 2015, New York, Tricia Spencer-DaSilva plucked one red long stemmed rose from the many bouquets around, kissed it and placed it on her husband's grave. As she did so she recalled the words she had written in a letter to Carlos, and placed in the casket.

My darling, as suddenly and unexpectedly as you came into my life, you left. I thank you for loving me, and for never once making me have to doubt that love for me. You made me laugh, and you made me so happy. You brought out the best in me, and my darling, most of all, you made me feel whole, complete.

The love you and I shared will never die. Sleep my love, until we meet again.

Christina, followed by her husband, Derek, and their two boys, Carlos, and Jonathan, plucked a rose and did the same as Tricia had. Gina and her husband, Tom, followed. Next, was Kirk, his wife Sharon, and their son, Justin. Katrina, her husband, Mike, and their twin girls Casey and Kelly followed, then Richard and Denise with their beautiful daughter they had named Tricia Ann-Marie, after their favourite aunt. Other mourners followed, then left after hugging family members.

After some time, Carlos' loved ones all walked away, still in shock that a healthy man could just go to sleep and not wake up. "Natural causes," the coroner had said.

Christina took Tricia's hand as they walked. "Tricia," she said through her tears. "Thank you for loving dad so much and for making him so very happy for the past nine years. I love you for that, and I'm sorry your time together was so short."

"Thank you, Christina, for everything, and for being a wonderful step-daughter. I thank you for your support when your Auntie Gina did not want me in your dad's life."

Christina stopped and hugged Tricia. "I know dad loved you and I've always trusted his judgement. If he loved you, that was good enough for me. Oh Tricia, I already miss him so much."

Wiping a tear, Tricia replied, "I do too, but he'll live in our hearts forever. And the love we shared, will never die."

They continued walking toward the cars. Tricia continued. "I loved your dad with all of my heart, and he showed me, every day, how much he loved me. Do you know that he bought me a dozen long stemmed red roses every week?"

"That's dad, he was so warm and generous."

"Your dad and I were both fortunate to see our families extended. We enjoyed two weddings and six christenings. I'm especially glad that he got to hold his grandchildren, and his beloved god-daughter, young Tricia, in his arms. They brought him so much joy. Between the two of us we've five grandchildren, and that's such a blessing. Christina, we may have had only nine years together, but they were the happiest years of my life. For that, I thank God."

BONE KEEPER
By Paula Smellie

Yesterday is ashes; tomorrow wood. Only today does the fire burn brightly.

- Inuit proverb

BONE KEEPER

March 4, 1991

"Dr. Beaujould?" The young man stood at the foot of Suzette's bed wearing a sheepish look. Whether this was for interrupting her breakfast or a reaction to the flirtatious overtures of the pretty nurse who had deposited him in her room, she couldn't tell.

Running her eyes over his mild face with its trim beard and patches of acne, she certainly didn't see what all the ooh-la-la was about. The man was of average height, with a narrow frame, and shoulder length hair that chafed at Suzette's traditional upbringing.

She sighed heavily. "Oui, c'est moi. Et vous?"

Hoping the stranger would not prolong their encounter, she perched a pair of reading glasses on the end of her nose and reached for the day's issue of Le Droit.

She was getting old and to her that was akin to rotting while still alive. She silently cursed the vertigo that confined her to bed long enough for pneumonia to set in; cursed the obnoxious ticking of the wall clock, the nurses who talked to her like she was a baby or deaf; and cursed, most of all, the passing of time for snatching away those she loved with its greedy hands, leaving her no one.

Suzette spread out the paper on her lap, smoothed it with her hands and looked up. The stranger offered her a closed-mouth smile that crinkled the skin at the corners of his eyes.

"Je m'appelle Evan Strauss... aaah... Je suis de... Toronto."

Suzette pooched out her lips and watched his eyes scan the tray of half-eaten toast and eggs in their salmon-coloured melamine dishes.

"Je suis... désolé... à... aaaah... à d'inter-rom-pre votre... petit...déjeuner... mais je... je..."

His French sounded like a thick finger plunking the keys of an old-fashioned typewriter. Suzette was determined to end this slow death by bad French.

"English is fine, please. I am fully fluent."

The young man exhaled and relaxed his grip on the black portfolio case he was clutching.

"Thank-you," he said, stepping around to the side of the bed. "Again, I'm Dr. Evan Strauss," he said, extending his hand to Suzette.

"I hope you don't mind," he continued after a brief handshake. His hand was warm and dry and his grip was firmer than Suzette expected from a person of such meager stature. "Your assistant, Stephanie, said you would want me to come see you in person about this. She advised me to come see you here."

Suzette wrinkled her brow. "Here"was a private room at St. Joseph's Hospital in the town of Belle Rivière, Quebec; where Suzette was recovering from a nasty case of pneumonia.

"Did she tell you I was coming?"

Suzette's back tightened. "No, actually, she didn't." The possibility that Stephanie had called while Suzette was asleep or down in Radiology getting her chest x-rayed made the situation no less irritating.

Strauss' cheeks reddened, but Suzette caught a glint of humor in his eyes.

"Well, then, I should explain myself, shouldn't I?" A lock of ruddy brown hair flopped over his face and he smoothed it back behind his ear. "I'm an immunologist from Toronto. I came across your name while doing research on the 1918 Spanish flu deaths in Nunavik."

Suzette closed her eyes and rested her head back against a pillow. "Let me guess," she said. *"Northern Medicine?* October 1968?"

"Yes, that's right," said Strauss, his voice tinged with excitement.

"God, that was ages ago. Where did you dig that up?"

"Robarts Library in Toronto. Microfilm." He looked pleased with himself. "It was an amazing feature."

"Oh, yes. It sure was." Suzette waved her boney brown arms for dramatic effect. *"Amazing Stories of Survival* or *Amazing Survivors' Stories* or some such nonsense. *Fifty Years Later...."* Her voice trailed off.

Strauss cocked his head and squinted his eyes. "I'm sorry. Nonsense?" He gestured towards the chair beside Suzette's bed and asked, "May I?" She nodded and he folded himself into the chair.

"Oh, yes," Suzette continued. "Wonderful nonsense. At least my part of it was. I gave them the interview and yes, my story is unique and touching and all that jazz, but it's hardly a story of *survival*, at least not in the context of that flu."

The truth was, she owed her survival to Claude and Marie Beaujould, the childless missionary couple, who adopted her after her birth mother died of influenza.

Suzette covered her mouth with a tissue and stifled a cough. Again, she silently cursed the vertigo that had put her on her back for days, allowing fluid to build up in her lungs and become infected. *Opportunistic.* That's what the doctor had called her pneumonia.

This was her most serious health crisis to date and it made her contemplate her own mortality more than she cared to admit. She no longer believed in "a better place" where she would be reunited with Claude and Marie. Nor did she believe in a spirit world where her birth mother and the rest of her deceased tribe would be waiting to receive her. For her, death was the promise of loneliness made complete.

Irritated by these thoughts, Suzette said, "You didn't find what you were looking for in the article? What was so important that you needed to come all the way here? I'm sure Stephanie could have helped you, no?"

Strauss shifted in the chair and leaned forward with his elbows on his knees.

"No, not really. As the last surviving member of your community, only you have the authority to help me with this."

Suzette smelled the remnants of her poached egg and tasted vomit in the back of her throat. She was sure impatience leaked from every pore in her face, but she didn't care. Strauss looked too young to be a scientist. Who was he to invade her personal space like this, poking around in the neglected closets of her life? She fought the urge to send the tray of half-eaten food flying to the other side of the room. She would find a way to make Stephanie pay for this intrusion.

"What exactly are your credentials?"

Strauss fidgeted with the zipper on his portfolio case. "I'm a postdoctoral fellow in the Department of Immunology at the University of Toronto. I work with Dr. Alan Webber."

Suzette stared, her small dark eyes unblinking.

"You've probably never heard of Dr. Webber."

Suzette blinked.

"He's quite well known in the infectious diseases community. His research on the efficacy of the flu vaccine after repeated vaccinations created quite a buzz last year. He was featured on CBC News not too long ago."

Suzette shrugged and hiked her eyebrows. "And where do you fit into all this?"

"Dr. Webber hired me to lead an investigation into the pathology of flu pandemics, in particular, the pandemic of 1918. I have funding from the Canadian Institutes of Health Research and I'm two-and-a-half years into my fellowship. I'll be wrapping things up over the next four months and then I'm off to the University of Edmonton where I'll be working in the Division of Infectious Diseases."

"Congratulations," Suzette said drily.

She stared down at the issue of Le Droit, still open in her lap. It was all bad news on the international scene: oil fields were on fire in Kuwait, Soviet troops had entered Lithuania, and the Sudanese people were stifling under the heat of Islamic law. Closer to home, someone had stolen a March of Dimes coin collection tin from the snack counter of the local ice rink. Shaking her head, Suzette reached for her teacup and looked out the window instead.

Strauss continued, "I could get a letter of introduction from Dr. Webber if you'd like. Stephanie didn't think" - but Suzette cut him off with a loud clearing of her throat.

She looked at him over the top of her reading glasses and said, "You're a long way from home, Dr. Strauss. What can I do for you?"

"Well, when I spoke to Stephanie, she didn't think waiting until you were home or phoning you here were good ideas. Due to the sensitive nature of my request, she recommended that I come here and see you straight away." He paused and his eyes searched her face. "It has to do with the burial ground at Wolf Point."

Suzette's heart clenched. She raised her eyebrows and said, "Oh?" Looking away, she felt his eyes on her like the red laser sight from a gun. Strauss seemed to be waiting for permission to continue. Her skin felt clammy. "Fire away," she said.

"Dr. Beaujould, I'm here to ask your permission to disturb one of the sites. It's not part of the main burial ground, but it's very significant."

⇒⊣⊢⇐

November 10, 1918 (Suk-Luk)

Captain Ludvik Brunner tugged at the sweat-soaked collar of his jacket and cold air stung his neck. The *S.S. Apolina* had come to port in Suk-Luk not more than thirty minutes hence and already her deck was lively with villagers making merry, for the arrival of vessels bearing goods was always a cause for celebration in such remote places.

"No, boys! Stay away from there!" Brunner lunged after two young boys who had dashed past him towards the ship's fore end. "Stop!" They didn't seem to hear or perhaps they didn't understand his feeble attempt at Inuktitut.

Brunner would normally have paid them no mind, but the passenger laid up in a tiny berth atop the *S.S. Apolina's* foredeck was ailing sorely and Brunner was concerned the man's illness might be the same one that had already claimed many lives in St. John's and its adjacent coastal villages. The sick man, Hans Mueller, was an Oblate missionary, charged with overseeing the dispersal of mail and supplies from the larger coastal missions to smaller communities like the one in Suk-Luk.

In all truth, Brunner was eager to get this man and his sickness off of the *Apolina*, but that would have to wait. Women with baskets of dried fish perched on their hips and men with furs and pelts slung over their shoulders already lined the docks, waiting patiently for an invitation to do trade.

Many of them had come from the new settlement at Wolf Point located a couple of miles upriver from Suk-Luk, right next to the water. Its small rocky shoreline had no port and could not receive any vessel larger than a modest sloop.

Topping 150 feet, the *Apolina's* hull would have to drop anchor far away from land. And so the residents of Wolf Point
made the trek to Suk-Luk on foot or with sled dogs. But
the collective joy among these resourceful people made it
impossible for Brunner to distinguish those who had made
the difficult journey from those who had not.

A few youths leapt on board, leaned over the ship's railing and shouted taunts to their friends down below who
lacked the courage to join them.

There was talk in St. John's of an armistice. The world
powers had tired of sending their young men to the slaugh-
ter. Or perhaps God himself had intervened, making the
world too sick to carry on with its bloodshed. The deaths of
so many seemed senseless to Brunner, but he supposed this
was the price of freedom. No, not freedom, but something
akin to Melville's *democratic dignity, which on all hands, radi-
ates without end from God; Himself.* Brunner's tattered copy of
Moby-Dick was the only bible he needed.

He side-stepped a clutch of barrels that had just been
carried up from the cargo hold and nearly knocked over an
old man, who was on his knees by the rigging, smiling up
at the sky.

It was unusual for any vessel to make the trip through
Ungava Bay and up the Koksoak River in winter, but the
mission in Suk-Luk required supplies that couldn't wait until summer.

Though not an icebreaker like Russia's vast and mighty
Svyatogor, the *Apolina* was a powerful steamship, built to
withstand blows from ice several feet thick – a far cry from
those ocean tramps that got stuck or stove-in by ice – and
her captain was no less stalwart.

The winter had been agreeable so far; only modest discs of new ice drifted on the water. Pack ice had only just begun to form along the shore, and that had cracked like sheets of hard candy beneath the *Apolina's* hull, reinforced as it was from prow to stern with extra planking and steel bands. Even so, Brunner did not want to linger here. By December first the entire bay could freeze up and he might be forced to winter at Fort Chimo.

His brows came together in a tight frown when he contemplated his chances of making it out of the bay before the freeze-up. He instinctively reached for the handkerchief in his coat pocket and caressed its embroidered edge. His fingers felt for the embossed initials of his love, waiting for him back at home. *She said she would wait.* He blinked rapidly and released the handkerchief. *She said she would.* He fixed his gaze ahead and lengthened his stride. *She will. She will. Wait for me, my love.*

A brass band, their brown faces contrasted against white parkas, boarded the ship and began playing. A Moravian by birth, Brunner recognized the hymn. Brunner was not himself a religious man. Nor did he care much for what the church was doing among these far north peoples, but the patron churches paid him well and never tried to cheat him out of his profits.

Brunner had almost reached the boys, when he had to pull up and make way for a girl chasing after a silver-coated puppy skittering among the crates of supplies now cluttering the deck. A pregnant woman holding a toddler with a large birth mark around one eye, stepped in front of Brunner and said something in Inuktitut. He shook his head and she switched to French, but he didn't understand that either. He was too preoccupied to extract any meaning from her words.

The woman followed Brunner's stare and called out, "*Oh*-kee!" The boys stopped and the older one looked over his shoulder. Just then, Mueller appeared on deck and approached the boys, holding out small packages that could have contained sweets or jacks and, no doubt, the little bibles distributed by missionaries wherever they went. Mueller bent over and shook hands with both boys. Brunner cursed under his breath.

The woman hiked the baby higher on her hip, which was no small feat with her belly jutting out as it was, and waddled over to Mueller. The smaller of the two boys tried without success to wrap his arms fully around the woman's middle. Mueller smiled weakly and reached out to pat the baby's cheek. His shoulders were stooped and his eye sockets looked dark and hollow against his pale skin. The tuba and trombone squawked from somewhere near the port side and Mueller coughed into his fist.

Brunner sighed and turned away. He clasped his hands behind his back and strolled to the starboard railing. With his back to the wind, the fresh air no longer stung, but soothed his neck where the coarse fabric of his collar had chafed it. He pulled the handkerchief from his pocket, pressed it to his lips and inhaled deeply, but the scent of lavender had long disappeared. His heart filled with longing. He stood erect and surveyed the gray water, his eyes reaching for that place where the river spilled out into the bay, and beyond that, the ocean.

The band played with more fervor and the villagers sang along in French. Brunner's French was not that good, but the words came to him in his native Moravian.

Our heaven-ly Fa-ther, source of love,
to Thee our hearts we raise
Thy all-sus-tain-ing power we prove,
and glad-ly sing Thy praise. A-men.

The hymn carried Brunner back in time, to his homeland, before the war, before the sickness. He closed his eyes and imagined the *Apolina* slicing through the surf beyond Ungava Bay. *I'm coming, my love.*

⸻

March 4, 1991
Strauss shifted in his seat and adjusted his glasses.

Suzette put down her teacup and frowned. She hadn't discussed Wolf Point with anyone in over twenty years. The *Northern Medicine* people had showed her some grainy black and white photographs of a barren patch of tundra, hemmed in by rocky outcrops on one side and the bank of a placid river on the other.

The interview came with an offer to fly her up there for a photo op, but she had panicked and lied to the *Northern Medicine* people that she was afraid of flying. For many months after that, Wolf Point had been for her the elephant in every room.

Suzette's heart raced and her lungs felt heavy as lead. Her hands were shaking so badly, she dared not raise the teacup to her lips. The flu pandemic of 1918 had scraped the people of Wolf Point from the earth, leaving her no roots to claim as her own. She was part of no tapestry, no family tree, and no circle of loved ones. Strauss was silent for a moment and Suzette detected a subtle movement of his eyes that seemed to acknowledge her discomfort.

After a few beats passed, he drew in a deep breath and said, "With your permission, I'd like to exhume the remains of a young woman, named *Anaaya*."

He emphasized the name as if Suzette might recognize it. She had never learned the names of any of the Wolf Point settlement people, not even her birth mother's. Suzette stared at her hands.

Strauss said, "I have reason to believe I can get a good DNA sample from Anaaya's remains, which could be used to isolate the flu virus and study it. I assure you, any remains exhumed will be laid to rest again according to whatever requirements you have."

Requirements? She never knew this Anaaya. It was a strange thing to Suzette to be designated as keeper of all these bones. Her chest tightened like a fist and she coughed, long and hoarse.

Strauss straightened. "Are you okay?'

Suzette gestured towards a pitcher of water on the nightstand. Strauss reached over and poured her a drink. "Here," he said, handing her the cup. "Shall I call the nurse?"

"Thank-you. No." She took a sip of water and said, "It's just that every now and then my body likes to remind me why I'm here." She cleared her throat and rested the Styrofoam cup in her petite lap, barely breathing, waiting for the painful spasms to subside. Three days of treatment had not fully doused the fire in her chest, but at least the coughing fits were shorter and less frequent. "There's a bag over there on the floor. Would you please pass it to me?"

Suzette patted a spot on the bed, right next to her hip and Strauss placed the black canvas duffle bag as directed. "Now, time for a treat." Suzette rummaged through the bag and pulled out two packages. "I hope you like black licorice. It's my favourite."

Strauss' eyes moved from the candy to the glucometer and test strips lying on the nightstand and back to Suzette. She cocked-and-readied herself to shoot down any challenge to her licorice habit, but none came.

She held out both packages and lifted her eyebrows. He smiled, pointed, and accepted a small handful of *Good & Plenty* candies. "Good choice. Love those," she said, popping a few of the pink and white capsules into her mouth. "You know, you can tell a lot about a person from what kind of candy they like."

"Really?"

"No." Suzette grimaced. "That was a joke." She fished a brown and black *Allsorts* candy from the other package and said, "Now, where were we? I think you were telling me about this.... Ana...Anana..."

"Anaaya."

"*Anaaya.* Yes. So, who was she?" Suzette reached up to adjust her reading glasses with both hands in an attempt to hide the flush that was rising up her cheeks. Why should she be ashamed of not knowing? Or was it shame that she now showed an interest after a lifetime of indifference?

Strauss said, "Well, what I know is that Anaaya was 22 years old when she became ill with the Spanish flu. She got sick in November of 1918 and died later that month."

Suzette remembered being 22. She was teaching in those days, but certain people in the Catholic school board didn't take too well to her. She had to admit there must have been a grating irony to it – an Inuit woman, in rayon, floral prints and lipstick, teaching the sacraments to white children.

With the Beaujoulds' full support she had pursued her doctorate in education. When she wasn't working or studying, she went out drinking and dancing with friends. Occasionally, she dated, but small-town men had small narrow minds. And now she was old, *too* old, for that fluff. The last thing she needed was an old fart to take care of.

"Only 22?" she asked.

"Yes," said Strauss. "She was quite a young woman, but I believe she had a husband and some children who also may have died from the flu."

Suzette said, "God, that's awful, isn't it? Can you imagine?" She wondered if Anaaya was related to her birth mother. In such a small community, it was likely. Had she assisted with Suzette's birth? Perhaps it was Anaaya who brought her to Claude and Marie. Suzette licked at her dentures and a muscle under her eye twitched.

Strauss leaned in and his voice became soft and intense. "We - my colleagues and I - believe her burial circumstances were different from the other victims at Wolf Point and that her body was well-preserved as a result." He held his hands up in front of his chest, palms facing each other, fingertips touching. "According to the written report from Father Patrice Ammon who pastored the church at Suk-Luk, Anaaya's body was discovered by missionaries."

"I see," said Suzette, hungry to hear more.

Strauss laced his fingers together and said, "Ammon's records show that Anaaya was the last flu victim at the Wolf

Point camp. Her husband and at least one of her children had also perished. He wrote that her other children were also sick and unlikely to survive. He was already quite ill by then, himself, and died before he could learn what became of them."

Suzette clucked her tongue and shook her head. "How very tragic," she said, staring off into space.

"I know," said Strauss. He swallowed and allowed a moment of silence before continuing. "The bodies of most of the other Wolf Point victims were stored in two houses, but..." Strauss paused for a beat, as if weighing out the wisdom in elaborating. "There was a problem with dogs."

⇥⇤

November 29, 1918 (Suk-Luk)

"Dogs.... help... mother... dogs.... sick," were the only words Claude Beaujould could understand between the boy's shivers and frantic hiccups. The boy, who had staggered into Suk-Luk with a smaller boy, was now wrapped in a blanket and trying to tell Father Patrice Ammon something about his family. He gestured urgently with his small hands, pointing somewhere upriver. Rivulets of white salt stained his cheeks where tears had cut paths and dried up.

The smaller of the two boys was also bundled in a wool blanket, his eyes wide with shock. Marie Beaujould was on her knees, rubbing his arms and back. Her movements were gentle, but Claude saw in her eyes a ferocious will, as though health and warmth and comfort could be transferred through her gaze.

She looked up at Tuuq and asked, "Can I please have some water?"

Tuuq nodded at a woman who was standing nearby and said something in Inuktitut. The Beaujoulds had purchased tinned goods and kerosene from the woman when they first arrived in Suk-Luk. It was she who had brought over the blankets the boys were now bundled in. She was tall for an Inuit woman. Her cheeks were sunken in and her face more lined than Claude remembered. Very few here had not been touched by hunger and sickness in recent weeks.

"Not cold," Marie added, making eye contact with the woman. "Warm it. Please." There was no need for Tuuq to translate. The Inuit here had learned much of French from missionaries in the region, but for Claude and Marie the acquisition of Inuktitut was proving to be a slow process.

The older boy had the hollow-eyed look of one who had just returned from the land of the dead. He was raving.

"Don't.... dogs... eat them! Don't let... dogs eat... sister!"

Both boys were skinny as sticks. They couldn't have been more than 6 and 4 years old. Skin prickled at the back of Claude's neck as thoughts of where the boys had come from and what had traumatized them raced through his mind. He could not fathom how they got here and how they were still standing.

Though the air inside Ammon's parlor was stiff with cold, sweat glistened on the top of the priest's bald head and he had to push his glasses up his nose more than once.

Finally, he removed his glasses, rubbed his eyes, and said, "They have come from Wolf Point. They are brothers."

He sighed heavily through his nose. "If what he is saying is accurate, the people there are... all lost."

═══ ═══

March 4, 1991

Suzette wrinkled her nose and said, "Yes, I know about the dogs. Terrible business." The *Northern Medicine* people had told her that 47 people died at Wolf Point, but only 27 bodies were found. Sled dogs, wild with hunger, had eaten the others before they could be buried. It had taken the survivors from the neighboring community of Suk-Luk four days and a huge supply of petrol to dig a mass grave in the permafrost.

Strauss nodded his head. "Yes," he said. "Must have been horrific. I think that's why the missionaries buried Anaaya so soon after discovering her body. They dug a shallow grave next to the house in which she was found. About three feet was as deep as they could go before hitting the permafrost." Strauss paused. "I'm sorry. I know this is probably a sensitive subject for you."

Pulling her best poker face, Suzette said, "I'm fine. Please go on."

"We," said Strauss, refilling Suzette's cup with water from the pitcher, "are also interested in Anaaya because of her age. One of the mysteries about this flu was its pattern of fatality. Usually, a flu virus will strike down the very young, the elderly, or people with compromised immune systems. But *this* flu killed mostly young adults. Ninety-nine percent of those who died were under the age of 65

281

and nearly half were between 20 and 40 years old. We need to understand why. How did this particular strain kill and why was it so lethal in young, otherwise healthy adults? If we get a well preserved tissue sample, we may be able to recreate the virus and study it."

Suzette clasped her hands together and wedged them under her chin. Closing her eyes, she took a few breaths. Then she opened her eyes and said, "Dr. Strauss, I am wondering if it would be possible" - she paused, wary of her own vulnerability.

"Yes?"

"Possible to determine if we are related. Anaaya and I." She could see in his expression that he was not expecting the question, but he seemed pleased by it. Her shoulders relaxed and she smiled.

He also smiled and said, "I... yes. If I can get a good sample with viable DNA, it would be fairly simple. I'm sure one of my colleagues at the university could do it if you're really that interested."

Inclining his head to one side, Strauss asked, "Does this mean I have your permission to exhume Anaaya's remains?"

"Yes, of course," Suzette said. "Do what needs to be done. You have my blessing."

Strauss seemed to be fighting with himself to not behave like someone who had just won the lottery, but it was no use. His eyes sparkled with new light and his cheeks blushed like ripe apples. He was surprisingly handsome with his emotions all out in the open.

"Thank-you so much, Dr. Beaujould. I can't tell you enough how much this means to me – to my team. And I promise you, we will do our very best to treat Anaaya's remains and the burial site with the utmost respect. We will take only what we need. Nothing more. And we will see to it that Anaaya's remains are laid to rest again in a proper fashion. You have my absolute word on that. And, of course, if you have any additional requirements, we will be happy to adhere to them."

There was that word again: *requirements.* Suzette thought for a moment before speaking. She had never imagined anyone needing her permission for anything regarding Wolf Point or what lay buried beneath it. She had always regarded herself as an anomaly - plucked out and cut off - but never as a remnant, bearing a legacy or a responsibility.

Her heart was swollen with emotion. Strauss could have easily exhumed Anaaya's body without coming all this way to seek her approval. She would never have known and it wouldn't have mattered. She found few qualities more pleasing in a person than integrity and respect. Tears stung her eyes and she looked up at the ceiling to keep them from falling.

"Do you need my approval in writing? Shall I sign something?"

"Do you mind?" His eyes widened and he clasped his hands in front of his chest. "I hadn't thought of that." He started to fumble with his portfolio case, presumably to find a blank sheet of paper.

"No, of course I don't mind. I've got something here..." She reached into her duffle bag and pulled out a spiral-bound notebook with a print of the Cherubim Putti Angels on the cover. It was the notebook she used to jot down story ideas for *The Catholic Voice.* Suzette was in her final months as editor-in-chief of the premier journal for Catholic educators. She was long retired from her work as an educator, which was for the best since she could no longer enter a Catholic Board building without feeling like an imposter.

A photograph slipped out from between the pages of her notebook. It was a colour photo of Claude, Marie and Suzette in front of the CN Tower in 1976 when it first opened in Toronto. The photo had not captured one of Suzette's more cherished memories. By the time they took the Toronto trip, Marie was wheelchair-bound and macular degeneration had nearly blinded Claude in one eye. But it was their last trip together as a family and this was the only photo she had left.

Claude died shortly after, in the winter of 1978. He was ninety. Marie followed in the spring of 1979, at 88. The family's photo albums had disappeared from Marie's room at the nursing home in Gatineau, along with Marie's watch, a locket containing a rare photograph of Marie's mother, and several articles of Marie's clothing. Of course, none of the staff could account for a single item.

"You *know* your mother had Alzheimer's. We often found her in other residents' rooms, wearing layers of clothes that didn't even belong to her. Who knows what she did with those things?"

Who indeed? Suzette's finger caressed Marie's likeness in the photograph and her thoughts drifted to the nurses' frequent complaints.

"Your *mother* needs to be watched constantly... your *mother* said the rudest thing yesterday... your *mother* is biting now..." *Mother.* She turned the word over in her mind as one holds a wine glass up to the light to check for spots.

Mother. She remembered like it was yesterday the one time she had called Marie that.

It was 1924 and Marie was in the kitchen, her happy fingers dancing through bread dough to the beat of George Gershwin's *Rhapsody in Blue.* The song was playing on the Radiola Grande, a birthday gift to Marie from Claude. Suzette had held the note from her kindergarten teacher up to Marie and said, "Here, *mother.*"

Marie turned and smiled down at her. Her smile was like the sun and it warmed Suzette so. It held such promise.

Suzette said, "Madame Babel asked me to give this to my *mother.*"

But Claude, who had been smoking and reading in an armchair in the tiny den next to the kitchen, shook out his newspaper with such violence, Suzette expected to see black letters falling out of the pages and onto his lap. She remembered how his jawline had tightened and bunched, as if marbles were under his skin.

Marie's smile flat-lined. She took the note from Suzette's hand and tucked it into the pocket of her apron. Glaring at the back of Claude's head, she said, "No, Suzette."

She turned her back and hunched her shoulders over the bread dough. Suzette's heart cracked and something bled out of her in that moment.

Marie's voice went cold. "Do not call me *mother.* Just... Marie."

Suzette had tried to think of what she did wrong. What bad thing had she said or done to make her parents so cross? Hadn't Claude, just last night, as every night before that one for as long as she could remember, carefully tucked the blankets around her and kissed her forehead and cheeks and nose? That very morning Marie had made Suzette's most favourite buttermilk pancake ever – an especially fluffy one with raisin eyes and a string of red licorice for a mouth. She was sure Marie's eyes had sparkled with delight when first presented with Madame Babel's note. Was the note very bad? What was so bad about the name *mother*? Wasn't that who Marie was?

Her heart beat frantically as she stood there, staring, barely breathing; waiting for an explanation or a lecture or punishment - anything but that cold silence. But Claude and Marie seemed to have thick glass walls around them. Nothing more was to be said. Suzette went into her bedroom closet, closed the door and cried herself to sleep.

She wished she could forget about it, but the memory stuck like burs on a dog's behind. Suzette tucked the photo into a pocket of her duffle bag and turned her attention to the blank page in front of her. She wrote a brief note, tore it from the notebook and handed it to Strauss. "I've signed and dated it. Will you keep in touch? Let me know how things turn out?"

"Of course," he said, a warm grin lighting up his face. "Absolutely." He quickly read the note, folded it in half and slipped it into a sleeve inside the cover of his day timer.

"And you'll remember about checking to see if Anaaya and I are related? Do you need a blood sample or something from me?"

"Tell you what, when we're done at Wolf Point, I'll stop by and see you on the way back to Toronto. I'll tell you how everything went and I'll get a swab from inside your cheek. That should be sufficient. I can show you pictures and you can ask me anything you want about the excavation."

"Sounds wonderful. When will you go up there?"

"We can be ready to fly out on Thursday."

"So soon?"

His cheeks reddened. "We were prepared for a positive outcome. The work is rather time-sensitive. We need some preliminary data in order to put together a solid proposal for funding for the rest of the project. Granting agencies are not flexible with their application deadlines and we don't want to miss our window."

"I see." As a retired academic, Suzette was well acquainted with the rigors of federal funding competitions for research in the arts and sciences. She certainly didn't miss that part of her career.

"We'll take a flight from Toronto to Kuujjuaq and go the rest of the way by ice plane and dog sled team on Friday morning." He smiled broadly. "I can't wait to inform Dr. Webber and the rest of the lab. This is so great."

"Well, good. I'm glad. And I'm glad you came to see me." It seemed that Stephanie's judgment wasn't as poor as Suzette had previously thought.

"So am I, Dr. Beaujould. So am I."

Strauss stayed with Suzette for another twenty minutes. When it was clear they had both run out of things to say, he stood up and held out his hand to her.

"Thank-you so much for your time," he said, letting her delicate hand linger in his for a moment. "I can't tell you enough how much I appreciate this."

"Oh, stop. You're welcome. You're welcome." She pushed her thick gray hair behind her ears, making no effort to conceal the blush rising to her cheeks.

"Please get well soon and when I see you again I hope it won't be in here. And I promise, I *will* come see you. I won't forget."

"Thank-you. You're too kind."

"Alright, well, good-bye."

"Good-bye, Evan. And good luck up there. I'm sure you'll need it."

"Thank-you," said Strauss, bobbing and dipping respectfully before slipping through the door.

The room seemed quieter and emptier than ever.

>=<+ +>=<

November 29, 1918 (Suk-Luk)

The woman from the store returned with a tin cup and bent down to help the boy drink. Marie stood up and faced Ammon.

Ammon coughed into his handkerchief and spoke with a scratchy voice. "They want us to help their mother and their baby sister who are still alive. Their younger brother and father have already died."

Claude swallowed and put his arm around Marie's waist. She was a nurse, but she could be sensitive about such matters, especially as they involved small children.

Ammon continued, "He says dogs attacked them and tried to eat them as they ran to the river, but their family's lead dog protected them and chased off the other dogs. They followed the river to get here."

The priest locked eyes with Claude. No words passed between them. Claude knew Ammon would never ask him to endanger himself, but the question hung silent in the air. Marie touched Claude's shoulder.

Claude said, "Tuuq and I will go." Glancing at Tuuq, he added, "That is, if you're willing."

The Beaujoulds had learned early on in their missionary visit that Tuuq was their most trusted resource for all things to do with Nunavik and its people. But more than that, he had become a dear friend. Claude had learned more from Tuuq's open heart and willing spirit than from the gospels themselves.

Tuuq nodded and said, "I will go, too." Like many of the Inuit in Nunavik, Tuuq's French was impressive.

The Inuit of Wolf Point were mostly Catholic converts who had traveled from the western coast of Ungava Bay to winter at a spot close to the mission in Suk-Luk, where they could attend church services. It was hard for Claude to reconcile how God could allow so much suffering among a people who had received the gospel and its ministers with such gentility and grace. He felt shamed by their personal sacrifice and would not refuse to endanger himself for the few survivors who might still benefit from his help.

Marie squeezed Claude's arm and said, "I'm coming with you." Claude's muscles tensed, but he knew it would do no good to resist. Besides, Marie's skill as a nurse might prove useful.

Francine Fleming, Maria Jemmott, Shirley Merith,
Manjit Singh and Paula Smellie

March 7, 1991

After dreaming that her dentures had trotted across the floor and leapt up onto the windowsill where they barked like a German shepherd, Suzette's eyes fluttered open to the sound of dishes clattering on trays. She recognized the familiar sound of the breakfast cart trundling down the hallway. The door swung open and a dietary aide dressed in blue scrubs and what looked like a large white shower cap nudged through the door carrying a tray. Ancient and scrawny, she reminded Suzette of a stick bug. Suzette glanced at her own stringy arms and thought, *God, do* I *look like that?* The aide deposited the tray on the table next to Suzette's bed and left without saying a word.

Seconds later, Gwen came lumbering into the room, her long micro braids bundled into a fashionable twist on the top of her head.

"Hello, my lady," she said as she pushed open the heavy avocado-coloured curtains covering the window.

Gwen was Haitian and wide as a house. And there was no question about it - she had full command of the floor, with its mix of young and old nurses.

Turning her extensive bulk in Suzette's direction, she clucked her tongue and shook her head. "No sunshine today, my lady."

Suzette's belly rumbled at the sight of the yellow yolk under the translucent skin of her poached egg and she thought that was sunshine enough for her. She held out her forefinger, which Gwen cleaned with an alcohol swab, before lancing it and drawing a tiny sample of blood.

The glucometer beeped and Gwen made a note in Suzette's log. She pulled two bottles of insulin out of her pocket and mixed them in a syringe. Suzette lifted her hospital gown to receive the injection in her abdomen. The mixture of long and slow-acting insulin would help her body metabolize the sugars in her breakfast and keep them stable at least until her next meal, if not longer.

"And here's your amoxicillin." Gwen passed Suzette a medicine cup with one large orange and red capsule.

Suzette swallowed it down with some water and said, "All gone."

"Okay, my lady. Have a good morning," Gwen said, heading with great effort towards the door.

Suzette scarfed down her poached egg, wiping the bowl clean with pieces of buttered toast. Then she ate the sugar-free jelly straight from the tiny plastic container. She drank all of her tea while it was still hot and asked for a refill, but before she could drink half of it, she was stricken with a sudden urge to leave. She tried to read, but memories of Evan Strauss' visit foiled her ability to concentrate on the Thursday issue of Le Droit. She pressed the call button on the bed's railing.

After a few minutes that felt like hours, Gwen returned. "Yes, my lady," she said, easing her girth over to Suzette's bedside. Her voice reminded Suzette of a warbling bird. "What can I do for you?"

"I want to go downstairs for a little while. Go for a bit of a walk."

Gwen pursed her lips and looked down at Suzette through gold-rimmed reading glasses. "A walk, eh?" She pinched Suzette's wrist between her meaty thumb and fingers, while looking at the watch she wore on a chain around her neck because her wrist was impossibly large to be enclosed by any watchstrap. "Mm," she said, still appraising Suzette in that suspicious way she had. Next, she pulled out a stethoscope and pressed it to Suzette's bony chest and back, listening. Suzette obeyed Gwen's commands to breath in here and out there, and in again here and out again there. Next she pulled the chart from the end of Suzette's bed and read it. Her lips moved, but no sound came out. She gave Suzette a wary look and said, "You feel okay?"

"Right as rain," said Suzette, drumming her fingertips on the tray table. She had been restless as a toddler ever since Evan Strauss came to see her three days ago.

⸺⊹ ⊹⸺

November 29, 1918 (Wolf Point)

Mangled corpses, some with their heads or hands missing, lay strewn about like trash. A few dogs stood guard over their bounty, snarling and snapping at others who came too close. It didn't seem real. Claude had seen his fair share of death, working in the mines, but nothing could prepare him for this. He looked up at the sky and drew in a deep breath, praying not to vomit.

He reached for Marie, but she had moved away from him, towards a group of small dwellings. If she was distressed by the carnage, she didn't show it.

Tuuq emerged from one of the larger houses opposite the group of smaller ones and yelled something to Claude and Marie. The wind was gusting and all Claude heard was, "Bodies piled inside..." Tuuq freed his rifle from the sling he wore diagonal across his back. He was waving and yelling at Claude and Marie to take shelter, as they were both unarmed.

Tuuq raised his rifle and fired several rounds into the air, which startled some of the dogs and set them to fleeing. Others refused to leave the bodies alone and had to be shot. Ravens quickly got to work on the corpses of the dogs and the human remains that were now free for the taking.

⊫⊰ ⊱⊪

March 7, 1991

Gwen raised her eyebrows at the tray of empty breakfast dishes and sighed heavily through her nose. "If you feel okay, I suppose it's fine for you to get up and walk about for a little while."

"Fantastic."

"Are you sure you don't want a wheelchair? I can get Irena to take you down."

Suzette nearly spat. "No, thank-you, dear." Irena had committed the unforgivable offense of sponge-bathing parts of Suzette's body no one had seen in years, while Suzette lay in a drug-induced stupor. "I can walk. *Alone.*"

"How about a walker? Just so you have something to support you."

Suzette shook her head.

Gwen backed up slowly, shrugged her humongous shoulders and said, "Okay, my lady, but take it easy. Please."

"Of course, I will," said Suzette, watching as Gwen squeezed herself back through the door and into the hallway. "Thank-you," she called out in a weak voice, careful not to trigger a coughing spell that might send Gwen stampeding back into the room.

She slid out of bed and put on her housecoat and slippers. The floor seemed to be tilting upward – she must have stood up too quickly. She sat on the edge of the bed and waited for the dizziness to pass. Her chest felt tight again and her mind wandered to her people. *Her* people? When did she start thinking of them as *her* people?

Strauss had mentioned that most of them would likely have died from pneumonia. She tried to imagine being as sick as she was now and having no medication and no nurses to help her. She thought of the nights she lay awake, wracked with chest pains or coughing until she barely had strength to raise a cup of water to her trembling lips. Was this how they had suffered?

Her thoughts drifted to Claude and Marie. Though at times her heart ached with longing for them, it was divided: one half loving and the other resentful, the two halves separated by a thin barrier across which Claude and Marie staggered back and forth like drunken soldiers.

In the months and years following their deaths, many difficult questions she dared not ask while they were alive had become impossible to ignore. Why did the Beaujoulds take her, only to designate "father", "mother", and "daughter" as words forbidden to pass between them? Was their adopting her truly a kindness or an act of pity or of piety or some selfish whim? At first she was shamed by what she considered to be pettiness and ingratitude on her part, but over time the questions seemed less trifling to her.

She knew little of the people of Wolf Point or those dreadful weeks during which they had all disappeared like the morning dew after the sun comes up. Her mind bore through that great nothingness, drilling deeper for some clue, some repressed memory of something the Beaujoulds might have told her - a name, a picture or an artifact they might have shared with her. But there was nothing.

➤+ +➤

November 29, 1918 (Wolf Point)
"Claude," Marie yelled into the wind. "Claude!"

"Yes, yes, Marie. I hear it, too." Claude's boots crunched in the snow as he clopped over to where his wife stood like a statue in her down parka. He flinched at the sound of Tuuq's rifle and the yelping and barking that followed each shot. The fur lining of Marie's hood was so thick he could barely see her face straining against the brisk wind to pinpoint the direction from which the sound was coming. Claude knew what Marie, tortured by the barrenness of her own womb, wanted desperately to hear.

"Shhh! Stop that," she snapped, flapping her gloved hand at Claude's noisy boots. "Over there. That house."

They both leaned into the wind and listened. "It's the baby. The baby girl," Marie shouted, her words broken by the cawing of hungry ravens. Claude reached for Marie's hand and led her slowly towards the entrance of the sod house.

➤+ +➤

March 7, 1991
Suzette's vision blurred and she felt something wet on her face. She dabbed at the tears with the sleeve of her housecoat

295

and looked at the wet spots in the fabric as though she had never seen such things before. She blew her nose and lifted her chin. Thanks to Evan Strauss, she now knew the name of at least one person from the Wolf Point settlement and that name burned itself into her brain as if by a white-hot branding iron. *Anaaya.*

She took a few wobbly steps and wondered if this was really a good idea. Her next couple of steps felt better and she decided to go ahead as planned. She took her change purse from the duffle bag and shoved it into the pocket of her robe. She managed the walk to the elevator and the ride down, but by the time she scuttled out into the hospital's bright lobby, she felt like she was inside a kaleidoscope of floors, walls, and people. She grabbed onto the railing that ran along one wall and closed her eyes, concentrating on her breathing, careful not to trigger a coughing fit.

The dizziness and nausea soon passed and Suzette set her sights on the tuck shop up at the end of the corridor. She surprised herself and made it all the way without having to stop and sit a while at the clinic located midway between the elevator and the shop. She smiled at the shop's layout of book tables; refrigerated bouquets; shelves of trinkets and greeting cards, all imprinted with encouraging messages. Everything was designed to give hope and comfort, and Lord knew she could use some of both.

She sidled over to a rotating jewelry display. Her breath caught in her throat when she spotted a silver angel pendant among the tiny replicas of crosses, hearts, and praying hands.

She reached out a shaky finger to touch the pendant and remembered the bible and soapstone angel she had buried Claude with. Marie was also buried with a bible and wearing a sterling silver angel pendant, similar to this one. Suzette had tended their graves regularly and when she could no longer manage the bending and kneeling, she paid a small fortune to have it done for her by the cemetery groundskeepers.

A sales clerk in a blue volunteer smock leaned over the counter and said, "Hello. Can I help you?" Her auburn hair was gathered in a French braid that reached just below her shoulders and her hazel eyes had an uncanny resplendence, as if lit from within. "The angels are beautiful, no? I bought one for my auntie. She has breast cancer."

"Oh, I am sorry to hear it," Suzette said.

"Don't be sorry. My auntie was only given six months to live, but she is still here with us, two years later." She smiled and said, "There must be a real angel watching over her." Nodding at the display, she asked, "Do you believe in angels?"

Although her faith had waned, especially in the years since the Beaujoulds had passed, Suzette was still in love with the idea of angels. Perhaps it was because she believed those beautiful powerful beings were as alienated from heaven as they were from earth and therefore, like her, had no sense of belonging. She was fascinated by stories of angels and their dalliance in human lives.

"I most certainly do," said Suzette, unhooking the angel from the display. "How much is this one?"

She handed it to the woman, who lifted her eyebrows and held it close so she could read the tiny writing on the price tag. "It is $7.99 plus tax." The woman tapped some keys on the cash register and said, "With the tax, your total is $9.29."

Suzette paid out the correct amount from her change purse and the woman asked her if she wanted it wrapped or placed in a small bag. She declined both, placing the pendant in her pocket instead, along with the payment receipt.

She was about to peruse the greeting cards when a high-pitched voice cried out, "Suzette!"

Startled, she pivoted awkwardly on one foot and saw Monique standing in the entrance to the tuck shop, with her weight balanced on one leg, her eyes round as saucers.

"*There* you are." Monique's long blonde hair was swept back in a ponytail, making her face seem wider and accentuating a jawline that was square, yet somehow delicate. "Gwen told me I might find you here. She sent me to check on you. See if you needed any assistance."

"Oh heavens, no. I'm fine," Suzette said, trying to catch her breath. She took note of the huge banana clip that sat somewhat askew on the back of Monique's head and thought she might try wearing one her self. It would keep the hair out of her face while she weeded her garden in the spring.

"Well, would you like me to help you back to your room?" Monique's soft brown eyes revealed a genuine concern that disarmed Suzette, just as Evan Strauss had done three days ago with his look of raw pleasure. And though Monique had startled Suzette, her presence was a relief. Besides, it could have been Irena who showed up and Suzette was in no mood to deal with her.

"Alright," said Suzette. "That would be nice. I am ready to go back now." She linked her left arm in the crook of Monique's right elbow and they strolled slowly towards the elevator. Monique's skin was smooth and soft and she smelled like soap. Suzette wondered how old she was.

In the casual tone one used for discussing the weather or the price of apples, Suzette asked, "How old are you?"

"Oh? Asking a woman her age? Isn't that a taboo?" Monique winked and gave Suzette's arm a gentle pat. They were so close Suzette could feel the warmth of Monique's body and this was surprisingly pleasant to her.

"For an old woman to ask a much younger woman? I should think not. What would it matter for me to know? I won't tell anyone."

"Oh, I know. It's not you, Suzette." Monique giggled and set her face in a mock frown. "It's just that the older nurses, well, I don't like to say my age around them. I think they already don't like me." She leaned in close to Suzette and whispered, "Especially Gwen." A few stray hairs from Monique's ponytail tickled Suzette's cheek.

Suzette sucked in air through her teeth. "Tsk. Tsk. Don't you worry about them. They're just jealous because you are young and pretty."

"No, it isn't that," Monique said as they walked into the elevator. She pressed the button for Floor 4. Her voice took on a serious tone. "They are afraid of the younger generation because they think we'll take away their jobs one day. More of us are getting degrees now." She shrugged her shoulders and said, "They're afraid and I don't blame them."

Patting Monique's arm, Suzette said, "They are afraid of the future – of progress. That's nothing new. But you can't stop progress." A wave of guilt washed over her as

she remembered her attitude towards Stephanie when Evan
had showed up unannounced.

Monique gave Suzette's arm a gentle squeeze and whispered, "I will be 22 next month."

Suzette took in a sharp breath and pain stabbed at
her lungs. Her knees buckled and Monique reached with
her free hand to help steady her just as the elevator door
opened. They shuffled out and Monique steered her towards a chair.

"Oh my God! Are you alright?"

Monique jerked her head right and left, looking for another nurse to call over, but before she could alert anyone,
"Code Blue!" rang out from the PA system. "Code Blue in
S-426! Code Blue! Code Blue in S-426!"

"Oh my God, Suzette! That's my patient! Are you okay
now?"

Suzette nodded.

"Stay here. I'll come back for you." And Monique ran
off in the direction of S-426.

⸻⊹ ⊹⸻

November 29, 1918 (Wolf Point)

The Beaujoulds stopped at the entrance to the house and
Claude tugged at Marie's hand. He looked at her over his
shoulder and raised a gloved hand to his mouth. Marie
obeyed his gesture, and kept silent. Claude leaned forward
and called out in a deep clear voice, "Hello?" No answer
from within, only the sound of an infant wailing. "Hello?"
he called, louder and switching from Inuktitut to French.

He looked at Marie again and signaled that they would enter. He pushed her firmly behind him, using his body to shield hers, and slowly opened the animal skin flap that covered the entrance.

Claude stepped into the dwelling and gagged. Marie followed, close behind. Her hand flew to her mouth and her eyes welled up with tears. The stench was unbearable. Claude grabbed hold of his wife and hugged her close, trying to contain his own sorrow.

➤✦ ✦◄

March 7, 1991

Despite all of the noise and chaos around her, Suzette barely heard a thing, apart from the thoughts racing wildly through her mind. *Monique is 22!* Anaaya was only 22 when she died. She had been a real person – just as real as Monique. Possibly even Suzette's blood relative. Suzette opened her hand and stared at the pin she had been clutching in her pocket. *Blood relative?* Her heart raced. A single thought blazed across her mind: she must catch up with Evan and his team. She had to make sure Anaaya received a proper burial just like Claude and Marie had. Just like family. This was her requirement.

Once in her room, she sat on the side of the bed, trying to calm her breathing. The last thing she needed was a coughing fit. Focusing, channeling all of her strength and mental discipline, she stood up straight. She waited a beat before moving just to make sure she was steady on her feet. The floor did not lurch upwards and her head felt fine. She shuffled over to the clothes cabinet and swung open the door.

As quickly as she could afford to move, she changed out of her hospital gown into the pants, sweater and overcoat she had worn to the hospital. She sat down in a chair and slipped on her boots. Plowing through a mental packing list, she stuffed her hat, scarf, and mittens into the duffle bag; along with her bathrobe, glucometer, test strips and the angel pin, wrapped in a pink Kleenex. Something was missing. *Insulin!* Could she manage without it? What about her antibiotics? She'd had no time to think this through. "No matter," she said under her breath. "I'm leaving."

Even though her pulse was pounding and her chest throbbing, the exhilaration she felt was well worth the discomfort. She tore open the drawer in the nightstand, giggling at the sight of a navy blue book lying inside. "Ah yes. Yes, yes, *yessss*," she said and pressed its hard cover to her lips. Nuns originally ran Saint Joseph's when it opened in the 1960's and every room still had a bible in it. "Thank-you, St. Jo's," she whispered, squeezing the bible into her bag, between her robe and underthings. Anaaya would be reburied with an angel and a bible, just like Claude and Marie.

Now that she was dressed and packed, she plunged her mind into phase two: how to get to the elevator without being noticed. The stairwell would be much better for stealth, but walking down three flights of stairs in her condition while carrying her heavy duffle bag was simply not a viable option. She cracked open the door and poked her head out just enough to see down the hallway. One old man shuffled along the hall, leaning on the arm of a younger man. A rotund lady dressed in several hospital gowns was having a heated conversation with herself, but Suzette saw no nurses. She leaned further out the door and confirmed her hunch: the nurses were not at their station. She offered up a silent prayer of thanksgiving for the Code Blue and one of supplication for the poor soul in S-426.

She hoisted her bag, and scooted the distance between her room and the elevator, passing the empty nurses' station. She glanced with longing at the door behind the nurses' station, but snooping around for her insulin and other medication was a risk her nerves wouldn't allow her to take.

She pressed the elevator call button and held her breath, expecting Monique or one of the other nurses to dart out into the hall and come charging after her. If it was Gwen, of course, there would be no darting or charging, just a slow stomping that might give Suzette time to get away.

The elevator arrived and Suzette stepped inside, shivering from a sensory cocktail of freedom and danger she hadn't felt since she was a teenager, drinking whisky out behind Mr. Panette's shed with some boy who must have had eight hands. Her own hands were shaking terribly now and she clenched them into fists. She half-expected the elevator to stop its descent and begin climbing back up to the fourth floor, where Gwen would be waiting with a troop of nurses, ready to put her back into bed. But when the elevator door slid open and Suzette stepped out into the lobby, she knew she would be in the clear as long as she kept moving.

She walked through the sliding glass doors and a brisk wind swooped behind her like a giant wing, urging her forward. She imagined this was how young birds felt when their mothers lured them to the edge of their nests and beyond. She inched forward obediently, squeezing her elbows in tight to her body as icy air rushed down her collar, through her corduroy pants and up under her sweater. Her long overcoat whipped around her and she was afraid she might join the soiled napkins and discarded sandwich wrappers she saw swirling around in the wind.

Snow banks piled on the inner curb of the semi-circular drive glistened with ice crystals, their rough edges buffed smooth by the prior evening's rain. In a few short weeks the snow and ice would yield themselves to the first vestiges of spring.

Suzette shrugged the duffle bag off of her shoulder onto the pavement. Her meager muscles smarted where the strap had dug into her shoulder and her fingers were so numb she could barely open and close them.

She felt the weight of the bag against her shin and contemplated dragging it to the taxi parked at one end of the drive, but there was no need. The cab eased away from the curb and pulled up in front of her. She looked over her shoulder, back through the glass doors. There was no commotion of nurses scouring the lobby in search of their missing patient. The reasonable part of her wished there was.

The stout cab driver was already out of the taxi and opening the rear passenger door when Suzette turned away from the doors and from the comfort and safety of St. Jo's.

She slid across the backseat.

The cab driver asked, "Where to?"

"VIA Rail, please."

Soon they were coasting down streets that Suzette almost didn't recognize. The day she had been admitted to the hospital, the air was cool and stiff, but the sky clear and bright. Now, the sky was gray and the roads were slick and soupy from tires that churned the sleet and road salt into brown slush.

The town of Belle Rivière sat in the cleft of two hills that stood like sentinels on Gatineau's northeastern cusp. It was large enough to have its own hospital, police station, and shopping mall. It even had a pretty decent public transit system. Here and there, modern low-rise apartment buildings asserted themselves between clusters of brick factory buildings and rows of century homes.

Perhaps of most worthy note, were the public elementary and secondary schools built just four years ago. People from Gatineau often joked about Belle Rivière, the town where even the weather was Catholic and the squirrels wore rosaries.

Suzette imagined the Floor 4 nurses would be in a panic soon. Gwen or Monique would come to her room to check her vitals and administer her lunchtime doses of insulin and antibiotics. There would be pandemonium. A "Code" of some sort would be announced and every place an elderly patient could go would be searched. She remembered Monique's concerns about the older nurses and hoped Gwen would not hold her responsible for Suzette's disappearance. She deeply regretted any distress her actions would cause the young nurse, but it simply couldn't be helped.

The cab crested a hill and a strip mall came into view. The tiny VIA station was situated between a Desjardins Credit Union and a Fairmount Bagel. Suzette glanced at the meter, pulled out her credit card, and thought through her next steps.

⊷⊹ ⊹⊶

After Suzette paid the driver, he opened her door and helped her onto the curb where she hunched against the chilly air. At her age, Suzette had little tolerance for cold, and even though the worst of winter was over, she found the current conditions hard to bear.

The driver snatched her bag from the backseat and gestured for her to walk ahead of him through the station's main entrance.

The smell of fresh-baked bagels hung in the air. Suzette's stomach growled and saliva pooled under her tongue.

The driver walked ahead of her and set her bag down on the floor, next to the counter. She started to wheeze and thought of her antibiotics. The driver doubled back and took her elbow until she had reached the counter. Suzette started to pull some loonies from her change purse, but the cab driver refused to take her money and disappeared through the exit.

Suzette wanted to look for a pharmacy, but the departure board showed that the next train to Dorval was scheduled to leave in only twenty-eight minutes and the next train after that wasn't due to pass through Belle Riviere for five hours. Evan said his team would leave Kuujjuaq first thing tomorrow morning. She had to get on this train or she might not make the last flight out of Dorval to Kuujjuaq. She pictured the small silver angel and the bible she had taken from her room in St. Jo's. Acquiring insulin and antibiotics would have to wait until she reached her next destination. Suzette used her credit card to purchase a ticket to Dorval.

The station's crewmembers were organizing the small crowd of travellers into a line. Families with small children were placed at the front, as were the elderly and passengers with disabilities. Suzette angled herself towards the front of the line and winced at a cramp in her lower back. She hadn't moved like this in days, perhaps even weeks.

She allowed herself to be ushered to the front by a female crewmember dressed in a navy blue skirt suit, white blouse and scarf with a VIA Rail pin. The name embossed on the tag pinned to her lapel was "Jeannie".

—◁+ +▷—

A young woman smelling of vanilla and berries sat next to Suzette. She reached down and her elbow grazed Suzette's calf. "Sorry," she said, wrangling something out of her backpack. "Excuse me."

Suzette was too tired to respond. She tried to read a complimentary travel magazine, but fatigue blurred her vision and she looked out the window instead.

Once out of the town's centre, snow-covered fields whipped by for miles, giving way to hills carpeted in forests of pine, spruce, and fir. She marveled at what lay beyond the brick and steel of Belle Riviere: the placid rivers, winding through meadows and pouring over rocky outcroppings; eddies spilling out into small green lakes, dotted with ice patches that looked like white lily pads; the carcasses of trees that died ages ago rising up out of ice-covered swamps. For many miles a wall of ancient rock that seemed hundreds of feet high lined one side of the track. Suzette's head drooped and she gave in to the train's sweet lullaby.

She was standing on a grave at Wolf Point, naked except for a pair of moccasin slippers. The ground rumbled beneath her. A crevice tore open and she was suspended in the air above it. An invisible force from below tugged at her moccasins. She tried to keep them from coming off, but she needed her hands to cover herself so off they came. Drums beat and there was moaning and ululating. Claude and Marie were there. Marie's wheelchair was dangerously close to the precipice and Suzette shouted at Claude to move her back, but it seemed that he couldn't hear. There were others standing around the edge of the crevice, dressed in traditional Inuit parkas, their long dark hair whipping in the air around their faces like tendrils of black ribbon. Then someone was beside her and took hold of her hand. She could not see the face, but she knew it was Anaaya and she was not afraid. Suzette heard drums beating and she descended slowly into the crevice.

A baby's cries transported Suzette from Wolf Point back to her seat on the train. The child fussed in the seat behind hers. The young woman who had been sitting beside her was gone. It was only four o'clock, but the sky outside her window was already a gray-blue smudge and many other passengers had turned on their overhead lights. There would be no sunset today, just a gradual darkening of the smudge. Within an hour or two, the world would disappear into thick blackness.

━◁ ▷━

Standing in the train's tiny bathroom wasn't easy – every bump and jerk threw her off balance. Squatting over the toilet bowl, Suzette cracked her elbow on the metal toilet paper holder. She rubbed her aching elbow and winced at the thought of trying to change her bottoms with the floor lurching beneath her. The Depend undergarment she had put on this morning after breakfast was damp and spongy; her bladder just couldn't stand up to the coughing fits. Rather than risking further injury, she lined her wet undergarment with as much toilet paper as she thought it would hold. She washed her hands, first one and then the other, having to hold onto the sink with one hand at all times to steady herself.

She patted her face with toffee-coloured mineral powder from her compact, dusted rouge onto her cheekbones, and applied lipstick. Eye makeup was out of the question; between the shaking of her hands and the rocking of the train, she would probably put her eye out with the mascara wand. Satisfied that she looked better than she felt, she slowly walked back to her seat, holding on to the backs of other passengers' seats.

She eased herself into her seat with a sigh of relief. Her ears tuned in to the sounds of clinking and rattling, which grew louder as Jeannie approached Suzette's section of the train car, pushing a snack cart.

Suzette paid for a bowl of chicken noodle soup and a cup of tea.

"Crackers?" Jeannie asked, holding out two packages of soda crackers.

"Yes, please." Suzette's fingers brushed Jeannie's as she took the crackers. The warmth of Jeannie's touch reminded her of Anaaya's hand in hers. "Thank-you," she said, smiling up at Jeannie.

On instinct, she reached for her bag in order to test her sugars. As her fingers closed around the glucometer she stopped and slumped back against her seat. She had no insulin to take with this meal. Her last injection had been right before breakfast.

Suzette's head hurt and her heartbeat quickened when she thought about missing her insulin injection and another dose of antibiotics. She imagined keeling over unconscious in her seat and poor Jeannie, green eyes filled with panic, notifying the conductor who would bring the train to an emergency stop at the nearest town where medical attention could be sought. She would die here in her seat before they could get her any kind of help.

Suzette told herself to stop being silly; she would be fine. The effect of her breakfast injection would have peaked by mid-morning and could last for the rest of the day if she ate very little. No use making herself sicker with worry. She would find a way to get insulin in Dorval or Kuujjuaq.

She drank the soup, leaving the noodles and the crackers, and drank her tea black.

Suzette breathed in slowly, checking to see how deep she could inhale before her lungs hurt and sputtered. She would be in Dorval in less than an hour and needed to think of a good strategy for getting her hands on medicine. A cold sweat broke out on her forehead and neck. Frowning, she swiped a napkin over her face and beneath the collar of her sweater. She fanned herself with the travel magazine and prayed for an idea to come to her. She needed to focus, not worry about things she couldn't help.

Her heel thumped against the duffle bag under her seat, triggering an idea. Suzette recalled a former colleague complaining that an airline had lost his luggage. He had gone as far as accusing the baggage handlers of theft.

Perhaps Suzette could claim that she had left the case containing her medicines in a washroom or passenger lounge at the station in Belle Rivière and had only realized it when the train was pulling into Dorval.

She knew it wouldn't be that easy; she imagined every possible question the pharmacist might ask her and how she might counter them. Naturally, the pharmacist would have to check with her doctor to confirm her prescriptions. She supposed leaving the hospital without her doctor's blessing made her a kind of fugitive and she imagined the worse case scenario: her doctor could insist that she terminate her trip and be escorted immediately to the nearest hospital, at which point she would flee the pharmacy, since turning back was not an option she was willing to consider. She wished she'd had more time to plan things out before leaving.

⊷⊶

"Dorval Station. We have arrived at Dorval," announced Jeannie, extending her arm to help Suzette out of her seat. Once Suzette was standing in the aisle, Jeannie bent down to get her bag from under the seat. Jeannie went through the open door of the train car and stepped onto the platform. She handed Suzette's bag to a porter and helped her out of the train. Jeannie gave Suzette's shoulder a gentle pat and said, "Good night."

The porter asked her if she had any checked baggage to claim.

"No," she said. "This is it. I am travelling light." She did not see how she could divide her time and energy between looking for a pharmacy and catching a flight out of Pierre Elliott Trudeau. She took a breath and asked, "Where can I get a bus or a taxi to the airport?"

⊷ ⊶

November 29, 1918 (Wolf Point)

The woman lay on a bed of animal furs with her eyes open. Her lips moved, but Claude could not hear what she was saying. Her chest rose and fell in jerking motions. She held on to the crying infant with one arm while the other arm lay limp at her side. A small boy, no more than a toddler, lay on top of her. Claude stared at the large birthmark that encircled one of his eyes. The boy's body was bloated and stiff and Claude knew what that meant. He leaned in for a closer look at the woman.

"Drink… please… drink," the woman whispered in Inuktitut.

Claude saw the dark spots inside her lips and on the palms of her hands. Death was imminent. He tore his eyes away and scanned the interior of the house for water.

Not seeing any drinking water, he leaned back with Marie still in his arms and turned his attention to the infant whose cries had drawn them there. Though Marie was a nurse, he did not want her to touch the woman for fear she too would become infected. He couldn't lose Marie; she was everything to him.

The baby's head was covered in thick black hair and her face was deeply flushed from crying. Marie pulled away from Claude before he could tighten his hold. "Marie, no," he commanded, but Marie knelt next to the woman and stared at the small bundle squirming in her mother's loose embrace. She reached for the baby and the woman's eyes followed her movements.

Claude's voice cracked as he urged Marie to leave the child alone. He laid a powerful hand on Marie's shoulder in warning, but Marie's back tightened and she leaned in closer.

⊷ ⊷

March 7, 1991 (Dorval)
Suzette lowered her eyes and slumped against the First Air ticket counter.

"I'm sorry, madam, but that is impossible. As I said, there are no more passenger flights to Kuujjuaq leaving this airport today."

First Air and Air Inuit were the only airlines flying to Nunavik out of Pierre Elliott Trudeau and neither had any flights to Kuujjuaq scheduled until tomorrow morning. Suzette closed her eyes and surrendered to the pain, tremors and tightness she had defied for hours. The ticket agent was speaking to her, but she couldn't make out what he was saying.

Suzette's skin was hot and damp and she really thought she might faint. Her pulse raced. She didn't want to pass out here. Or die. She needed to get to Kuujjuaq. Evan would be there. Evan would be able to help her. She believed in Evan - remembered his smile and trusted the heart behind it. It was Evan who told her of Anaaya. *Evan will be there.*

Suzette's vision was so blurry she couldn't make out the writing on the agent's nametag. Her thoughts became frantic and crashed into each other like bumper cars.

"Madam!" Suddenly, the agent's voice cut through loud and clear. She looked up and locked eyes with him. He laid a hand on the receiver of a telephone on his side of the counter.

"No!" snapped Suzette. "Don't." Breathing. "You." More breathing. "Dare."

His eyes grew round and his cheeks coloured. "Excuse me, madam, but you are sick, no? You almost fainted here."

She squinted at the nametag pinned to his purple blazer and said, "Pierre, I don't need a doctor. I am not going to the hospital."

"But" –

"What I *need*," said Suzette, looking him squarely in the eye, "is to get to Kuujjuaq by dawn tomorrow morning."

"But I told you, madam. There are no planes flying out of here to Kuujjuaq until tomorrow morning, *after* dawn. The earliest you can arrive in Kuujjuaq is 10:30 a.m. There is nothing better you can do."

"There is always something better a person can do. Now *think*. Please." Her stomach twisted at the thought of Anaaya's grave being opened without her being there.

Pierre sighed and drummed his fingers on the counter. The teacher in Suzette recognized his body language. Everything in his posture was directed downwards – shoulders, hands, chin, and eyes. He could be pushed. Persuaded, even. These thoughts strengthened Suzette and she stood straighter.

"Do you understand what I'm saying? I can't wait until tomorrow. I must leave tonight."

"Forgive me, madam, but may I ask why?"

Suzette's body stiffened. It was an excellent question and it echoed in her mind. Why *was* she so driven to do this? She was about to panic at the seeming insanity that must have come over her, when the answer came through with perfect clarity.

"I have family business to attend to."

Pierre inclined his head slightly and said, "I see."

"A funeral, actually. I'm in charge of something special in the ceremony. I have to be there."

"Well, madam, I am very, very sorry for your loss." Suzette looked into his eyes and believed him. "Can you call the other members of your family who are already there and ask them to wait?"

"No," she said, shaking her head. She had no idea how to reach Evan Strauss. "What about driving? Is there a bus or a train I can take?"

"Unfortunately, there is no rail service into Nunavik and you cannot drive into Kuujjuaq or anywhere close to it."

"What? This is Quebec, not Antarctica." Did he think she was daft? "There is a road to go everywhere in Quebec." She snapped her fingers a few times and asked, "What's that road that goes north?"

"The James Bay Road?"

"Yes! That's it. The James Bay Road. Is there no bus I can take up there?"

"No, ma'am. There has been talk about extending the road from Shefferville into Kuujjuaq, but so far that's all there is – *talk*."

"How can there not be a road? Or a rail service?"

"Well, madam" –

Suzette's hands flew to her face and she groaned.

"Madam?"

"Good *God!*" She uncovered her face and looked up at the ceiling. "This is ridiculous."

She heard a low rattling in her chest and blinked back the tears that so desperately wanted to fall.

A man in blue work coveralls rolled a mop bucket over to the adjoining ticket counter and began mopping up a puddle of brown liquid that could have been cola or black coffee. Stunned at her bad luck, she watched him work. Keys and white plastic cards jangled from a ring fastened to his belt. He was completely bald, and his face reminded Suzette of a walrus. Both of his forearms were covered in a colourful tangle of fantastical creatures.

"I am truly sorry," Pierre said, "but I cannot make a miracle happen."

Suzette oscillated between the compulsion to fight on and the thought of surrender. The word "miracle" flickered in her mind like a faint Morse code and she tried to hone in on it, but it was like trying to catch a little butterfly in her hands.

The janitor worked the mop closer to Suzette's coordinates and she caught a glimpse of wings feathered in blue, green and gold. Then she realized what she was looking at. *Angels.* Spiritual warfare inked on muscular forearms. She could have parted the long bristles of his moustache and kissed him on the lips.

Suzette studied the angel tattoos and formulated a plan that was so crazy it just might work.

She stood on her toes and leaned closer to Pierre. "Do you believe in angels?"

Pierre's eyes once again grew round and he opened and closed his mouth a few times without saying anything. He seemed unsure as to how or even whether to answer her question. Then he straightened his shoulders and said, "Yes, I do."

Bingo! Suzette felt like she was back in the classroom, coaxing young minds across the rickety rope-and-plank bridge that spanned the gap between ignorance and enlightenment.

Pierre furrowed his brow and asked, "Why?"

"It is important that we believe in *something*. Personally, I believe we can see angels in everyday life. What do you believe?"

He lifted his chin and said, "Actually, I am a firm believer in the presence and work of angels." His head drew back slightly, as if he was unsure whether to expect reward or criticism for his confession. A muscle in his cheek twitched.

Suzette's eyes bore into his. "What if *I* am an angel?"

"Madam?" A fresh sheen of perspiration coated his face. He licked his lips and took a long sip from the ceramic mug next to his keyboard.

"Does the bible not say that when entertaining strangers you could be entertaining angels?"

Pierre remained silent for a moment, resuming his earlier posture: shoulders, hands, chin, and eyes all turned down. "Well, yes, I think that is in the bible somewhere" -

"And am I not a stranger?"

"Well, yes. Yes, you are. I mean...we've never met, but... I don't know."

"What if I *am* an angel?"

"But you are *not*," he said, his voice slightly higher. "I don't think an angel would... well..."

317

He seemed flustered. It was a good sign. Suzette knew he had reached the point where he would have to fully accept her rationale or deny it. The odds were even.

"Are you saying you believe you are an angel?"

"What I am saying is simple." She leaned back, gripped the edge of the counter and pulled herself close again. "Help me because I might be an angel and if I am, you would not want me to go back to God and point you out as the man who did not help me. Don't be that man, Pierre. Simple as that."

Pierre rested his elbows on the counter and clasped his hands together. There were dark hairs on his knuckles. He shook his head and said, "This is the strangest conversation I have had in a very long time."

"Have a little faith, Pierre. Just as small as a mustard seed. That's all you need." She touched his forearm and said, "I have faith in you."

Nicely done, she thought, smoothing out her clothes and putting both hands on the handle of the cart. She pursed her lips and hiked her eyebrows. Fixing him with her most authoritative look, she said, "I'm going to use the restroom." She held that eye contact with him for a couple of beats and said with her eyes only, *and when I get back, I expect a solution.* She turned and left Pierre to wrestle with her unspoken demand.

⇥⇤

November 29, 1918 (Wolf Point)

The sick woman lifted her chin and tried to speak. Her eyes blinked rapidly. At Marie's touch, her grip on the infant tensed slightly. Claude noticed it. Marie must have noticed it, too, for she looked away briefly and drew in a deep breath before easing the baby girl out of her mother's embrace.

Claude moved to Marie's side and held his face so close to hers that the fur on her hood brushed his cheeks and eyelashes.

"Give it back," he demanded in a furtive whisper.

But Marie refused to meet his gaze. She began wrapping the child more tightly in the soft animal skin and looking for additional coverings to shield the tiny body from the cold outside.

"No, Marie! I will not allow you to do this." He grabbed her shoulders, forcing her to face him. "I forbid it!"

Just then a gurgling sound came from the woman's throat. Her eyes opened wide and her chest rose in one final heave. Claude held his own breath, and searched her waxen face for some sign of life, but found none. His muscles bristled with rage. How could a divine God be so negligent?

Marie put her lips close to the baby's face, and said, "I am your mother now. Yes, that's right. Your *mother.*"

Claude's jaw tightened and he stormed out into the biting cold.

⇥⇤

March 7, 1991
Suzette leaned against the counter in the restroom and concentrated on her breathing. Her legs felt like rubber and she didn't know how much longer she would last. She

could stave off hyperglycemia by eating little, but hunger was taking its toll. Even if there was a way for her to get to Kuujjuaq tonight, she could go into a crisis while there or die along the way. There was no pharmacy in the airport and she did not have the strength to travel into the city and look for one. Who was she kidding? She was no nurse. She didn't know what she was doing.

She shuddered and warm tears filled her eyes. But it wasn't despair that moved her. It was gratitude that flooded her soul and spilled down her cheeks. She thought of Claude and Marie, and how they had loved her; of the birth mother she never knew, that brave Inuit woman who died on the cold shores of a Nunavik river after giving birth to her; of Evan, whose bold visit had opened her mind to things she never thought possible; and of the nurses at St. Jo's, especially sweet Monique who she hoped would forgive her for all the grief she had surely caused. And, she could not forget Stephanie, who worked so hard for her; a job that up until now, Suzette realized with remorse had been completely thankless.

She used some quarters from her change purse to buy feminine napkins from the dispenser. Inside a stall, she took off her pants and hung them on a hook. Next, she removed the soggy Depend undergarment, and none too soon because the gel-like stuffing was erupting from inside of it. She took a pair of clean underpants from her bag and lined them with the feminine napkins.

Once she was cleaned and dressed, Suzette stood for a moment, regarding herself in the mirror. She frowned and wondered if the pneumonia had affected her brain. What was she doing running away from the hospital, further and

further from the medicine and care she desperately needed, and trying to manipulate people into moving moun-
tains for her? She closed her eyes and admitted to herself
that she was acting like a fool.

She opened her eyes and stared at her reflection. It
was time to stop this. She had come as far as she could.
Pierre had said there were no more flights and no buses or
trains. It was time to take no for an answer. She had tried
her best to be there for Anaaya, but she needed to end this
journey now and look after her health. She lifted her chin
and walked back to the First Air ticket counter, so depleted
of strength that she could barely keep her shoulders from
drooping.

At the counter, Pierre was leaning forward on his elbows with his chin resting on his knuckles. His expression was somber, but just as Suzette was about to begin
her apology a brilliant grin parted his face, leaving her
speechless.

"I called a friend," he said.

⚊ ⚊

December 2, 1918 (Kuujjuaq)

Claude rubbed his chin, his fingers exploring the ridges
of pockmarks his dark beard did not cover. Marie sat beside him in a matching wing-backed chair with the baby
girl asleep in her arms. Chairs of such elegance and comfort belonged in the homes of wealthy people. It amazed
Claude that even in an isolated, barren place like this, the
Church could acquire such luxuries and he struggled to
conceal his disapproval.

Father James Babineaux sat across from them, his smooth white hands clasped atop a massive wooden desk. Babineaux was the rector for the Catholic mission in Kuujjuaq.

His eyes moved from Claude to Marie and back to Claude. He cleared his throat and asked, "Are you sure?"

Marie placed her left hand on top of Claude's right and gave it a gentle squeeze. Claude swallowed and said, "Yes." He shifted in his seat, and gestured with his left hand. "We have given this decision much thought."

Babineaux pursed his lips and turned his face towards a tall arched window. A dust-mottled beam of sunlight cast a radiant glow on the rector's narrow face. He leaned forward with his elbows on the desk and locked eyes with Claude. "It's barely been three days since you found the child. Are you sure this is really what you *both* want?" He stared at Claude, his tiny blue eyes piercing Claude's conscience.

Claude's mouth went dry. He was about to speak when Marie leaned forward in her chair and said, "Father."

Babineaux moved his gaze to Marie.

"You know Claude and I have been married for nearly ten years and we have had no children of our own. I *know* this child is a gift from God." She squeezed Claude's hand. "And Claude agrees. This is a miracle."

Claude did agree. The baby's survival was indeed a miracle and in this short time, Claude already found himself overcome by a powerful urge to protect and provide for the helpless infant. But every instinct to love was followed by a hammer blow of shame. Marie should not have lied – *they* should not have lied - to the people back in Suk-Luk.

Babineaux looked at Claude again. Claude forced a weak smile and said, "It's true. The child is a gift. A beautiful little miracle."

"Well, then," Babineaux said, throwing his hands up and letting them fall lightly on the desk. "I commend you both for making such a resolution. Raising any child is a sacrifice, but *this*" - he drew in a deep breath - "this will change your lives forever."

Claude thought he saw a flicker of sadness in Babineaux's eyes.

"Undoubtedly, you will face, among other things, challenges of a... *social* nature."

Claude cleared his throat and reached for the cup of tea Father Babineaux had set before him earlier. *Social* challenges were the least of his worries, for as he sipped the tea he was reminded that *all liars shall have their part in the lake which burneth with fire and brimstone.* The tea was cold by now, but it did not cool the painful burn of those words blazing a white-hot trail through his mind. It did, however, keep his tongue from sticking to the roof of his mouth.

Babineaux leaned back in his chair and crossed his legs.

"But," he said, resting his hands in his lap and smiling warmly, "I have no doubt the two of you will do a fine job of raising the child. You have a strong faith in God and in *each other.*"

To Claude, who was sure the priest must possess a measure of the Holy Spirit adequate to see the truth in men's faces, that last part seemed more of an admonishment than a compliment. Did the rector somehow know that Marie had not respected a dying woman's final wish to hold her child? Could he see in Claude's eyes a dark shadow of guilt for taking the child to Kuujjuaq under false pretenses? If Babineaux had suddenly cried out, "Liars! Hell awaits thee!" Claude would not have been surprised.

Marie smiled and squeezed Claude's hand triumphantly. "Yes, Father. Faith is the key to salvation and to a lasting marriage. We are *very*" - but Claude gripped her hand so hard that she stopped talking.

Remorse for hurting her pecked at him like a sharp finger, and he struggled to keep his composure. He had longed for a child, too, but he saw little faith and certainly no dignity in this affair. He had failed as miserably as Adam in the Garden of Eden. He was without excuse. Husbands were expected to lead their wives. Had it been too much for God to ask? No. God would surely hold him accountable.

"I must admit," Babineaux said, looking at the bundle in Marie's lap and shaking his head, "I do believe it was only by the grace of God that you found this little one."

Marie smiled faintly and lowered her head.

Babineaux's voice sobered. "I do need to ask you both something before we move ahead."

The muscles in Claude's neck and shoulders stiffened.

"Yes, of course, Father," Marie said, stroking the infant. "Ask us anything. Anything at all."

"To the best of your knowledge, does the child have any surviving relatives?"

Claude pictured the two sick boys from Wolf Point and his pulse quickened.

"No," Marie said, before Claude could answer. "A search was conducted and no relatives were found. Father Ammon was at a loss and... well... that's where we came in."

Claude's jaw tightened and he stared at his hands. There had been no search. When Claude and Marie had returned to Suk-Luk with the child, Father Ammon was too sick to receive them. The elderly relatives that were now caring for the child's brothers were in no shape to assume responsibility for a baby. Claude had promised to take the girl to Kuujjuaq, a more established community, less ravaged by the flu, where the Church would be able to take care of her and see that she was reunited with loved ones when the situation in Suk-Luk had improved. But Marie had something else in mind. Perhaps if Claude had not wanted a child so badly himself or had been a stronger better man, he would not have broken so easily. He still couldn't understand how he had let this happen.

"Claude?" Babineaux's voice sounded like it was coming from far away. "Is everything alright? Forgive my many questions, but I do take my role in such matters quite seriously." He waved his hand in the air and said, "But not to worry. You are fine, fine people and under these extenuating circumstances I am happy to endorse your adoption of this special little girl."

At this, Marie began to laugh and cry and cuddle the tiny infant. With equal enthusiasm, Babineaux rifled through his desk drawers for paper and ink to register the birth.

"Look at you, Marie," Babineaux said, gesturing towards the child, who was beginning to squirm inside her swaddling. "I can see already how well motherhood suits you."

Claude looked out the window, but all he saw was the face of a dying Inuit woman.

⊨⊨ ⊨⊨

325

March 7, 1991

A frigid wind nearly tore the clothing from Suzette's frail body, turning her marrow into hard butter. Road salt crunched under her boots as she made her way across the tarmac.

While Suzette had been in the restroom contemplating the easiest way to undo the mess she had gotten herself into, Pierre had arrived at a most unexpected solution to her flight problem.

"I have a friend in the cargo office," he had said. "He told me there is a flight coming in tonight around 10:00 p.m. It just so happens that this plane will be heading back out around midnight, making mail drops to all the major towns en route to Kangiqsujuaq."

Suzette didn't make a sound.

Pierre said, "Including Kuujjuaq. *And* the pilot has agreed to take you."

She had nearly fainted.

"You'll have a bit of a wait, though. The crew will need a couple of hours to unload some cargo, refuel, and load up the mailbags. It'll be close to two in the morning when you get to Kuujjuaq, but at least you'll make it in time for the funeral."

He had blushed when she took both his hands in hers and kissed them. They said little to each other after that and moved about in quiet joy – a reverent silence in honor of whatever power had worked to bring about this superb outcome.

Pierre had escorted her up to the VIP lounge where she was able to eat a little something and rest until it was time to board. Adrenalin made her sleep fitful. One minute she was marveling at her luck and the next she was worried it was all a dream – that she wasn't really going anywhere – or that she would have a deadly crisis before she reached Evan.

Out on the tarmac, darkness pressed in like a vise. Suzette was so tired she could barely put one foot in front of the other. Snowflakes drifted like dust motes in the air around the floodlights and Suzette strained to make out dark shapes concealed in the night, beyond the reach of the lights: a few planes parked in an L-shape, a large object suspended from a winch, and huge pumps.

She leaned against the tall slender woman who had come to collect her from the lounge. The woman, who had introduced herself as Mary, wore a bright pink parka and acid wash jeans. She didn't resemble any of the Inuit women Suzette had ever seen in pictures or on television. With her impeccable make-up and elegant up-do, she looked more like an exotic supermodel. Suzette almost cried when she considered her own ignorance and all the lost and lonely years, when she could have been seeking out women like Mary. Women like herself.

Cold invaded every gap in her clothing and even the snow landing lightly on her face was painful. She coughed so hard, her eyes watered, and Mary reached out an arm to steady her.

An image of Pierre's grinning face flashed in her mind. She had been too tired and weak to say all the things she wanted to say to him, but hoped he would know how much she appreciated all he had done for her.

Suzette's limbs wobbled and jerked as she walked up the metal steps to the plane. By the time she crossed the plane's threshold, she felt as if sandbags were strapped to her body and gravel stuck under her eyelids.

A crewmember appeared and said, "Welcome aboard."

He secured her bag in an overhead compartment at the rear of the plane and helped her get strapped into her seat. "I'm Johnson. I see you've already met Mary. You're lucky she was with us tonight. She's off duty now, but she'll be able to help you with anything you need back here. She's a pro. *And*," he said, winking at Mary, "she's a real sweetheart."

Mary gave him a playful bump as she squeezed past them and dropped down into a seat across the aisle from Suzette's. A purple skirt suit and white blouse hung on a hanger from a hook above the seat in front of Mary's. Draped over the uniform was a scarf in colours matching those Suzette had seen on the tail of the plane.

Johnson crouched down and fiddled with something under Suzette's seat. His brown face was round and cratered like the moon. He had the most pleasing smile Suzette had ever seen.

She had never been in a plane like this before. It was small and had no more than a dozen passenger seats separated from the front of the plane by a wall. Mary reclined back in her seat, put on headphones from some kind of music player device, and closed her eyes.

Johnson gestured towards the wall and said, "That's a movable bulkhead. All the Hawker Sidley 748s have them." He might as well have been talking about a part of his own house. His pride in the plane's condition was overflowing. "We can make room for up to 44 passengers in here."

The walkie-talkie in his belt crackled intermittently.

"Six passengers flew in with us," he said, nodding towards Mary. "That's why we needed a flight attendant. She's deadheading back to Kangiqsujuaq now."

Suzette wrinkled her nose and Johnson grinned.

"We also carried animal feed on our last trip. It's pretty smelly, but you'll get used to it."

He straightened up to his full height, which wasn't much, and said, "You'll probably get a lot of noise and vibration back here, but it's nothing to be concerned about. It's par for the course with these turboprops." He went through some safety instructions, which Suzette barely registered, and told her they would be in Kuujjuaq by half past two.

She reached for his hand and said, "I can't tell you how much I appreciate this. I'd like to give something to you and the other pilot," but Johnson held up his hand and shook his head.

"No need for that. We're happy to help a member of the community."

Suzette smiled. She didn't know what to say to that. *A member of the community?* This was not how Suzette ever imagined her first encounter with other Inuit people would be. She expected to be treated as a curiosity or an outsider, which was certainly how she had always regarded herself.

Johnson gave her shoulder a reassuring touch and said, "You remind me of an old Inuit proverb my father used to tell me. 'If you are going to walk on thin ice, you might as well dance.'" He winked and disappeared through the door of the plane.

Exhausted, Suzette squeezed her eyes shut and imagined the woman from her dreams chasing children over a snow-covered knoll. All thoughts of insulin, antibiotics, cross nurses and failure faded away. Suzette's muscles relaxed and for the first time since her journey began she was at peace.

≈÷ ÷≈

December 11, 1991 (Pingualuit National Park)

Irniq pulled up the fishing line, unhooked the Brook trout and lay it down in the snow covering the frozen surface of the tiny lake. He muttered a small prayer of thanks for the fish and stuck a knife into its brain. The lake was one of dozens dotting the plateau surrounding the Pingualuit Crater. He whistled and Anyu stopped his sniffing in the ice hole and capered over, his long white tale curling over his back. A small patch of brown behind his left ear was the only part of the husky that wasn't white. Anyu barked a few times, but Irniq's mind was made up. It was time to head back. He packed up his tackle and gear, hoisted his catch and walked back towards the igloo he had built earlier that morning. As was his custom, Anyu trotted a little ahead of his master, head high, alert for any danger. Oki always said Anyu took pride in his job.

"He is just a dog," Irniq would say in retort.

"Stubborn. One day, you'll see."

I do see now, brother.

Irniq did not know how many more expeditions he had left in him, but his body had not yet told him to quit. Tomorrow, he would trek a mile or so north, to the banks of the Vachon River, where he would receive a party of extreme anglers, eager to ice-fish the river's world-famous

Arctic char. Irniq clucked his tongue. July, now that was the sensible time to fish the Vachon. Stay at a beautiful lodge like that one up on the Payne River. But now? Now the river was treacherous - frozen in some places, roiling like a rabid animal in others - and the char elusive. There were only six hours of daylight in which to fish, strike camp and take shelter before darkness and harsh Arctic winds made it dangerous to be outside.

In the summer, he would fly southeast, across Ungava Bay, and lead tourists on hunting expeditions. They would track the George River caribou herds, migrating downriver, and a variety of small game thriving in the boreal forests lining the Koksoak River. He and Oki had lost their entire family somewhere along that river and sometimes, while stalking a caribou or searching for tracks, he thought he caught a glimpse of one of them in the rustling of a leaf, the flash of a wing, the sun glinting off the water or reflected in a patch of ice-covered rock.

Within minutes, Irniq had scaled and gutted the fish.

He threw a clump of sphagnum moss into a stone *kudlik*, and retrieved flint and pyrite from his pack. He held the pyrite over the moss and struck it two times with the flint. Sparks flew like fireflies and ignited the tinder. He snatched a burning tuft of moss from the *kudlik* and dropped it into the small fire pit he would use to roast his lunch and warm his bones.

The fire grew and cast a cozy glow that flickered off the curved walls and vaulted ceiling of Irniq's igloo. He inhaled the earthy aromas of moss and larch and thought the only thing missing was Oki. He ran his tongue over his teeth and remembered fondly his big brother's gap-toothed grin. It would soon be four years since Oki's death and Irniq missed him no less with the passage of time.

Irniq was sinewy and strong, but when he stretched out his legs, his knees complained, accusing him of forgetting that at seventy-six, he was as far from the spry youth he had once been as the moon is from the earth.

He shifted his weight on the fur blanket and felt a jab from the corner of a folded paper in the breast pocket of his undershirt. It was the telegram he received at the Kangiqsujuaq post office nearly two weeks ago. He reached under his sweater and pulled out the yellow sheet of paper. Unfolding it with care, he read it again. *You don't know me, but we may be related. Long story. More details to come. Will visit you soon. Keep well. S. Beaujould.*

He put the paper down on the blanket, giving it a protective pat as if he feared the same dark spirit that had devoured his past might swallow this also. As he turned the fish over the fire, memories of his early childhood flashed and flickered, melting away like tiny shards of ice in the palm of his hand. He knew he'd had another brother, younger than him, and a baby sister, but he couldn't remember their names or what happened to them. As far as he knew, they had died like all the others at Wolf Point.

He wished he could talk to Oki. Oki's body had been weak in the end, but his mind was strong. He had always been the smarter of the two, a star student for the Oblate missionaries who had taught them to read and write in French after they fled further upriver to Kotsiktok with some distant relatives. Oki would have remembered more than him.

On a chain around Irniq's neck hung a tiny gold crucifix and a white gold angel. He pulled them out now from beneath his sweater and closing his eyes, kissed them both, first the cross and then the angel, which he pressed to his lips for the longest time. "Anernerk", he whispered. He could not explain it, but that Inuktitut word, meaning "angel", blazed in his mind like the fire in his *kudlik*.

He turned the fish again and repeated the word until it ignited a recollection from his distant past. He slapped his thigh and laughed at the long-forgotten memory that now warmed him more than any fire ever could.

"Anernerk," he said. "That was your *name*, baby sister!" He gently stroked the telegram's yellow paper and said it again in English. "Angel."

NOTES ON CONTRIBUTORS

Francine Fleming, a student at the University of Toronto's School of Continuing Studies, will complete her Creative Writing Certificate in the summer of 2017. You may connect with her on Facebook.

Maria Jemmott is a member of the Writers' Community of Durham Region. A retired public service worker, she also enjoys working with children and is a volunteer with an after school program. You may connect with her on Facebook.

Shirley Merith is a college professor who holds a Masters Degree in Education. She has authored several travel related articles and educational manuals. You may connect with her on Facebook.

Manjit Singh is a high school teacher and has hosted Multicultural Radio. An earlier version of *Buckets of Wonderment* placed as a finalist in the '2016 Open Season Award for Fiction' in *The Malahat Review.* To connect with her, please visit: **www.manjitsinghauthor.com**

Paula Smellie is a creative writing student at the University of Toronto, where she also works. You may connect with her on Facebook.

www.walkingthroughstories.com